The Blameless

The Blameless

RYAN KENEDY

THE UNIVERSITY OF WISCONSIN PRESS

The University of Wisconsin Press
728 State Street, Suite 443
Madison, Wisconsin 53706
uwpress.wisc.edu

Gray's Inn House, 127 Clerkenwell Road
London ECIR 5DB, United Kingdom
eurospanbookstore.com

Printed in the United States of America
This book may be available in a digital edition.

Library of Congress Cataloging-in-Publication Data
Names: Kenedy, Ryan, author.
Title: The blameless / Ryan Kenedy.
Description: Madison, Wisconsin : The University of Wisconsin Press, 2023.
Identifiers: LCCN 2023015010 | ISBN 9780299345044 (paperback)
Subjects: LCGFT: Fiction. | Novels.
Classification: LCC PS3611.E544 B53 2023 | DDC 813/.6--dc23/eng/20230425
LC record available at https://lccn.loc.gov/2023015010

This is a work of fiction. Names, characters, places, and incidents either are
the product of the author's imagination or are used fictitiously, and any
resemblance to actual persons living or dead, businesses, companies,
events, or locales is entirely coincidental.

For
SUSIE

PART I

PART I

Chapter 1

Her son was a tapper and every morning he tapped his pancakes with a fork three times before each bite. Never once or twice, never more than three times. Three pancakes, three taps. Frequently he tapped his right index finger on the palm of his left hand and stared at the floor. Always the right finger and the left hand. And the rocking. He was a rocker. Back and forth for hours, rocking the upper body with an empty gaze, rocking outside of time or against it.

Virginia was still learning when to intervene and when to leave him to his routines. She did not allow bouts of violence. The head banging, for example. Or if he started scratching himself. These were the darker horrors of Timothy's condition, the self-inflicted wounds, the unimaginable frustrations.

He was five and she was still waiting for him to speak. It had to be a real word, one of the eight parts of speech, or an obvious variation. And like a science experiment it had to be repeatable. Nothing uttered by way of scrabbled consonants and random vowels.

Pancake. Two syllables. If they were overcooked or slightly disproportionate Timothy would not eat. He might pick at them instead or stare at their imperfections. She learned to measure the batter before pouring. And if you cooked them carefully, on medium low, you could achieve a texture softer than skin.

Her strategy was simple. Follow the program. Avoid complications. But there was something in the order of events that always upset the balance, some disruption at the molecular level that only Timothy perceived.

This morning he refused to wear clothes. It happened occasionally. Virginia dressed him and immediately he took them off.

"Stop it," she said. "I mean it. We'll be late."

She dressed him again, the clothes came off, she tried again with a different shirt and a new pair of pants. He panicked and cried. He screamed and fluttered his hands.

"What, Timothy? What is it?"

She knew the theory about clothing. It was not so much the contact between the fabric and his skin that disturbed him, but the variable spaces in between. In other words, some areas touching and others not touching.

She served Timothy at the breakfast table. Fork on the right side. Milk in the smooth plastic cup. Adapt to his needs. Which is why Virginia started early every morning. Why every day she prepared her mind before getting out of bed. With a normal child you could teach certain responsibilities, establish a set of age-appropriate expectations.

She watched as he sat naked at the table, his body in uniform relation to all objects in the room, tapping with his fork three times between bites.

In the shower she turned the knob as hot as she could stand it. She felt the water overtake the chill. She closed her eyes and stood very still under the showerhead. Before the body wash and the shampoo, before the salt scrub, before the razor, she held her hands together under her chin and turned so that the water ran down her back. No need to rush this, she thought. These first few seconds. Avoid all reflection. Listen to water crashing on tiles. Listen to water circling the drain.

She wrapped a towel around her hair and another around her body. She would check on Timothy in the kitchen. Still not finished with his breakfast. In the bathroom she rubbed lotion on her face and neck, her shoulders, both arms, enough for the front and back, legs to feet. A downward automated motion of the hands. She put on underwear and a bra. She zipped the skirt and pulled a blouse on overhead. She used the blow dryer on her hair, stopping now and again to listen for her son. A smudge of toothpaste was glued to the sink. Virginia rubbed it with her finger and rinsed the basin. She used a wad of tissue paper to clean around the edge of the toilet bowl where Timothy often missed. In the mirror she put on makeup and eyeliner.

When she came out he was lying under the window in a diamond of warm sunlight. His body pearlescent, he lay in the fetal position with one side of his face pressed against the hard laminate floor.

She turned the fan off in the kitchen.

"I have this for you," she said.

It was a blue and silver wetsuit made of soft scuba material. She kept it on a hanger in the hall closet. Dr. Bremmer, the psychiatrist, had suggested this remedy because it closes the space between the body and the world.

"Let's put it on."

Timothy appeared to ignore her. They were five years into this. That's how many days and hours? That's how many words spoken to no reply? She knew he heard the sounds. What she did not know is if he understood them as words.

There were others like him but each child represented something unique. You had to understand the general condition first, the nature of the disorder, and then work on the specific variation of your child, this person in front of you. Virginia had given more than three years of her life to books and articles, to group counseling sessions, discussion boards, social media. She had gone to workshops and seminars seeking a cure, waiting for a breakthrough. She knew who the experts were and what they had written. She had studied the competing theories. And if anyone asked she could list the early warning signs by stages of progression or by rates of occurrence. She had personal contacts at the nonprofit groups, at the offices of the corporate sponsors, at the government agencies. She understood the bureaucratic protocols. She had written letters, made phone calls, she had even led an organization of volunteers.

Then Neil left.

Three words she would say for the rest of her life. She used them in conversation. It was a way of putting it that signified an abrupt shift in living arrangements. A way of thinking about herself in relation to everyone else. *Then Neil left.*

He rented an apartment downtown to be closer to work. That was more than a year ago. Late winter of the year before. They were divorced now and he was seeing someone else. Virginia didn't know her name or how long he had been with her. She was a figure in the background, a body in the blurred distance, and Neil never talked about her. Once when it was Virginia's turn to pick up Timothy she was there in the apartment. Virginia didn't go inside. She waited in the hallway next to the elevator and the fire extinguisher.

Neil had Timothy one weekend a month, which was more than he wanted. Virginia called him a weekend warrior, as in one weekend a month and two weeks a year, a part-time soldier equipped with battle fatigues and body armor. But he had let her decide the terms of their divorce, not out of guilt, and not simply because he wanted things to remain productive and amicable. He was merely indifferent. He had no way of dealing. Timothy was not like a son, more like an expensive and complicated house cat, a creature that appeared in doorways and rubbed up against the walls.

When they divorced she dumped Neil's last name and went back to Bigelow. It was agreed she would keep the apartment. Neil would pay for it. He would pay for all things Timothy. Schools and specialists, treatments, medications, afternoon snacks. He would pay alimony to supplement Virginia's income. He would pay for the gym membership until it expired. He would pay for the *don't make this difficult*. He would pay for the *I want us both to be happy*. Then came trouble at work. Losses led to layoffs and restructuring, cutbacks or rollbacks, she couldn't remember what he called them. Neil was lucky to keep his job. Virginia, who always thought of herself as unlucky, moved to an apartment in Hollywood with views of the freeway. She took on an extra class at another campus to pay the bills. Now she taught Composition five days a week in Los Angeles, Santa Monica, and Pasadena. She cursed the drive between campuses. The routine traffic delays, the crowded parking lots, the breathless effort to beat the clock.

After Neil left, Virginia quit the disorder. It was the thing that ruined their marriage, according to Neil. She cancelled subscriptions to several psychiatric and medical journals. She pulled over a hundred books off the shelves, boxed them up for donation. Without offering an explanation to anyone she abandoned the online support groups that had sustained her during her worst moments of fear and confusion. She stopped visiting the web pages and discussion boards, removed her postings, emptied her inbox, shuttered the Facebook account.

It was not an admission of guilt on her part. This radical shift in her behavior. It did not in any way whatsoever vindicate her former husband or validate his accusations. Vindicate, validate. Neil left her, left his son. She had married a weak man, a coward, and now they were divorced.

Virginia quit the disorder because she had reached the end. All her research had come to nothing. Look at the facts. Nothing had changed for Timothy. She knew nothing, she could change nothing. Timothy was Timothy. He *is* Timothy. This was their life and it was never going to change.

"Put this on," she said to him.

She raised her son to his feet but he wouldn't stand. He wouldn't support his own weight. He was like someone who didn't know how or why, as though the purpose of legs and feet never occurred to him.

"This is really awful," she said, "what you're doing. The way you're acting."

She sat on the sofa and angled his body across her lap. She jammed one leg into the suit and then the other. His feet were limp. He did nothing to help her. She stood him up in front of her, trapped him between her knees, held him upright. She pulled up the top of the wetsuit and guided his arms through tight sleeves. She did not care if she was being too rough with him.

"You're *you*," she said, "and I'm *me*."

The wetsuit was sewn with flat stitches and included a zipper in the back. Virginia had cut off the long pull-cord attached to the zipper because the first time Timothy wore the suit he discovered the cord and wrapped it around his neck.

When she finished he dropped down to the floor again. She put his socks and shoes on. She brushed his white hair hurriedly while he lay on the floor in the sunlight.

Timothy's school was less than a mile away. Often when her schedule permitted they walked there counting the steps. She said all the words to him. *Curb, car, stoplight.* She said *crosswalk, birds, flag.* He never looked where she pointed. He either ignored her completely or watched her hand. She said *hand.* She said *band, land, stand,* or things that rhymed with a word. Sometimes he walked the entire distance. Other times he stopped and sat down or followed a completely different course. She had read about savants and wondered if Timothy was one of these, or would someday emerge as one. They said it could come later, the development of mysterious pathways. She wondered if complex arrangements passed through his mind at any given moment. She had an image, a fantasy, of someday waking up to find him playing Mozart on the piano in the living room, although she had no piano and there was not room for one in her small apartment.

At school they worked on behavioral modification. They worked on recognizing visual stimuli. They worked on video modeling and eye contact. Responding to cues. But today her son was despondent. Today Virginia had to drive him in the car and carry him to the classroom. At the school she explained about the wetsuit. She had packed an overnight bag with his blanket and pillow. Tonight he was going to Neil's. Virginia asked if she could leave the bag until she picked him up. They were accommodating, naturally. Every parent had a special request. Always *could you do this*, or *can I ask a small favor*. The staff was accommodating. They were people with astonishing capacities for accommodation.

Timothy rested against her chest, his head on her shoulder. Let's not call it an embrace. Hold him tight but don't wait for him to return the feeling. She smelled his white hair which still smelled like baby blankets and morning cartoons. Virginia kissed his unresponsive mouth before leaving. She would pick him up after school and take him downtown on the train. It was Neil's weekend. Neil and the girl he was with. And then Virginia wouldn't see him again until Sunday afternoon. It was what she longed for all month, her time alone, two days. When it came she did not want to let Timothy go.

~

She kept her things locked inside the trunk of her car. They were organized in plastic bins. Lecture notes, bluebook exams, syllabi. Every morning she stood in the campus parking lot with her trunk wide open to gather whatever she needed for class. She was an adjunct instructor, a part-timer. In other words, no office space, no benefits, crushing wages. She owed eighty thousand on student loans and worked out of the trunk of a Honda.

The English Department was clear across campus. Virginia carried her purse and a black leather book bag heavy with various texts, attendance records, graded papers, whiteboard markers. She walked at a militant pace in her two-inch heels, wearing the skirt with the white blouse, shouldering the two bags. The copy machines were in a private room next to the main office. She had to enter a code for the machines to work. Five hundred copies for the entire semester was her limit. The full-timers, the tenured professors, had unlimited access but the adjuncts taught on various campuses, could presumably make copies for students at other institutions, and the deans were worried about their budgets.

Virginia placed the handout on the glass, closed the cover of the machine, pressed the green button. She had all of ten minutes until class. Timing was key. Wake up, get the kid off to school, battle the traffic, find parking, walk across campus, make copies, hurry to class. She had no pity for students who arrived late, the drag-steppers with their coffee cups and jingling keys. When they came in after five minutes she knocked points off their grade.

It was petty and she resented it. As a student she imagined what kind of teacher she would become. The professor who didn't take attendance, the popular one who flouted all the rules, the provocative unpredictable genius. She did not know then that her students, the vast majority of them, would behave in all the wrong ways. They would not engage. They would not respond. Only graded assignments mattered to them. *Are you collecting this?* they would ask. *How many points is it worth?* Her students needed guidelines, prohibitions, penalties. Forget about intellectual curiosity and speculative pleasures. They needed routine structure and a passing grade to advance.

The Chair, Ellen Parks, came into the copy room holding a handful of papers. Virginia did not want to see Ellen, much less speak to her. She was hoping to avoid anyone on the hiring committee, especially Ellen. It was two weeks since the interview for the full-time position. Earlier in the week Virginia received the official letter signed by the Chair and the Dean regretfully informing her that she had not been selected as one of three finalists. She was not going to read the letter, but then she did and afterward regretted it. She had sacrificed the pleasure of throwing it into the trash can unopened. The letter only confirmed the obvious. At the interview they told her they would call in three days if she was selected to meet with the college president. Nobody called.

"One more week," Ellen said. "Then I'm off to Nepal with my husband. Have you any plans for summer?"

Virginia offered no reply. She wanted Ellen Parks to go away.

Ellen said, "Oh, you poor thing. You look so tired. Are you still grading research papers?"

Virginia turned and gave Ellen a malicious look.

"Seriously, Ellen, don't you think it's rude to say that to a person? *You look so tired.*"

Ellen laughed awkwardly.

"I didn't mean anything."

"Of course I'm tired," Virginia said. "And I get it, Ellen, I look like shit. What am I supposed to say, *thank you? Thanks for noticing?*"

"I'll come back."

"You don't have to," Virginia said, "mine's finished."

She raised the lid and grabbed the sheet of paper off the glass. She crammed the copies into her bag and slung the bag over her shoulder.

"I'm sorry I caught you at a bad moment."

"A bad moment? Ellen, this is not a bad moment. This is every day. I'm teaching on three campuses this semester. You have no idea what that's like."

Ellen stood with her arms crossed, lifting one eyebrow. Her face was tense, her mouth rigid. "I'm sure it's difficult for you."

"No, *difficult* I can do. This is not difficult. This is degrading. It's unfair. I've been teaching for how long, a decade? And I'm still at ground zero. I don't know what else to do, Ellen. Or how else to prove myself. I teach whatever shit schedule is available, I sit on committees, I tutor in the writing center. But for some reason I can't get a full-time job. And they tell me I'm supposed to feel lucky. Lucky I even got an interview. Which I'm sure will be my last."

"I'm sorry, Virginia. I'm sorry you feel this way."

"What have I done wrong? That's all I want to know. What is my *lack*? Really, what is it? I want to know, Ellen. Obviously I need to improve. Was it something I said? Did I say something dumb in the interview? This is the second time you've interviewed me. So tell me, please. What am I doing wrong? I came prepared. I thought I answered the questions well. My teaching demonstration. My timing. And I'm looking at the committee and you're all nodding your heads. Where's the disconnect? I don't understand."

Ellen was silent, her mouth formed an embarrassed half-smile, and behind her eyeglasses she blinked rapidly.

"Who are the finalists, anyway? I'd like to know who you put forward."

"Virginia, we can't talk about this."

"Are they so much better than me? You know my teaching, Ellen. You've observed me how many times? You've always rated me excellent. So tell me, please, you'd be doing me a great favor. What is my *lack*?"

"This conversation is making me uncomfortable."

Virginia wanted to punch this woman, hit her in the mouth.

"Oh, *you're* uncomfortable," she said.

"I understand your frustration. I do, Virginia. I take it very seriously. But you know as well as I."

"I'm thirty-seven," Virginia said, "and I can't make a decent living. I'm a good teacher, Ellen, and you know it. Is full-time employment too much to ask? I would like to teach on one campus for a change. Is that fair? To have an office of my own? To be respected and appreciated? To get paid what I'm worth?"

Ellen placed her papers in the sheet feeder.

"I would love to see more full-time openings," she said. "You of all people know how hard I fight for priority."

"I could understand if my student evaluations were poor. Or if I was unprofessional in some way."

"We're hoping next year."

Virginia repositioned her bag. She would never get hired full-time at this college. She would never understand why and no one would tell. The word, the almighty word, was *confidentiality*. But the truth was Ellen didn't like her and that was probably the reason. Anyway, they did not need a reason. She was in the adjunct pool, drowning in the deep end, her hair caught in the drain.

"I have to go to class," she said. "My students are waiting."

"One more week. We can do this."

"You already said that, Ellen."

~

In class she reviewed the proper methods of research documentation. Her students' final papers were due in a week. With the lights off she lectured on examples of good and bad. She pointed to the bright screen in front of the class showing a student's paper from last semester.

"What should it say?"

She folded her arms and waited for a response.

"Look at the parenthetical citation. Who knows this? Anyone? By now everyone should know it."

Her students were looking at the screen and not seeing the errors. Or else they were seeing the errors but did not care to verbalize their answers. In any case she had explained this material already and they were still getting it wrong in their drafts.

"Look at it," she said. "Look at the Works Cited page. How is it sup-posed to be organized? Someone remind me."

Finally a hand went up. A student offered the correct answer.

"That's right," said Virginia. "Are these entries alphabetized? Obviously not. So that's one problem. What else?"

The freshman research paper, a requirement, a rite of passage. Do this, not that. Virginia waited. She paced in front of the classroom. Then she looked up at the screen and folded her arms. She dreaded teaching this material. The page on display was typical of the kind of work students submitted. It was sloppy and full of indolent mistakes.

"You can see how confusing this is, can't you? Please say yes."

She turned to her students. Outside of class they were all writing lengthy papers riddled with inaccuracies and errors.

"Pause for a moment," she said, "and consider what it's like for me to read your papers. Imagine my task. Or do this. Imagine you're a world-class chef. In front of you, on the stove, are several pots and pans. On the counter there are bowls, mixing dishes, open containers. What you're attempting to do is make a good meal, which means multitasking, which means you must pay extremely close attention to detail. Your job as a chef is to taste and evaluate. People are waiting. Now, imagine the kitchen is full of flies. Flies are everywhere, swarming, landing on everything. You're trying to do your job and do it well. But there are flies all over the kitchen, crawling on the food, swarming around your face, and quite frankly they're fucking everything up!"

Her students laughed. In the classroom profanity always procured laughter. She could not understand why.

"Don't you see?" she asked.

Next week she would labor over their ten-page essays, the awkward phrases, the flaccid arguments. Because they didn't listen, because they simply did not care. And not this class only, but all her classes. Certain stu-dents would fail these basic courses and one or two would have the audac-ity to file a formal complaint against her.

On the board she wrote the Latin phrase *et al.*

"What does it mean?" she said. "We went over this last week."

Eleven students had skipped class and the room felt hollow. She knew who was absent, who had missed the review. Not that it mattered. A day after submitting final grades she would utterly forget their names. She would see them on campus in the fall and not remember their names.

"Et al.," she said.

She wrote the translation on the board and said in a quiet voice, a voice no one else could hear, *"and others."*

~

On her way out to the car she saw Ellen Parks. Ellen was crossing toward the library. Virginia walked past her without saying hello, without apologizing. She did not owe Ellen or anyone else an apology. Virginia packed her things into the trunk and slammed it shut. She would drive home, eat the salad from last night, grade papers from another class on another campus. Her mother had called while she was in class. On the highway she inserted earbuds and dialed.

"Where are you?" her mother said.

"On my way home, what's up?"

"We'll talk about it later."

"Later? Why later, are you dying? Do you have cancer?"

"Let's not talk while you're driving. It's dangerous."

"Mother, I do this all the time. I drive and talk. It's what I do. The car is my office. Think of this as my office hours."

"Did you watch the news?"

"You mean the road rage? The shooting? It happened south of where I live, so you don't have to worry."

"It used to be the people on drugs."

"Now it's everyone."

"It's best to stay clear of it. Don't get involved."

"I'm in a car on the highway, I'm already involved."

"What I'm saying is watch out for the maniacs."

"And what I'm saying is I *am* a maniac. Is this what you wanted to talk about?"

"I'll call you later."

"No, absolutely not. I have work to do this afternoon. I have to concentrate. I can't be worrying about anything, it's distracting."

"It's nothing to worry about."

"Then why are you calling?"

"To tell you Travis Hilliard is out of prison. He's been released. He's out on parole."

A shove, a gut-punch. Virginia didn't say anything. The name Travis Lee Hilliard was buried in the middle of her chest.

"They let him go?"

"I got a letter in the mail from the parole board."

"Why'd they let him out? Did they give a reason?"

"No, they just said."

She had certain memories of the man. The day he killed her father he was fixing an old car, the hood raised, the engine spread out in parts. Virginia remembered his greasy fingers and forearms. She was riding her bike on the smooth blacktop behind the church. The trick was to keep her dress from getting caught in the chain, or worse, her toes. Travis Hilliard had a moustache and her father was clean-shaven. She remembered the difference. He smoked cigarettes and she saw him once without his shirt.

Virginia asked her mother, "And you're okay with this?"

"I have no say in the matter."

"You should've had a voice. They should've notified you of the hearing."

"They did."

"And you didn't go?"

"It wasn't the first hearing. He's been up for parole once or twice. I never wanted to go."

"Why not? I would've gone."

"I don't want anything to do with it."

"Well, now he's out of prison. Maybe if you'd said something."

"Maybe, Virginia, but I didn't."

"Does Amanda know?"

"I called your sister this morning."

"What did she say?"

"She doesn't know what to think. I told her he's not a threat to anyone."

"You don't know that. She lives right there in Citrus Heights. How far is that?"

"He doesn't even know she's alive. How would he know? Anyway, they wouldn't have let him out if they thought he might do something. They don't let out dangerous people."

"Do you know anything about the prison system?"

"No, Virginia. I don't know anything about anything."

"Where is he now?"

"I don't have a clue, the letter didn't say."

"Don't they have to disclose his whereabouts?"

"I'm told that only applies to sex offenders."

"It's ludicrous," she said. "He shouldn't be alive. They should've given him the chair. He should've been electrocuted."

"I thought you were against the death penalty."

"In theory, yes, but not in this case. I'm reversing my position on a lot of things. I'm undergoing a major reevaluation if you want to know."

"That happens to everyone."

"It's happening to *me*."

"Try not to worry about this. I didn't call to make you worry."

"I'm not worried. If he comes near me I'll blow his brains out."

"You're too volatile," her mother said. "I don't like you having a gun. You shouldn't even own a gun."

"You've seen the news. It's mayhem down here."

"You really need to move."

"There's nowhere else to go, Mother. This is where it ends."

"Where what ends?"

"The whole goddamn world."

~

At home she poured a vodka and tonic and stirred the ice with her finger. She put a stack of papers on the kitchen table to grade. A dog was barking in the apartment next door, a dingy mutt with a nervous bite. She wanted to shoot the dog in the mouth. Virginia had complained about the barking, but the woman who lived there, the woman whose balcony was forested with plants, was the property manager, June Flauss. It was a mistake to move in next to the manager. She was always sitting on a striped lawn chair outside her screen door, and whenever Virginia got home the woman greeted her with an assertive smirk.

Virginia poured another drink and stuffed her ears with cotton. An effort to concentrate first required a deliberate layering of certain sounds, a muffling of others. She turned on the fan and started some music. She kept hearing the name in her mind. Travis Lee Hilliard. Still the details of his face eluded her. Something of the Burt Reynolds look about him, consistent with the times, like the magazine ads for Marlboro cigarettes.

The dark hair and thick moustache, the olive complexion and light-colored eyes. Travis Lee Hilliard. He would look different now, of course, older and gray. She remembered his teeth. He was missing a tooth, an incisor. It was something she noticed whenever he smiled.

She drank the vodka and chewed on a piece of ice. If the dog was barking she could no longer hear it. She started reading the first essay, the paper on top of the stack. She had to fight her way into it, reading and rereading certain sentences and paragraphs to get the gist. It was a D paper at best. By the end of the first page she knew what every grade would be. Her tendency was to over-comment and she had to resist this urge. It was too late, anyway. The semester was nearly finished, the window for revision had closed, and the student was failing the course.

She advanced through the stack of papers wrestling with inept sentences, with incoherent paragraphs, marking errors, scribbling comments in the margins. There was a rhythm to it and the grading became easier for a while, but after a few hours it grew more demanding again. It was ruining her neck and it would probably ruin her eyesight. Among other things, grading papers had destroyed her desire to read. She did not blame her students entirely. They did not know their best efforts were so dreary and disheartening to her. It was the word itself that discouraged her, the habit and burden of language, Virginia's insistence on things having names and meanings, and her son's inability to learn them. The fact that she could find no alternative to words, and the fact of his incapacity.

Lately, and for the first time in her life, she wasn't reading anything in her spare time. In graduate school she had studied the Romantics. Blake, Wordsworth, Shelley. She published two sections of her dissertation and delivered papers at several conferences. For a while it was total submersion, reading everything, night and day, but that was years ago. Scholarly pursuit no longer held any interest for her. It required too much energy and focus, too many hours of uninterrupted study. Anyway, she had nothing new to add, nothing original to say. She tried reading a handful of contemporary novels, prizewinners mostly, titles other people were reading, but nothing caught on. Instead, she watched foreign films without subtitles and stupid YouTube videos. She binged on Netflix and nightly news. It did not matter if Timothy played on the floor or looked at the screen. Whatever he saw he did not know it as sex and violence, he did not hear it as inappropriate language. He liked cartoons because of the colors and sounds. Narrative meant nothing to him. Only images, raw and plotless, captured his attention. Most nights after Timothy went to bed Virginia stepped outside onto the balcony and leaned against the iron rail, cocktail in hand, in view of all the cars on the Hollywood Freeway.

~

It was best to take the Red Line downtown. Otherwise the traffic and the problem of where to park the car. They would catch the train at Hollywood and Vine and take the short ride to Neil's. On the way to the station Virginia held Timothy's hand and carried his bag. While they waited for the train Timothy looked up at the film reels painted on the ceiling or else at the pattern of tiles beneath his looping strides. There was a sign on the wall. If You See Something, Say Something.

She said *tickets, turnstiles, tunnel.*

The train stopped and started at precise intervals, 7:25, 7:32, 7:37, when bodies moved in predictable ways, suddenly, and without thinking. On hot days the body odor was something to contend with. The sweaty underarms. The rather heavy breathing. Timothy pressed his face to the glass. That was his thing on the train. To press his whole face against the window. There could be graffiti, or something like snot. She tried to make him stop, pulling him away from the glass, Timothy, pulling him away. Then for a while, maybe a few months or longer, she carried antibacterial spray and went about spraying and wiping. Examining surfaces and contacts. Watching where people placed their hands, where they touched.

Something about riding the subway, she didn't know what exactly, reminded her of crouching under the table at an old Italian restaurant, dimly lit, in a quiet booth. The dark sticky floor, a thick metal pole that her hands could not fully clasp, and the grownup's legs, their pants and nylons, their fat and skinny shoes. *Don't touch anything, Virginia. Come out of there. Show me your hands.* Even now as an adult the undersides of restaurant tables represented something mysterious and revolting to her psyche.

As a child she wanted to be underneath everything, chairs, desks, beds, or somewhere inside if it were possible. A cabinet or a closet. She had discovered a crawlspace amid the blue hydrangea bushes growing alongside the house. Secretly she had collected a small assortment of cigarette butts from where the smokers gathered on Sunday mornings. Virginia separated the filters into yellow for men and white for women. She especially liked the white cigarettes with traces of pink lipstick. These she kept entirely for herself.

Timothy held his face to the glass and together they watched the tube lights and blurry surfaces and the crowds at each new stop as they came into sharp focus. She told Timothy he was going to his father's and won't that be fun. She said *forward, motion, rumble*. But the sadness was setting in. That feeling of loss. She pointed to his face in the glass and said *reflection*.

They walked to Neil's building, still plenty of light in the sky, and rode the elevator up. The bag she was carrying was not heavy but it was beginning to feel that way. At the door she knocked and waited. There was something humiliating about knocking on the door of your former husband and waiting. Something about certain rights being revoked, a refusal of the right to enter. Virginia did not want him back. That wasn't the thing that bothered her. He would never understand that it was riding the train and carrying the bag. It was knocking first and then waiting outside the door.

The girl came to the door dressed in her gym clothes. Mid-to-late twenties, young, pretty, et cetera. A slim figure in the background coming into full view. She introduced herself as Kendal and held out her hand. Awkward, cheerful. Someone from the office maybe, or the friend of a friend, a setup.

"Neil's on his way," she said. "I just got off the phone." Her voice carried an apology, an acknowledgment that men did not create the problem, they were the problem.

Kendal offered her a drink. A glass of wine, a bottle of water. Timothy slowly circled the room. He put his hand out and lightly touched the walls.

"Hi, Tim," Kendal said. "That's a really cool wetsuit you're wearing."

Timothy walked past her. As hot as it was he would not give up the wetsuit after school. Now the wetsuit was Neil's problem.

"I'll bet you're ready for a fun weekend," Kendal said.

She extended certain vowels, like musical notes, for emphasis. Something about her tone suggested clean freeways and bright sandy beaches. Timothy touched the plants and the furniture. He circled the room.

"What do you have planned?" Virginia asked.

"Neil's bringing Thai food," she said. "Tomorrow we'll walk the pier and hang out. Get some ice cream. Fun stuff like that."

Kendal had runner's legs, the body of an early riser. As she spoke she followed Timothy with her eyes.

"How was school today, buddy?" she asked him.

He walked past her and circled the room touching lightly. The apartment had decent windows. Views of downtown.

"I packed his clothes," Virginia said. "This morning the wetsuit. He takes off his clothes. Long story."

"Neil told me about that."

It was Neil and it was not Neil. It was asking where to set the bag. It was not wanting to stay and not wanting to leave Timothy with the girlfriend.

"It's not all the time," Virginia said. "Anyway. If he refuses to wear clothes tomorrow, he can just wear the wetsuit again."

"Oh, totally."

"But it zips in the back so he'll need help going to the bathroom. You'll have to watch him. He'll put his hand there when he needs to go. Otherwise you'll have no way of knowing."

"No worries," she said. Then to Timothy she said, "Wetsuits are awesome! We should totally go surfing."

The girl did not exist as he circled past her. He was doing his laps around the room. Touching the windows and walls. Touching the television and the chair.

"I guess I can go," Virginia said, "if Neil's on his way."

"He should be here any minute. I can call him if you want."

"No, it's fine."

Virginia moved into Timothy's path. She kneeled in front of him and opened her arms making it impossible for him to go around. She hugged him. Timothy. She placed his arms around her neck. Do this for him. She said *love, love, love*. She smelled his hair and the wetsuit. She kissed. She felt the loneliness setting in, the hard goodbye. She saw the train ride and how everything seems different when you enter the apartment alone at night. She said *Sunday* and kissed him again. They would see each other on Sunday. A brief absence was a good thing. People need this. She kissed her son. She squeezed him once more and said goodbye. When she let go he continued around the room, touching everything in its place, leaving no mark.

She did not see Neil on her way out of the building. She watched for him as she neared the subway. She was determined to not worry. Everything was fine. Neil was probably home by now. The time it takes to walk to Pershing Square.

She bought a coffee on the corner and found a seat on the train. The train was crowded with eyes. Everyone glancing at everyone else. Who are we riding with tonight? They looked at Virginia, unintentionally. They turned away, she turned away. An occasional half-smile. Certain people and only some of the time. She tried to avert her gaze whenever possible. She read the advertising, the public service announcements. Quit smoking, feet off the seats, stop beating your child. She tried to decipher a name written in graffiti, Papi or Tati, written in a black Aztec scrawl.

People standing. Others staring at phones and tablets, or wearing headphones, settling in. As the train started forward Virginia felt the momentum overtake her. The way the body carries every surge, every countless vibration.

With arms folded she held the cup close to her mouth and sipped through a hole in the lid. The caffeine would keep her awake. She stared at knees and shoes. She said to herself, *rubber, plastic, metal.*

Eight stops, twenty-six minutes.

Chapter 2

There were noises outside his room. People walking past the window, a clattering of voices, then doors slamming. L.T. reached for the bedside lamp and the room went dark. It was then he noticed the rattling sound coming from the air unit below the curtains. He realized it now only because the television was off and the room was quiet. In bed he worked to get comfortable. The two pillows were large, the mattress wide and very soft, and he did not especially like this. In prison he slept on a narrow mattress with a thin pillow, always on his right shoulder, facing the wall. But the walls in this motel seemed far apart. L.T. closed his eyes and tried to forget about the walls.

He found sleep in littered forms, scraps of dream memory, the slow routine of route-step and painted lines. He heard a guard's voice on the loudspeaker and the sound of an electric buzzer signaling the movement of compliant souls. L.T. moved when the men in front of him moved. He followed the single-file march down a spiral staircase, a narrow column of iron steps that grew steeper with each turn until at last they were unreasonably steep and impossibly high above the ground, and as there was no handrail to grab, nor anything within reach, L.T. started to fall.

When he came awake he sat up and put his feet on the carpet and braced himself on the edge of the bed. He moved from the bed to the window, and back to the bed. Then from the bed to the toilet, which was not stainless steel, and therefore did not refract the sound of his own familiar stream. He pissed and did not flush. He stood before his shape in the mirror.

He wanted a cigarette. The thought of it quickened his senses: the quiet float of smoke in a dark room. He had quit smoking some eight or nine years ago when the State took the cigarettes out of the prisons. For a time it was agony inside the cages. There were shakedowns and drag-offs, and outside on the yard inmates were taking flight at each other. L.T. had prayed through the night sweats until they were gone but he had shouldered the craving ever since. And he was feeling it now, that hoary crawl under his skin, that human ache.

Of course, it was not smart to pick up the habit again. The morning cough was part of it. The stale fingers and smoky clothes. Then the price in dollars and cents. How much these days for a pack of cigarettes? Not to mention the nervous urge, the ritual gestures, the fire requirement. To start something was easy, to get out of it was quite another matter.

What's more, he knew better than to venture out at night. The night belonged to criminals and delinquents, and to women with corrupt hearts. Still, he began to dress himself wearing the stiff white shirt and the khaki pants afforded to him at processing. These were his only clothes. He pulled on his socks, adjusting the seams. He straightened the toe. He did not like to feel the stitch when he walked. He reached for a shoe, the left one, lifted up its tongue and forced his foot inside, then pulled the laces tight. The brogans were new and the leather was stiff. He flexed his foot, then reached for the other shoe and repeated the slow, deliberate process.

The keycard was on the desk beside the telephone. He had used a card instead of a key to open the room, something new to him. He put the keycard into his shirt pocket with his debit card. Both cards in the same pocket so that he could keep track of them together.

He was careful to close the door quietly. The parking lot was full of cars and in some of the rooms the people were still awake on their beds. Lamplight shone behind those curtains. All the other rooms were dark. He did not wish to disturb anyone. Downstairs the surface of the swimming pool was like a solid pane of glass. There were eight or ten empty chairs arranged around the water's edge. A bright red soda machine was plugged into the wall by the pump, but the pump itself was quiet. He heard trucks on the highway and the sound of a freight train passing through town. Otherwise nothing, no movement at all. The sky was clear. Although he could not find the moon, he saw for the first time in many years a scattering of pale stars.

The motel was not far from the Greyhound station between the river and the state capitol. He would find the nearest liquor store, whatever was open at this hour, buy a pack of smokes and come straight back to the motel. Simple enough. He went downstairs and cut across the parking lot to the road and looked down the street both ways. Nothing in sight. He chose a direction, call it east, and started walking.

The air was clean and damp and it felt good to be out walking at night. He was surefooted, that was the word, and unfettered. He walked past a row of sturdy buildings made of brick and heavy masonry. He was fully awake, under no man's watch, and he was free to walk at his own pace. His stride was swift and natural, and his vision was sharp at the edges, and he could feel the solid ground underfoot. The shoes were breaking in nicely and he knew they would be comfortable soon because they were made of cowhide and the soles were made of slip-resistant rubber. Most men received only one pair of shoes to last the duration of their sentence. L.T. had worn through many pairs before these. They were thick as boots and made for work and for long hours of standing, but you had to break them in first, the way he was doing now.

Around the corner and down the street, two blocks in that direction, he found a liquor store, Jinn's Wine & Spirits. Iron bars protected the glass door and the storefront window. A crowd of neon signs illuminated the darkness. When he pushed through the door he set off the motion detector. An electronic tone sounded and the man behind the counter looked up and nodded, *I see you*. The man looked Indian, like the desk clerk at the motel, only this one wore an orange turban, a blue collared shirt, a pair of tan slacks. The Sikhs wore turbans. Seeing a bearded man in a turban reminded L.T. of the old Hills Brothers coffee can in the kitchen cabinet at home. The one his mother kept her tips in. Although, if he remembered correctly, the man pictured on the can was an Ethiopian, not an Indian.

The man behind the counter had dark eyes and a long black beard. Maybe he was a Saudi, or else Pakistani. Osama Bin Laden wore a turban and he was a Saudi, not a Sikh. The clerk was reading a newspaper. He had a television going in the back. L.T. could hear applause followed by laughter. The man had hairy arms and wore a gold wristwatch. He was alone in the store and this is how he passed the time.

The walls were shelved with wine bottles and every hue of hard liquor. The expensive bottles on top, the cheap mash in wicker baskets on the endcaps. He looked at the beer behind the refrigerated glass. A hundred names he had never heard of. He was not interested in trying new beers. He reached for a six-pack of Miller High Life and closed the door on the cold. A drink would put him in violation of his parole. There were many such conditions. Nevertheless, he carried the carton of bottles through the candy aisle and set the beer on the counter in front of the clerk.

"Soft pack of Winston's," L.T. said, "and matches if you've got them."

The man in the turban folded his paper and stood up.

"Regular or one-hundreds?" the man said. Clearly it was all routine to him. Nothing but ordering and reordering, thought L.T., and the daily deliveries through the back door, the beer trucks every Tuesday and Friday, stacks of cardboard boxes, restocking the shelves, replacing the receipt tape, and the nickels and dimes and filthy bills, the quick-picks and penny scratchers, and chasing out the mumbling bums and the kids with grabby hands.

"Regular," L.T. said. He did not want to complicate matters.

The man put cigarettes on the counter with the beer and reached below the register for the matches. L.T. wondered how often the man got robbed and what kind of weapon he kept under the counter. A cudgel? A little snub-nose revolver? On the cash register was a sticker of the American flag with the words *Never Forget*.

L.T. had no cash and the debit card was still a clumsy item. He positioned the card strip-side down in reverse, according to the diagram, and swiped the card. The trick was to swipe it properly, neither too fast nor too slow. L.T. felt like a man who could not spell words.

"Can I get cash?"

"Forty max," the man said.

"I'll take the forty."

The plan was to draw his money out of the account gradually, first in smaller sums, then larger. He worried they would take his money or freeze his account. The government had that kind of power. But it was his money, he had worked for it, earning scrap wages and building up savings. The parole board had considered this fact at L.T.'s hearing.

The man put the bottles in a plastic sack. L.T. collected the matches and cigarettes in one hand and carried the sack by the loops. The security tone sounded as he passed through the glass doors a second time.

He looked up the street. He could walk that way again, retracing his steps back to the motel, or else he could turn right and walk the other way around, which appeared to be the shorter route. He decided on this direction, as it seemed the faster of the two.

Rounding the corner he saw a girl, a young woman, standing alone under the streetlight. She wore very high heels and a skirt that hardly covered her backside. Her legs were gangly, all bones and ankles, and she wore a tube-top over her knobby chest. A full-length tattoo covered one shoulder and arm. Vines and flowers it looked like. An ugly thing, whatever it was. L.T. was sure there was a record of it somewhere, a photograph clipped inside a police file. Her eyes were painted green and her hair fell down in ratty strands. She was loitering beside a phone booth, under the streetlamp, clutching a small purse under one arm. It appeared she was waiting for an urgent phone call. But the booth was empty, the payphone removed or stolen, even the directory was missing. The glass doors were scratched white and the metal surface from top to bottom was defaced with gang tags and lewd drawings and every known obscenity.

Parked along the curb was a red Mazda with black windows and no hubcaps. L.T. glanced at the license plate.

"Hold up," the girl said. "Let me get a light."

The cigarettes were in his hand. L.T. paused and looked at the girl. Here was a situation. Maybe it was nothing. In any case he felt a spike in his chest, a small thorn of worry. He glanced in two directions.

"Is that your car?" she said.

He did not answer. He looked back to see if anyone was coming up behind him.

"That's not your car?"

L.T. looked at the car. The rear window was tinted. He didn't see anybody inside.

"Give me a light real quick," she said.

He studied the bushes and the corners. He looked for any place a person might hide. He listened intently. Up the street he saw a figure, the shadow of a man, sitting on the sidewalk with his back against a brick wall. The traffic light at the intersection was red.

"Who's up there?" said L.T.

The woman looked up the street.

"That guy?" she said. "Shit if I know."

"What are you doing here? You waiting for somebody?"

"Yeah, I'm waiting for somebody," she said, like it was nobody's business.

L.T. took a slow look around. Say someone came out of the shadows. The six-pack in his left hand could do some damage. He was glad they were bottles and not aluminum cans. You could use a bottle like a club, if necessary. You could smash a bottle, if you absolutely had to, and cut somebody.

L.T. said, "You want a light or not?"

The girl opened her purse.

"You got a cigarette I can borrow?" she asked.

"You ask me for a light and you don't even have a cigarette?"

"I gave away my last one."

"So you want a cigarette and a light. Is this what you're saying?"

"*Holy mother of God*," she said, "forget I asked."

The woman was a user, crystal meth or heroin, a chronic nosebleeder, a prostitute. Feeling both disgust and pity L.T. relented. He looped the bag over his left forearm to keep both hands free as he tore the film off the pack of cigarettes and opened the foil wrapper. He tapped out a cigarette and gave it to the woman.

"Appreciate it," she said. "What's your name?"

He tucked the pack into his shirt pocket. He struck a match and met her cigarette with the glow of the flame.

"Goodnight," he said, tossing the match into the street.

"Hang on a minute," she said. "Let me walk with you."

"You don't know where I'm going."

"Just to the corner," she said, "past that guy up there."

"What are you afraid of?"

"I don't know, look at him. What's he doing?"

"He's a bum, it looks like."

"What if he tries something? I can't run in these shoes."

"Those aren't shoes," he said.

"What's wrong with my shoes?"

"Listen," he said to her, "I don't want anything."

She took a drag from her cigarette.

"You what?"

"I don't want anything," he told her. "You understand?"

"What's that supposed to mean?"

"Listen, I just got out of the joint. A cop rolls up and sees me with you? See what I'm saying? They run me back inside."

"Let me walk with you is all I'm asking. What's the crime in that?"

"Look at you, dressed the way you're dressed, out here in the middle of the night."

"How am I dressed?"

"Come on," he said. "What do you want from me? You want me to walk you somewhere? To the stoplight, the intersection?"

"Past that guy is all. At the light you go one way, I go the other," she said. "Why are you looking at me like that?"

L.T. carried the bag in his left hand. The girl's shoes were loud, clopping on the sidewalk. He pulled the bag tight, looping the straps around his fist. He was ready with the bottles. The word that came to mind was *circumspect*. As in *walk circumspectly*. He could swing the bag if he had to.

"Why were you in jail?"

"I committed a crime."

"What crime?"

"That's my business."

"I didn't know it was a secret," she said. "How long were you in? Or is that another secret?"

"A long time."

"And you don't want a friend?"

He glanced at her without answering. Her heels clopped on the sidewalk. They were so tall she could hardly walk straight. Her body wobbled with each step.

"You got weird priorities," she said, "getting out of jail and all. Any man I know would be all over it."

"I don't doubt that."

"Why would you? It's the first thing, right? You got to take care of first things first."

"Is that the rule?"

"I'm only saying."

"I know what you're saying."

As they approached the bum on the sidewalk, the girl danced behind L.T. and walked on the street side. But the drunk was passed out, harmless. An old man in piss trousers.

"You know him?"

"I've seen him around," she said. "I don't like him. He tried to grab me one time."

"You're making it up."

They reached the intersection where the girl tossed her cigarette in the street.

"Let me write down my number," she said.

"I'm walking the other way."

"What do I owe you?" he heard her say, "for the cigarette?"

"Go home," he said.

When he reached the motel he crept up the stairwell and used the key-card to open his room. It took three tries to make the door work. Everything involved a card and a swipe. He was out of breath now. He closed the door and locked the bolt. He turned on the yellow lamp, set the beer on the table next to the television, and rested in the armchair by the curtains.

When his heart calmed down he turned on the television and muted the volume. He made himself comfortable in the chair, reached into the sack for a bottle, twisted the cap, and set it on the table. This was how he had always imagined it. First the cigarette, then the beer. He pulled the cigarettes out of his shirt front and tapped one out. He set the pack on the table. The beer was sparkling and cold. He could smell the cigarette, the dry tobacco.

He was about to light the cigarette when he heard a knock at the door. The police, he thought, who else could it be? Someone saw him with the girl, a known streetwalker, and phoned it in. L.T. did not move. He regretted turning on the lamps. The rule to observe was *lights out*. Now the knock sounded again. He could feel the blood-drum deep inside his ears. He stood up and parted the curtains with one finger. He was only half relieved to discover no police were outside his door. It was the girl. She frowned at him. Gesturing at the door impatiently she banged on it a third time.

The muscles in his stomach tightened. He turned the deadbolt and opened the door.

"What's wrong with you?" he said. "Why are you following me?"

"Let me in," she said.

L.T. scanned the stairs and the rooms down either side of the corridor. Every orange door had a metal number affixed to it and the windows of all the rooms were dark. He looked over her shoulder at the parking lot below.

"Open the door, please. I'm asking you."

28

She tried pushing against the door but L.T. held her back.

"You're not coming inside," he told her. "What are you thinking?"

"Hear me out," she said.

"No, I won't, I won't hear you out. You don't know me. We don't have any business together."

She stared at him like a part of her brain was on hold, like somebody had knocked her in the head.

"Go on," he said. "Get out of here."

"All right," she said, "I'll go. Just let me use the bathroom first."

"Not here you won't."

"Then I'll leave you alone, swear to God. That's what you want, right?"

"I told you I'm a convict. It's a violation."

"It's not a violation," she said. "What violation? It's a free country."

"I'm on parole."

"So what *parole*. No one cares about *parole*."

"Are you stupid or something?"

"I'll be quiet. You want me to be quiet, don't you? Because I can be a crazy loud bitch if given half a reason."

"I want you to go, please."

"Not until I use the bathroom," she said. "Then I'll go. You'll never see me again."

Any other man at any other time would slam the door in her face or else call the police. That's what a normal person would do. Call the authorities and let them sort it out. Every cop in town probably knew her by name, or whatever name she used, whatever she called herself. But how would it look for him, a convict on parole, to get mixed up like this with a hooker his first night out of the joint? How could he explain it to them? There would be handcuffs, a backseat ride to the county jail, a hearing, a review of his parole.

He pleaded with her. "Listen," he said, "I don't want trouble. You're giving me grief here."

"I'm doing what you said."

"What's that supposed to mean?"

"I'll tell you in a minute."

"God damnit," he said. "Help me here!"

L.T. let the door swing open. He yielded to her as she pushed through. He was being played, it was obvious, but he didn't know what else to do.

The girl stormed inside and L.T. closed the door behind her. He locked the bolt and secured the chain in its slot, and then he waited for the next thing.

He could see the tattoo on her arm clearly now, a pattern of roses, each about the size of a quarter. The ink started above her wrist and crawled up her arm and twisted over her right shoulder. A climbing vine of rose petals and green thorns.

"My man's looking for me," she said.

"Don't tell me about your man. I don't want to hear about your man. There's the bathroom. Hurry it up."

"You don't believe me? If you want I can describe his car."

"Just do your thing and leave," he said. "I'm not interested in details."

"I owe him money. I got to work tonight or else I can't go home." She ran her fingers through her hair. "You told me to go home, but what about my debt? I got to work, simple as that. I got to make money. Then I pay my man and go home."

She waited for a response.

"Do I look stupid to you?" L.T. said. "Why are you doing this? What did I do to you? I helped you is what I did. Didn't I help you? Didn't I give you a cigarette and let you walk with me?"

"You think I'm lying."

"Look at me. Do I care if you're lying or not? I'm not involved here. Go to the bathroom. Do whatever you need to do and then leave me the hell alone."

"You said that already."

"But you're still here. That's what I can't understand."

She closed the bathroom door behind her and turned the lock. L.T. switched off the television set. He reached under the shade and turned off the lamp. It was dark in the room. He pulled the curtain and surveyed the parking lot through the window. He looked for a guy sitting in a parked car or out roaming the lot. He saw no one, but he was not pleased. He was not at all pleased. His first day out and things were already a mess. He closed the curtain again and turned on the lamp. He put a cigarette in his mouth but did not light it. He would wait until after the girl was gone. He hitched his pants and sat down in the chair again. He knew better than to go out at night. He had violated a basic rule. And this is what happens when you violate it.

When the girl came out of the bathroom L.T. bolted up from his chair. The girl was stark naked, scraggy limbs and all.

"No, no," L.T. said. The cigarette fell out of his mouth. "What are you doing? Don't do that!"

The girl was flat-chested and hairless. She looked like a child standing awkwardly tall in her mother's shoes. Only she was not a child and did not resemble one by any means. Her body was gangly and pale, starved at the waist, and one leg was badly bruised. She was bony in the shoulders and hips, a white corrugated thing with a scab habit.

What he tried to do was look away. He saw her clothes lying in a loose pile on the bathroom floor. An old scripture came to mind, *do not sow among thorns*.

"Put your clothes on."

"A hundred dollars," she said. "Whatever you want."

He was losing his balance. The room tipped one way and then the other. L.T. braced himself. He tried to draw an easy breath.

"You get dressed," he said.

"What's wrong with you?"

"Do what I said."

"You just got out of jail."

"That's right. Now, get dressed like I told you."

"I'll take sixty-five."

"It's not the money."

"You're an asshole is what it is," she said. "What are you, *queer*?"

She grabbed her clothes off the floor and as she began to dress she let her words fly. L.T. glanced at her but did not stare. This was her scheme. To work herself inside and put him to it.

She picked up her purse and came toward him.

"I don't strip for free," she said.

"What are you talking about?"

"You heard me. I don't strip for less than fifty dollars."

"You want fifty dollars? Get the hell out of my room!"

"I'll call the cops."

"You're out of your mind."

"You don't think I'll call?" she said. "I'll tell them you tried to rape me."

"Rape you!"

"Let's have it."

He wanted to drag her outside and throw her over the rail. But he couldn't do that, he wouldn't do it. He only wanted her to leave. It was his motel room and he wanted her out. L.T. shoved his fist into his pocket. He had the two twenty-dollar bills. He tossed the money on the bed.

"That's all I've got," he said. "Forty bucks."

"I said fifty. Did I not strip for you? That was the deal or I'm calling the cops."

"I told you. It's all the cash I've got. What else do you want?"

"You ain't got nothing else," she said.

She took the money off the bed and grabbed the plastic bag with the beer inside. The bag and its contents belonged to her now. L.T. did not move. She unlocked the chain on the door. The cigarettes and matches on the table were hers also. Whatever she wanted. The open bottle of beer, she took that too. She slammed the door behind her and clopped down the stairwell.

L.T.'s hands were shaky. He felt sick all over and unsteady. His whole body was trembling. He had broken a sweat and feeling soft in the head he thought he should sit down now or else lie down.

The woman was gone but there was a chance she might return. In the dark he listened for the sound of her shoes on the stairs. He would not open the door again or even draw back the curtains.

Twenty-nine years, ten months, and fourteen days. He was back in the world.

Chapter 3

Virginia walked into the whiskey bar on Vine. No reason to rush home. She had given her coffee, a half-cup, to a homeless man with scabby lips.

She liked the woodwork in this place, the bottles on the shelves under the lighted archways, the brick walls, the hanging lamps. A band was setting up to play. Virginia took an open chair at the end of the crowded bar and ordered an Irish whiskey neat. She knew the bartender, Jason, or knew his name anyway. He was a cute guy and he recognized her and that was enough. Walking into a bar alone made her feel middle-aged. The thought of flirting with a hardworking bartender every time he came around was simply too much. Someone else could take him home.

She did not want to dwell on certain facts of her existence. Her lack of genuine friendships, for example. Her friends were mothers with children, people from the support groups, and she wasn't in contact with them anymore. Either you were in the group or you were off the radar. Virginia was off the radar. On campus she had colleagues. Colleagues were acquaintances, not friends. They were the people you sat next to in meetings, people you waved at in passing on the way to class, people you smiled at, politely, in the copy room. And then of course the dating issue, or non-issue as it were. Virginia's days were marked by an absence of life-dialogue, her nights by an empty bed.

For now this little corner of the bar belonged to her exclusively. It was noisy in the back, crowd volume, everybody facing the other way and talking. Virginia glanced at a wall of backs and asses. She was the woman at the end of the bar taking up treasured space. She tossed back the whiskey and ordered the same. At sixteen dollars a glass she'd have to nurse the second drink. She couldn't see the band from where she was sitting but the music was good and loud. Daydream music with an echo pop. Heavy synth and cloud-drift vocals.

Virginia wanted to get drunk but she knew she could not afford to hold the corner all night. After the second glass of Redbreast she sent a text to her sister in Citrus Heights. Amanda worked with her husband, Justin, in the door business. They installed doors. They had twin girls, Gilda and Hadley. Babies with old names. That was the new trend and the photo stream was endless. The girls in the pool. The girls eating and sleeping. The girls wearing their new outfits. At this hour they would be asleep in their cribs and Amanda would be watching a movie with her husband, something with stripper's tits and crude humor. They were small-business Republicans, under thirty and debt free, do-it-yourselfers who drove four-wheel-drive pickups. They spent whole vacations riding dirt bikes and posting photos of craft brews and porterhouse steaks.

"What are you doing?" Virginia wrote.

"Hi. Watching a movie."

"Girls asleep?"

"They're both sick again."

"Poor darlings," she said. "Timothy's with Neil this weekend."

"I'm sure you can use the break."

"Did mom tell you about Travis Hilliard?"

"Any plans?"

"No. Too much work. Finals next week."

"Yeah, she told."

"How do you feel about it?"

"I don't know. It's kind of weird. You?"

"Mom didn't even go to the parole hearing. I would've gone if I'd known about it."

"She's coming down next weekend to stay overnight with the girls. We're going to a business convention in San Fran."

"Door convention? How exciting."

"Shut up."

"Seriously, what goes on at a door convention?"

"Networking," her sister said.

Virginia ordered another drink and closed out her tab. Three drinks, fifty-five dollars including the tip. She was not really surprised by her sister's lack of concern. It was different for Amanda. She never knew their father. To her the man was no more than a photograph, a name seldom mentioned, a story their mother never wanted to tell. If there was any sense of loss Amanda was only vaguely aware of it. The circumstances surrounding his death remained abstract, unformulated. Amanda was only three when their mother remarried, and while she knew growing up that Ed West was not her biological father, Ed was her dad and she called him that. He adopted her and gave her his last name before she was old enough to choose for herself. Amanda West and Virginia Bigelow, two sisters eight years apart. They were so unlike each other in age, appearance, and temperament that it seemed fitting to grow up with different last names.

During the long pause Virginia set her phone on the bar. She listened to the music and heard parts of conversations. She watched the two bartenders, Jason and the other one, coordinate their movements behind the bar. The specialty drinks were popular. Drinks mixed with egg whites and chocolate bitters, sweet vermouth and cinnamon. She read the labels on the whiskey bottles shelved across from her. Whistle Pig Rye. Monkey Shoulder Malt. More people crowded into the bar looking for table space or room to stand. Dressed in all black, three tall waitresses floated through the crowd carrying drinks on trays.

A blond guy in a tight blue shirt leaned in next to her. He wedged himself between Virginia and the girl to her left and waited for the bartender. He smelled good. Virginia picked up her phone.

"Mind if I squeeze in?" he asked.

"No, you're fine," she said. "It's perfectly fine."

He tried to signal the bartender. Then he turned and smiled at Virginia. He stared at her.

"Matt," he said.

"That can't be your real name," she said. "Matts always have dark hair."

He smiled. "Matthias."

"Matthias," she said. "I like that much better. Matthias is fantastic, an amazing name. Congratulations. Never go by Matt. Matt is so depressing. Matthias, however."

In high school they called her Virgin, but by that time she was already familiar with sex. Her first time was with Brian Lepke in ninth grade. She was the girl climbing quietly out the bedroom window at night, the girl behind the roller rink on East Seventh Street waiting for the boy to show. Vodka and orange juice, a couple of cigarettes. Because it was bound to happen eventually. Two kids behind a wall.

Matthias asked, "Are you waiting for someone?"

Virginia shook her head. She could feel the whiskey. She had let Brian Lepke feel under her bra, his hand both hard and soft on her chest, and she did not stop him later when he reached his fingers under her skirt.

"You're in my corner," she said.

"Am I?"

Matthias laughed.

"What's in the glass?" he asked.

"Redbreast, it's Irish."

"Like another?"

Virginia shrugged. Who could say no? Matthias ordered the two drinks. She remembered making out with Brian Lepke with cinematic fervor. It was a grownup thing they were doing, absolutely forbidden, but it was almost infantile in its pleasures, the way hard tongues mingle with soft mouths, or the primal company of finger and cleft.

"I would offer you a chair," she said.

"No worries. I like standing. It's the whole reason for shoes."

"What's the point of pants then if you're not sitting down?"

"What?"

"I said, what's the point of wearing pants if you're not sitting down."

"Should I take them off? Take off my pants?"

"I don't think you need them. Not if you plan on standing."

She could tell what it looked like, she could describe its size and shape, by the way it felt in her hand. She tried to figure out how best to do this. She wanted to get it right the first time.

"My friends are over there," he said. "You should come over."

Sex on the ground behind the roller rink. She assumed it would go in no problem, just lay on the blanket and wait for it. But it didn't fit or didn't glide so easily and she was forced to maneuver it herself, to find the correct angle, with Brian Lepke on top bracing himself, leaning this way and that.

"I can't do it," she said.

"Why not?"

"I can't give up my chair."

Her first real boyfriend. Vital to the excitement, a crucial element, was finding a place to have sex. At home or at a friend's house. Parents at work or out of town. Sex in different beds.

The drinks came and they touched glasses.

"We have a table, plenty of room."

"I'm kidding," she said. "It's not that. Actually, I was about to leave. I already closed out my tab."

She showed him the receipt.

"That's no reason to leave," he said. "Come say hello."

"Where are they? Your friends."

He reached for her hand.

"Wait, I have to use the restroom first."

"Can you see where I'm pointing?"

Virginia stood on her toes and looked. "I see two guys with a girl. Are they your friends?"

He nodded.

"I'll take your drink," he said.

Lepke, Lepke, Lepke.

Virginia cut through the crowd. At the restroom she took her place in line behind two girls on their phones. Matthias. He was what, thirty? Incredibly good looking. Stupidly handsome. A swimmer maybe. An oarsman. Long powerful limbs overreaching the length of her bed. This was him trying to get laid, she thought. He had no idea. She would take him home, like Calypso, and keep him until the gods raged against her.

On the toilet, however, she discovered she was bleeding. *Oh no, no, no. Oh shit, no!* She wasn't carrying anything in her purse. *You've got to be kidding.* She tried to remember her last period and counted the weeks between. It was definitely early. She looked through her purse again. There was a line outside the door. Matthias was waiting at the table.

Virginia sat pale-legged on the toilet, under the hard fluorescent lights, stunned with whiteness. There was blood on her underwear. She felt faint, a little dizzy. She could taste the alcohol in her mouth. She improvised a thick humiliating wad of toilet paper, fixed it underneath, and flushed.

Moving sidelong through the crowded bar she slipped outside without saying goodbye. Because there would be this whole thing otherwise. A fabricated excuse, a phone number, the awkward pressure to stay. The risk was too high. She might leak through the tissue and then what? Anyway, whatever connection they might have had, whatever attraction, no longer mattered. What mattered was sex, every which way, sex in a dark room, the smell of a man's body, his weight upon her, and this was no longer an option.

Virginia let go of the heavy door. Gone were the warm lights, the music, the cocktails and festive voices. Matthias would look for her coming out of the bathroom, wait for her until it became weirdly obvious. Then he'd shrug his shoulders and laugh about it because what else can you do? The odd girl in the corner of the bar.

She practically ran home to her apartment, cutting through traffic, crossing against red and yellow lights. When a Metro driver laid on the horn, Virginia threw her hands up in bold defiance. It almost hit her, the bus, almost knocked her flat. After that she wanted to scream, she wanted to hurt somebody.

At home she wiped between her legs and flushed the gob of tissue down the toilet. She got undressed and ran the shower. Early in life she learned the best place to cry was in the shower with the door locked. The nearly scalding water, the smell of steam and bodywash. Virginia got in and fixed the curtain like always. Under the showerhead, she pulled back her wet hair and began to cry deliberate tears, violent tears. As the water washed over, she thought of her own sprawling death. Her body laid out on the avenue, the police cars and paramedics, the horrifically shitty end.

Chapter 4

L.T. moved from the bed to the window carrying all the soreness of poor sleep. Pulling aside the heavy curtain he peered at a cloudless sky. Across the way he saw two women pushing a service cart with white towels and plastic spray bottles. He would forget about last night, try to put the shame of it behind him.

Soon he showered in hot water and steam, washed his hair, shaved afterward. Day two wearing the same clothes. He was hungry, almost sick with appetite. He had forgotten what it felt like to walk outside in the morning, to cross a busy street against traffic, to visit a diner and sidle into a red vinyl booth with a window view of the avenue. He set his bag snug against the wall. Three old men were sitting at the counter reading newspapers and talking. Behind him sat a young couple with a baby in a highchair. They were speaking an Asian language, although he could not say which one. L.T. looked at the cakes and pies displayed in a glass case near the cash register. Behind the counter the waitress was fixing a pot of coffee. It occurred to him that he could sit here alone without posing a threat to anyone. He could eat without looking over his shoulder like an animal.

The waitress, a woman in her fifties, wore a gold-colored outfit with a large diamond pattern. She had a decent figure, a sturdy hourglass shape aided by the design of her dress which made her waist look smaller than it was. She set a menu in front of L.T. and a glass of ice water with a straw. *Lynette* was the name on her tag. L.T. examined the faded photographs on the menu. Swedish pancakes, Belgian waffles, omelets with fried potatoes. The idea of ordering what you liked, and then to eat it at your own pace, was something to remark. He drank the water, which tasted like the chlorinated stuff of swimming pools, the kind you choked on when you swam up for air too quickly.

The waitress came over with a pad in her hand. L.T. tried to remember if he had ever known anyone named Lynette. He thought of Tammy Wynette and Loretta Lynn, but he could not recall anyone named Lynette. He ordered bacon and eggs, biscuits and gravy, black coffee.

"How do you like your eggs?"

"I've eaten scrambled eggs every morning for as long as I can remember. So let's change it up, Lynette."

"Over easy?"

"I like the sound of that," L.T. said.

She wrote it all down.

"Anything else?"

"No, that's more than enough," he said. "Food served on a round plate is a privilege where I'm from."

"Where's that?"

"I shouldn't tell."

"Would I be worried?"

"You're the first real woman I've spoken to in decades."

"You don't look like a monk," she said. "What are you drinking?"

The cup on the table was upside down. L.T. turned it over.

"Black," he said.

These were not his words. The sound of his own voice seemed unfamiliar to him, disingenuous—his impersonation of another man. He was quiet by nature and disciplined in the art of hard silence. He knew these were dull things to say to a strange woman. He could hold long conversations with a concrete wall but a woman was a different matter. He had embarrassed himself by addressing the woman by name. How long had she worked in places like this, lunch cafés and all-night diners, and how many dim-witted conversations had she suffered in the company of lonely men?

The woman reminded him of his mother, Darlene. She had been a waitress too, in a nightclub, which L.T. was never allowed to enter. Later he understood it was a strip joint. More than once he sat alone in the car for hours, late into the night, waiting for his mother to take him home. She slept while he dressed for school. He would see her sprawled under the covers, a glimpse through the open bedroom door, her hair tossed, one foot uncovered. Then all afternoon she moved around the kitchen in her bathrobe smoking cigarettes and talking on the telephone. There would be a bottle of nail polish on the table and a glass of beer or wine. She was always short on money, always counting out dollar bills hoping they would add up to something. Mostly she depended on her good looks, her curly blond hair and sweet perfume.

Maybe that's why this waitress, Lynette, reminded him of her. She was blond also, although it was all color added. He supposed, in her last years, his mother did the same. But his mother was pretty when she was young. Pretty enough to bring a man home when she wanted. Some free bird with shaggy sideburns walking around the house in his undershorts. Or else leaning under the hood of some grease machine out on the driveway. His mother always talked about marrying a rich man, but she only dated shoeless types who fit a certain description, guys who lived according to her schedule, who played solitaire on the coffee table and drank all the beer in the refrigerator.

She drove a 1964 Plymouth, a silver Barracuda, with twin black racing stripes extending from hood to trunk. Everyone liked her in that car and L.T. was always proud to see her in it. Twice during the first year of L.T.'s confinement she came up to San Quentin. Once in the summer, and then again around Christmas. She sent letters after that, two or three every year, always apologizing for not visiting enough, or for not being a better mother. Five years into his term she committed suicide in her apartment in San Bernardino—*single white female, age fifty-four, dead of an overdose, no notes.*

There was more to it, more to her life, but L.T. could never lay hold of it. He had spent plenty of time trying to figure it out, years and years in fact, only to realize in the end how little he knew the woman, and he decided that was normal. He dropped out of high school sophomore year, 1971, left home to work in an oil field with his two friends Richey Muncy and Lyle Durst, and never lived with his mother again. She married and divorced a man named Ron Wilby, who once had money and lost it, and then she remained unmarried for the rest of her life. An alcoholic, always near an ashtray of stubby menthols, awake by night wherever the lights were dim and the music was loud and there was laughter. She had known too many men and had learned never to rely on them. And she died before L.T.'s conversion, so he never had a chance to write her a letter addressing the deeper issues of the soul. His mother didn't talk about God, did not attend church. She had her palm read from time to time, but like following the horoscope in the Sunday newspaper, this was merely an entertainment. He knew there was no point in trying to intercede for her soul now that she had passed on. And although he wanted to think of his mother as reborn, refashioned according to some glorified form, it never matched. Still, he refused to interpret his lack of imagination as a sign of knowing, and he resolved never to think of her as a lost soul.

In prison he read his Bible several times through. He read it and studied it and came to depend on it like a man who looks daily into the mirror. He desired to know it inside and out and wanted to believe it, to immerse the weary heart in that wisdom which quiets the mind. He did not know exactly why or how he came to believe. It was partly irrational. His faith emerged from his foolishness, and his faith made foolishness of all the rest. It was a man's choice to believe or not to believe, but faith was also a thing given to a man, inexplicably, and not to him alone. L.T. had witnessed many conversions on the inside. For most it was an act of despair but that fact did not rob the experience of its truth or meaning. And when men fell away, as they sometimes did, their apostasy did not negate the faith. Their misery was ever present. It circulated the cellblock in various forms, guilt, fear, isolation. Even the boredom inside the penitentiary, the monotony, was suffocating to the point of death. And then there was time itself, the low crawl of every day, the empty hands, the stomach rumble, a dry mouth in a dry cell. L.T. needed a God who could walk through the walls, a God whose wounds he could reach out and touch.

It was that radical. The first days and months of conversion. A teary-eyed sin-cleansing prayer. It was a measure of faith given by God himself. A crystal vision of the sacred and divine, of powers and principalities of the air, of bodies raised from graves. Soul clarity and the beginning of revelation. Bind the strong man and plunder his possessions. This was prison ministry. It was the great purpose of the man in chains, the upward call of God that Wayne Scott had talked about.

Wayne Scott was a black TV preacher doing six years for embezzlement. He robbed his flock to snort cocaine and jack-ramble the hookers on Sunset Boulevard. That was his testimony. Temptation and perversion and the fall of man. He had a wife and four children, preached three services every Sunday morning, two thousand souls rocking in the pews. They watched Wayne Scott wipe his forehead under the bright lights. He shouted *Glory Hallelujah!* He preached, heated up the auditorium. In prophetic outrage he paced the carpeted stage and flapped the winged scriptures and fell into fits of holy laughter. *Wayne Scott was pimped out and golden*: his own words, speaking in the third person. He had become Satan's minion, an instrument of hypocrisy. The velvet money groper, the midnight prowler in red polyester.

He would say the word, *Redeemed!* He would say it to the men gathering around the prison yard. The other word was *Sanctified!* Sanctified by the blood of the Lamb. Because the Almighty had broken him over the stone. *Behold the terrible hand of God*, he would say. Because Wayne Scott deserved AIDS and dying, or a gunshot to the heart, or a suicide syringe. Like every man in that prison, in that tomb, Wayne Scott deserved death and the fiery furnace. It was God's mercy alone that brought him to this place. *The law is for the lawless*, he would say, *punishment for creeps and thieves.*

L.T. remembered clearly the day Wayne Scott surveyed the small crowd of men gathering around the yard and started to speak to them. *I know you needy*, he said. *Y'all some needy folk. I ain't no different. This is Wayne Scott I'm talking about. Wayne Scott's the neediest of the needy. Hypocrite of the hypocrites. You tell me you got words to speak. I say, speak! You say, I got some sorrows you wouldn't believe. I hear you, brother. I hear you. Wayne Scott's got me some sorrows too. But I got the Word in me and the word of God says he knows my sorrows.*

L.T. was among those who came near to hear the man preach.

What you want then? he said. *A word of purpose? Search your rotten hearts, dear brothers. The heart is wicked above all things. Look upon your bloodshed and devastation. That's the word. Repent of your sins is the word. Follow the path of righteousness, which is the same for all men, black or white don't matter. I mean, shit, look around. The cell, the yard, chow hall, work detail. It's howlin' up in here, man! All this hatred and pain. And the violence*, he said, *of an evil man's hands. Who here knows what I'm talking about? The sickass thrill of it. You dig what I'm saying? This is the valley of shadows I'm talking about. You alone in here, motherfucker. That's right. And you better wipe that smirk off your face. Am I right?*

Yes, Wayne Scott was right. Men gathered around and listened intently. Hard men, men of bloodshed, the world's merciless bastards.

Wayne Scott pleaded with them. *You men are brothers of the light*, he said, *but you don't know it yet because you slaves to the enemy, blind to the Serpent of Old. Men like wheat on the threshing floor is what I'm saying. Men like grapes in the winepress. Hear me? What you need is the blood. That's what I'm talking about. The blood sacrifice. That's all that separates life and death, my brothers.*

The blood. Who here got it? Any y'all got the blood? That's what I thought. Ain't none of you got it. Go on then and weep, you goddamn sinners, chew your bitter herbs, for the shadow of death is upon you.

And how they were like the first disciples that year, proclaiming the message of the cross to raise up dead souls. L.T. had become something unrecognizable to himself, an evangelist in prison blues, talking it up to the inmates and guards in the chow hall and out around the dirt track. And some would hear what he had to say and others would turn him back, sometimes with threat of bodily harm, but he was free to turn the other cheek, free to walk away in shame. It was the last beatitude, the joy of persecution.

Wayne Scott called it a spirit of revival. It was a wildfire that burned through a season of drought and wind, and then it was like smoke and scorched hills, and then it was over. Wayne Scott was released on good behavior, others transferred out, new men came and joined the effort, but that first feeling of power and urgency was gone. The word is *unction*. L.T. had tried to get it back. He fasted and prayed for more *unction*. He read deeply into the scriptures, spent whole days studying history and context. He became familiar with special lexicons and concordances borrowed from the prison library. He had nothing but time. Time for obsessive cross-referencing, time to turn the papery pages, time for targeted study and verse recital. But where the knowledge increased, the ministry grew quiet, ineffective on a large scale, reduced finally to a small remnant of men drinking coffee and praying for courage.

They were there now, as a matter of fact, sitting at the regular table during the usual hour. Carlos Esposito and Ron Wannamaker and Chris Fritz. L.T.'s cellmate, Frank Teller. The bowler, Carl Woolley. Today they would covet his freedom. Together they would tell stories about life on the outside, stories about food and women.

L.T. stared at his breakfast. Soon even the novelty of fried eggs would fade into the routine of every day. He listened to the silver sound of his own utensils. Behind him the baby fussed and cried and that was fine. *Suffer the little children.* Occasionally the waitress came over to fill his cup with coffee. She wore nude pantyhose. He imagined her pulling them up to her waist in the morning dark.

Chapter 5

It was Saturday and she felt untethered, a little dreamy after a long night of broken sleep and an early morning run. She would finish grading papers this afternoon, gear up for finals week, cut out the drinking. No word from Neil, which meant Timothy was fine. They would take him to the pier and feed him ice cream, and the girl, the girlfriend, would tie a balloon around Timothy's wrist and babble into his ear.

Tomorrow Virginia would take him back. Until then she would have to tolerate an empty apartment. Not empty, but inanimate. Timothy's absence, his nonappearance, left the air undisturbed. The effect was unsettling. Virginia missed his small roving body, how he maneuvered between furnishings, claiming the territory, forming patterns of attachment to solid objects. He avoided anything soft. Pillows, stuffed animals, his mother's embrace. He preferred hard surfaces, the flat aspects of counters and walls. In the living room he tapped the black television screen and the fish tank. Passing the bookshelves he tapped the spines and edges of his mother's books. They were short and tall, thick and thin, but the words inside were irrelevant. Timothy had no patience for books of any kind. He could not sit still on his mother's lap enduring the turned pages. In the kitchen he tapped the lower cupboards and drawers, the oven door, the stainless-steel refrigerator. There he stood with his mouth pressed against the cold metal, staring at his blank reflection and making the fog appear. Or else he continued past the refrigerator to the sliding glass door where he paused, pressed his face against the window, and made the fog with his breath. Sometimes he tapped the palm of his left hand with his right finger, other times he stuck his fingers in his ears and made tiny pulsating thrusts. If he grew tired or bored he might sprawl on the linoleum floor with both eyes shut maintaining a stillness close to death. But mostly he drifted in and out of rooms, opening and closing the doors. Often Virginia followed his movements, analyzing his routines and practices, trying to understand why some situations, like doors left open, were so intolerable to him. Other times she did her own thing, fixed dinner or watched television or graded papers, aware but not entirely aware of what Timothy was doing, acknowledging his presence, on some level, and noting his absence, or confusing one for the other. He was there and he was not there.

Virginia glanced at her watch. It was one of those rare mornings when time passed slowly, when she kept looking at her watch thinking it must be later.

Her path that morning had taken her by the public library and a banner promoting a photo exhibit and art sale. There was a book Virginia wanted to borrow, Eckman's study of facial expressions called *Unmasking the Face*. For weeks she had been meaning to search the library for it, so after the run she showered, had coffee, and drove back to the library where she parked in the garage across the street.

Beyond the entryway were signs marking the event, arrows pointing downstairs, people filing down. But first, following the call numbers, Virginia found the book in the stacks and stood in line at the circulation desk. The cover was dreadful, seven headshots of a woman making ugly faces. The woman looked insane, like a person with rival personalities. Inside the book were more photos like these. People expressing emotion. Disgust, anger, sadness. The book was cheaply printed and colorless but that wasn't the point. The point was to learn how to read a face, how to pick up on visual cues. Virginia thought it might help her decode Timothy's moods. Often his demeanor was flat, unreadable, unless perhaps she was missing something, an elusive set of clues available only to the qualified eye.

Virginia put the book into her handbag, crossed the strap over her shoulder, and followed several people into the exhibit room where long cafeteria tables were loaded end to end with boxed photographs. Some were displayed in metal frames, others meticulously organized in heavy albums. Most were stacked in random piles.

On one table sat an unattended box of aged black and white portraits. These were mixed with tinted photographs of women in flowery dresses and men in black shoes and dungarees. Seeing these photos reminded her of the old words, the language of old people, their odd dialects, how people used to speak of things. The photos in the box were jumbled, generations of people displaced in time, their names missing. These were mixed with color prints of cars and Christmas trees and newborn babies. Virginia liked how the tones had faded, how the colors had aged, the rosy hues of past decades. She saw Polaroids of fishing trips and pink birthday cakes and sunbathers in full-bodied swimsuits.

People closed in around her, a man's hand reaching over to grab a stack, another man shouldering up to the same table. Virginia's privacy existed in the space between her hands. Three by five and four by six. These were older photos, early twentieth century, before people were made to smile. Large rural families, one of them an Ozark clan, standing before the camera, parents and grandparents and their posse of children all shacked up for a time, now saturated in rusty iodine and grim despair. But she knew it wasn't that awful. From what she had learned, from the stories she'd heard told, photos like these conveyed the wrong impression of past generations. Their lives were not as miserable as their dour portraits suggested. The real issue was technical, involving light sensitivity and shutter speeds. It was a matter of having to hold still for so many seconds to avoid blurring the image. But this photo was sharp and clear, each face etched in fabulous detail, eyes in perfect focus. Virginia admired the hard stare. It required discipline. It was pure technique.

She moved to another table. She said excuse me and squeezed in between. These photos were also in boxes but they were organized by subject. Circus photos, pictures of children, portraits of soldiers at war. There was an entire box of photos with someone's finger in the way of the lens. A face blotted out, or some part of the landscape. There were blurry photos, or photos focused incorrectly, so that the girl in the foreground was blurry but the blue flowers behind her were perfectly clear. Virginia recognized the flowers. They were hydrangeas. How much for this one? She held on to it.

There were photos of people running, and sometimes it was the runner who was blurry and other times it was people in the background. There were photos of women. Photos of brown afros, golden bobs, and red beehives. Photos of ashtrays and people holding cigarettes. Passport photos and mug shots. Photos with a man removed, an ex-boyfriend or husband, a missing father. Photos strategically torn to exclude an unwanted person.

"What are you interested in?" the man said to her. He was eightyish and balding, wearing glasses. Before this he was busying himself with the contents of an open trunk. "What do you like? In life, I mean. What are your interests?"

It was a business question. Whatever she liked he had something for her.

"I've never seen this before," Virginia said. "It's my first time."

"Fabulous," he said. "Welcome to my strange obsession. Let me explain something that might be of interest to you."

He leaned forward to share something, a piece of advice, a secret between like-minded individuals. Virginia listened.

"You'll find basically two types of dealers. Ones that consider themselves serious businessmen, the real money changers, and drummers like me who got nothing better to do. I don't have business cards, see? I'm an old elevator mechanic retired. I can't make change for large bills. I'm selling pictures at two bits, four bits, and a dollar. But you're just a kid, you don't know what a bit is."

Virginia laughed.

"Two bits is twenty-five cents," she said. "I'm not that young."

"And four bits will get you two," he said. "Figure that one out."

"I'll take this one," she said. She gave the man a quarter from her purse. "Where did you get all these pictures?"

"I started collecting in I want to say nineteen hundred and seventy-eight. For my own personal taste. I put 'em up on the walls."

"It's crowded here. I never would have thought."

"People collect for different reasons. They find something they like. Pictures of old furniture. Or women on motorcycles. Had a guy come in here this morning asking if I had any women on motorcycles. It's like they get something in their head and they got to have every picture of it in the world. It's crazy. You got to be a psychiatrist to understand it."

"What kind do you like?"

"Who, me?" he said. "That's easy. Pretty girls. See what I mean? I'm simple as they come. Pretty girls from the olden days. I got a million of 'em."

"I'm not looking for anything particular. I came to the library for a book and sort of wandered down here."

"Some of these guys, and gals I might add, they got pictures selling a hundred bucks for a five by seven. They got the long tables and everything arranged in photo albums. The rule is don't touch. They use these little white gloves, see? Everything's precious. They drape black sheets over the tables to enhance their formal appearance. The rest of us get maybe one table, or a table with a cart on wheels. Some take the hodgepodge approach.

They got everything mixed up. I like a little order myself. This is what I do for fun. I organize, I separate."

"You have an interesting collection," she said.

"I like to think so, sure. But you've got to touch. You've got to feel the paper. So what if they get a little wrinkled. They're old, they ought to be wrinkled."

"Do you have any favorites?"

"Sure, I got a lot of favorites, I got a lot of favorites. Ask me about it some time."

"Well, it was nice talking to you," Virginia said.

They shook hands. The man had a soft grip. Rough hands and a gentle grip.

"Arnold Epstein," he said. "You probably know three people by that name."

"You're the first," she said. "I'm Virginia."

"Virginia, you're a beautiful girl if you don't mind my saying. And you have a lovely name. I'm very pleased to make your acquaintance."

"Have a pleasant day, Mr. Epstein."

"It's what I been having," he said. "Call me Arnie next time you see me."

Virginia moved down the line looking left and right at what was offered along both sides of the walkway. She checked her watch, still plenty of time. The room was crowded with people looking at photos, forming value assessments, haggling and bartering.

She saw a man with a camera taking pictures of her, not of her specifically, but of everyone. That man over there, with the camera, roaming. He was taking pictures of people looking at pictures, and Virginia was among them. Maybe he was from the *Times* covering a local event. Or maybe he was someone else, unaffiliated, and maybe he *was* taking pictures of her specifically. Virginia acknowledged the man with a glare, and without making too much of it he pointed his camera in another direction.

She looked at pictures of screaming people on roller coasters. She saw women wearing dresses on blustery days, skirts and hair flying, and men smoking pipes or sitting in a barber's chair. There were pictures of women with their arms raised, and self-portraits taken in a mirror. She saw photos of people with mustaches drawn on their faces in various colors of ink. She saw women in the act of stripping. Honeymoon pictures, dance lessons, people playing music or else mooning the camera. She saw funeral pictures and pictures of caskets and headstones. People sticking out their tongues or flipping the bird. Pictures taken in August 1960. Pictures of kitchen appliances and home furnishings. She saw babies crawling on the carpet or out on the front lawn. Summer pictures and snowstorms. Pictures of crashing waves and flooded roads. Pictures of bodies buried in the sand with heads exposed. Pictures of people jumping or falling. People making out on park benches, petting or necking as it was once called. People caught on the toilet or behind a tree. Someone squatting in the woods with a roll of tissue in his hand. She saw photos of soldiers in Vietnam. Men on motorcycles. A teenage boy flexing his muscles. There were double exposures and composite prints. Photos marked by vignetting, photos illuminated by a lens flare. She saw one person feeding another with a spoon. People at home and in hospitals. She saw beer cans and human pyramids. Skinny dippers and tree climbers.

Occasionally she came to a photo and paused, something in it she liked. What was it? Maybe a person's expression, or the way they were standing or seated, an awkward pose, or something in the processing, a technical mishap, a fortuitous accident, some inconsistency that gave the photograph its presence. She paused and looked at it for several seconds. Twenty seconds is a long time. If a photograph captivated her for twenty seconds it might be worth keeping. Slowly she was starting to put aside certain photos for further evaluation. At fifty cents or dollar apiece. Photos she would return to, or revisit, to see if they could stand up to a second viewing.

She saw prints that were oblivious of their own value, discards or rejects, throwaways, yet somehow they had survived the boxed decades. She put them aside and continued looking, shuffling quickly through bikini photos and baby pictures and family holidays. The vacation photos and the soft-focus portraits. Kids playing sports, or horsing around, which was a phrase she'd never understood. And the theme of shyness or embarrassment, how resistance to the camera, to having a picture taken, was nearly universal.

And then she discovered another box, the contents listed as *blanks*. Inside were photos of people with blank gazes. Pictures taken when no one else was looking. They were not images of contemplation, or the mind at work. There was no hint of depth to any of them, nothing intimated, nothing revealed. They were bereft of longing. What was it then that captured her attention, that made her want to pause and stare?

Virginia looked through them slowly, one at a time, shuffling from the top. Close-ups taken with a telephoto lens, a homeless woman at the park, the green space around her compressed and blurred, a man sitting alone at a lunch counter, someone else in the backseat of a yellow taxicab. There were subway photos and people in crowded places, but always the face of utter stillness, the lost view.

They were ordinary people with vacant expressions and she was fascinated by them. Their eyes were fixed in a certain direction, but the object of their gaze, whatever it was, had disappeared. They were not looking past, or through, or beyond, they simply were not looking. Eyes open and not looking, not seeing.

She saw a child in the corner of a room, a small girl wearing a tattered dress, the light falling from a window. She saw a black man sitting on his front porch, somewhere down South, long ago, a little roadside house on the edge of a cotton field, and she was reminded of a phrase she once read in a book—*the human crop*.

There was someone lying ill on a blanketed couch, and someone else in bed, and an obese woman waiting for a bus, a boy on a tire swing, a man sitting at a kitchen table with his glasses off. She saw a woman in a bathtub oblivious to her husband's camera.

They were photos of not-seeing, not-hearing.

She wondered how they all got here, how they fell together in this one box. Perhaps they had meant nothing at one time, when each existed separately, separate moments, but now they formed a collection, identified, chosen from numerous others.

Virginia looked intently. There was isolation, obviously, she could see that. And she could see the voyeurism at work, the theft of a thousand private moments. The masculine element informing the point of view, eroticizing it. Hadn't she written a paper on the male gaze? Hadn't everyone?

Or maybe it was absence, finally, that captivates, that takes the gaze hostage. They were blanks, these photographs, empty casings. Twenty dollars for the entire box.

Chapter 6

The bus to Palm Springs pitched sideways and swayed, a rocking massive heaving thing on wheels, sluggish and heavy as a blue whale in the deep ocean. L.T. had drunk too much coffee, eaten too much breakfast. He read the legal papers again, which he kept in the original envelope. *Designated transferee to receive mobile home residence on ten-acre parcel,* and so on. He now owned a ranch, or whatever you call ten acres of remote desert land. The mobile home was parked at the end of a dirt road somewhere between Yucca Valley and Twenty-nine Palms. It belonged to his uncle Morris who had died a year ago at the age of eighty.

It was Morris who had started calling L.T. by his initials. His real name was Travis Lee Hilliard—Travis after his father. But from birth no one called him that. It was always Lee, which is what his mother preferred and was the name by which he was known until *L.T.* caught on. Morris never explained why he reversed the boy's initials. Perhaps it was an oversight. By the time L.T. entered high school, only his mother still called him Lee.

L.T. knew almost nothing about his own father, except he was stabbed to death outside a bar in Chino. His parents were separated by then, all but divorced, according to his mother. There were a few stories retold by the people who knew him, that he was rowdy and rough-spoken, that he had fought in Korea. When the war ended he came home on a hot-wire, battle-sharp, full of cunning and mistrust. He came back drinking whiskey, inventing rumors, and plotting retaliation against those who had unknowingly insulted him. That was all L.T. knew about his father. So maybe there was some genetic disfigurement in L.T.'s blood, an error in the code which made a man capable of killing, even a man like L.T. who never felt prone toward it.

He thought about the girl from last night and how he let himself get conned. He tried not to think about her appearance or replay the words of their conversation. There was a parable in the Bible about a servant who received forgiveness but who refused to forgive others. The girl was a thief and a whore, this much was true, but murderers must forgive thieves.

At the trial they found him guilty of murder and the judge incarcerated him for life. Two deputies took him from the jailhouse in Madera up to the prison in San Quentin. Wearing a new pair of orange overalls, wearing cuffs on his hands and chains around his shuffling feet, he rode for three hours in a van without windows, with stomach shits and nerves and bad breath. In a white van with no windows, swaying and bouncing, and the taste of blood on his tongue. He could feel the tires on the highway. He listened to whatever the grooved surfaces were saying, something like *hive* or *live*. He had about three hours to come up with a plan to fight and survive, or to hang himself from his bunk, or to starve himself hollow. His plan for the yard, the chow hall, and the crapper. His plan for the shower.

After serving six years on the bay where they taught him how to eat, speak, and walk, they put him on a bus to Folsom where he worked on the line in the factory. Every license plate in the state came out of Folsom Prison. Fifty thousand a day and how many millions of cars on the road. They fed big rolls of thin aluminum into the machines and blanks came out the other end ready for the presses. To punch the plate he had to hold down two buttons simultaneously. Hands raised in the air, one button to push for each hand, to prevent injury. At one time or another L.T. had worked every job on the floor. Most recently die setup and press. And before that he operated the painting machine and the drying racks. He worked in clear coats and inks, sorted, stacked, and inspected for errors. If work was a curse it was also a privilege. It kept the body moving, the blood running, and the pay, though meager, was something to accumulate over time.

And time was the one thing that never ran out. It was always in abundance, wherever you looked, always too much of it, every man serving his own time while adding his years to the aggregated total, so that each man carried the years of every other man until all men carried every minute of every sentence to pay for every crime ever committed.

To be outside of prison then was to be outside of time. He experienced it now as an external force running hard against the gray highway, skipping fast and loose across the river outside his window. He saw it through the gaps in the trees. The way time stirred the surface of the waters. How it

53

moved in the shadows. It was the force that blurred the roadside when you stared through your own glassy reflection.

When he got up to use the toilet he noticed only a handful of open seats on the bus. He lumbered to the rear, eyes down and clumsy-footed, attentive to each awkward step. He made no eye contact. The goal was simply to walk and not fall. In the lavatory he locked the door and lifted the toilet seat. Deep in the very center of his chest there was a stirring, a sick tremble. He saw himself in the small mirror. His face was thick. His hair needed a trim.

He thought about Morris again, and about his two sons, Jeff and Johnny, who were both dead. L.T. had grown up knowing them. They were kids with buzzcuts and smeared faces who lived in an old house on the out-skirts of Riverside. Morris kept a garage full of tools and car parts and motorcycle frames. He owned a horse named Shiloh upon whom the boys rode bareback on the shoulder of the road, three in line with Johnny hold-ing the mane.

Morris alone raised the two boys, or at least kept them alive with food and clothes and housing. L.T. remembered him as a scavenger for ciga-rettes and work. He drove freight trucks and fixed cars on the weekends, leaving Jeff and Johnny to sweat out the days. Their wife and mother, Adeline, left them when Jeff was only three. No one seemed to know where she'd gone or why. Morris might have known, but he never spoke of her. And Jeff and Johnny never said anything either. Their mother's absence was an unspeakable shame to them—a woman who walks away from the toilet without flushing.

L.T. remembered the summertime flies and a screen door clapping hard against the house. At the end of every day, Morris would sit alone under a porchlight swarm of gnats and flying insects, clouded in cigarette smoke, a can of Blue Ribbon beer in one hand. Hank Williams played on the turn-table, the same old songs, the same scorched bleating voice, night after night. In winter the house smelled like cold ashes and furnace dust and the garbage sack under the kitchen sink was always wet with rot.

Eventually Morris sold that house and moved out to the desert. L.T. never thought anything about him until he received notice of Morris's death and the legal papers transferring his estate into L.T.'s name. He could not say that he and Morris were very close, or that Morris was like a father to him. Morris was not that way. But Morris had let him sleep over when he was young, mostly during the summers, let him eat whatever food was in the refrigerator, and treated him the same as his own sons.

The plan was to take this letter, these documents, to a certain law office in Palm Springs, indicated by the business card enclosed, sign whatever papers they required, pay whatever fees, and find a way out to the house. The attorney, Darren P. Williams, had arranged to meet L.T. at the office tomorrow morning. He was leaving town for a week, but he knew L.T.'s situation and did not wish to leave him stranded. The two men had spoken briefly on the telephone a day before L.T.'s release. The man had been a friend of Morris's.

L.T. staggered back to his seat near the front of the bus. His body absorbed the motion, the momentum, the onward thrust of pastureland and pickup trucks and black cattle, acres of low-planted fields with irrigated rows, and the laborers who watered and harvested them. Outside the window lay an otherwise empty plain, and beyond this, on either side of the valley, were distant hills and steep rugged mountains. He saw brown fields plowed in long furrows, vineyards and wineries, the machinery of cultivation. He read the license plates of passing cars. He read billboards and road signs. The names of small towns. Turlock, Atwater, and Merced. He saw a row of white silos and working granaries with open chutes dumping grain into a line of rusty railcars. Trucks carrying caged chickens and crates of lemons and tankers hauling milk and gasoline. It was the whole world in motion, and everything was both new and familiar to him, at once ordinary and astonishing. It was a passing glimpse of the life L.T. had missed out on, the life he might have otherwise taken for granted.

He did not wish to revisit the past, but there it was, closeted in his mind. The girl's name was Terri Avalon and it sort of started with her. She was a waitress at an Irish pub in Venice Beach back when L.T. worked at Melvin's Tire & Wheel lifting cars all day, busting tires off the front and back ends. This is where he met Terri Avalon, a beachfront girl with a lipstick grin whose car arrived on a tow truck one afternoon with a two-inch screw through one tire. L.T. fixed the tire himself, twenty minutes, free of charge. He wrote up the order, smudging his fingerprints on the paperwork.

Terri Avalon offered to repay the favor if L.T. ever dropped by the pub where she worked. So okay, he went to see her at the pub, ordered pastrami and a draft beer and made whatever small talk. Terri lingered at his table near the bar, laughed and touched his shoulder. That was how it began, in pursuit of small curiosities. They met at the beach where she polished her nails. Terri wore cat's eye sunglasses, pulled her swimsuit high over the hip, rubbed coconut oil on her stomach and legs. They listened to music on a portable radio. It was spring and then summer in Venice Beach.

By August they were living together with Terri's roommate, whose name he had forgotten. In fact he had forgotten most everything. He remembered drinking tequila sunrises and smoking each other's cigarettes and dancing. There were parties and many people coming around. Terri knew them all. He could not recall a single topic of conversation, only certain images of sunburned shoulders and tan lines, and beer cans and liquor bottles crowding the countertops in the kitchen. And the days passing like that, weeks at a time, and so it was hard to say who started the fights and why, but there was a fair amount of bickering between hangovers and cravings. Everybody wanted inside Terri's pants. That was one problem.

And there was one guy in particular, a preppy boy, a little Malibu worm who worked as a waiter at the pub. L.T. had seen him at several parties. Sometimes after his shift at Melvin's, L.T. would walk down to the bar and grill and watch from the outside. He loitered on street corners, smoking, watching the sun go down over the Pacific. He established a vantage point in the dark, a view of Terri through the glass. That's how it started. And then one night L.T. waited in the parking lot till the place cleared out. The worm's name was Robby or Rodney. Maybe he was a college kid. In any case, fear of pain was not an issue for L.T. When the back door opened a group came out, flooded in light. Terri was with this new guy of hers, and with them was the dishwasher carrying the last of the garbage and a bartender named Rick Osaka. And there were two other girls, both waitresses, whose names L.T. could not recall. The whole crew came out together and L.T. made his move. He scrambled out from behind the dumpsters, ran up to the kid and with one punch knocked him flat on the parking lot, and that was the end of it.

Terri screamed at him. It was over between them, and when one of the waitresses ran back inside the restaurant to call the cops, L.T. split for home. Whatever clothes he could find he shoved into a duffle bag. He cradled the carton of beer in the refrigerator and took Terri's cigarettes from the freezer where she stored them. To hell with Melvin's Tire at eight dollars an hour and the so-called Venice scene. To hell with Terri, he thought. Scuff-knuckled and shaking with rage, he hurled the duffle into the pickup and lit a cigarette.

His plan was to drive over the Grapevine and down into the valley because there was always oil work to be found around Bakersfield. He had worked a few years over in Whittier as a roughneck and knew all about pumpjacks and drilling. And he thought about those things as he drove up the grade.

But those were recessionary times, he remembered, days of bank failures and budget cuts, inflation and record unemployment. L.T. tried the oil fields, the construction sites, the packing houses. He arrived early, spoke to the foreman on duty, the office secretary, and the man in back of the line. He worked a day here and a week there, scrap labor for low wages, cashed his measly checks at the supermarket. He ate dinner at the gas station where he squatted in filthy stalls and brushed his teeth in the sink. Most nights he parked outside the Super 8 Motel and slept in the Chevy. On the coldest nights he rented a cheap room with a hot shower and a television where he drank beer from a tall can and smoked a few cigarettes in the lamplight. There was Terri to think about, and he thought about her all the time, thinking maybe he might go back now that things had settled down. Twice he tried calling her. *Terri, honey, it's me.* But she told him not to call anymore. *Don't ever call here*, she said.

Things were falling apart and L.T. needed a job. On the way up to Fresno, outside the town of Delano, the water pump went out on the pickup. He knew it was the water pump when he heard the shrieking sound and saw the coolant leak and wiggled the fan. And when you change the pump you might as well change the cracked belts and hoses and replace the thermostat.

Life was okay when everything worked, and now nothing was working. L.T. left the truck on the side of the highway and walked along the shoulder of the road under a heartbreaking sky. The fruit orchards were stripped bare. Their cold thin branches were crowded with blackbirds and sparrows. Out in the weedy fields he saw slanted barns and muddy tractors and miles of fallow acreage. Things traveled backward until they became nothing again.

By nightfall the pickup was running. L.T. put the heater on his feet and listened to country music on the AM radio. Earlimart, Pixley, Tipton. He was traveling northbound to nowhere and when he reached Fresno it was more of the same. He scored drugs on Belmont Avenue from a kid named Tweety. He swallowed the pills with a fifth of bourbon, smoked some sweet reefer, watched the late-night lineup on HBO in his Parkway motel. Denny's for coffee in the morning and all day at Roeding Park collecting beer bottles and aluminum cans. He used the money to buy cigarettes and a loaf of white bread while the Christmas tweakers rode their bicycles in the midnight rain.

On New Year's Eve they stole his Chevy. They picked the lock and jacked the steering column. L.T.'s tools were behind the seat. He needed those tools. He searched the neighborhoods on both sides of the highway, passing a sign that said *Welcome to Fresno*. Dogs barking and clawing the fences, an empty storefront, some mountains in the far distance. *Welcome to Fresno*. He walked all day looking for his pickup and his tools and at night he buried his face in his hands and cried.

He was too afraid to call the police. He'd have to give his full name and he did not want to go to jail if there were warrants issued for his arrest. He didn't know how it all worked, he just knew it never worked in his favor. The Chevy was gone and so were his tools. He was a bum now, a transient, a drifter with no jokes to tell. He used the grimy sinks in park bathrooms and gas stations to keep a clean appearance. He labored for pocket change, preferring cash under the table. He rinsed garbage cans with a pressure washer, scrubbed grease stains with a wire brush, stacked sheet metal and firewood, sorted screws and bolts into separate piles, cleaned up scraps of wood and masonry. He pulled weeds for free. Whatever money he earned he spent on Hostess cupcakes and a variety of medicinal cures, including a brown powder he could snuff up his nose.

Those were days of nausea and fading. Wayne Scott called it the land of Nod, which means wandering, and L.T. wandered for miles, hitchhiking with his thumb in the air, striding backward on the shoulder of every road. Hard to get a lift these days. He followed the railroad tracks along the state highway and watched freight trains rumble past. They were moving too hard and fast to hop aboard. He smoked and drank and snorted his last tab of dope. He ate sweet Twinkies and chocolate cupcakes until all his money was gone. Then he curled up on the gravel beside the railroad tracks and napped, dreaming of that old horse, Shiloh, that he was chasing the steed in a field of tall grass.

In Madera he walked along Gateway Drive. The quiet of a Sunday evening, Mexican cafes on various street corners painted green, orange, and white. Smoke bulging out of the rooftop stacks and the whole town smelling like seasoned meat. L.T.'s stomach clinched and churned. He pissed in a park toilet on Yosemite Avenue. There he tried to bum a smoke from an old Mexican passing through the park who played deaf, muttered something in Spanish, then said in English that it was his last smoke and kept walking. L.T. passed a feed lot, a video store, a shop full of western wear. Signs hanging in storefronts. Items on sale, prices marked down. He looked for coins on the street. He searched the gutters for the meanest reflection of light.

Twenty-nine and drifting, walking gingerly on blistered soles, he continued north on D Street. He was sober but he felt soft in the head, out of focus. He passed through a residential neighborhood full of small homes with broad porches and low fences, with dead grass and leafless winter trees and yapping dogs. A brittle wind blew against his face. He heard wind chimes and a squeaky gate as the darkness came on. In the distance he noticed a water tower, its tank crowned in a halo of bright lights. He walked toward it until he came to a bridge spanning a shallow river with long sloping banks and a path running through willow reeds and wild shrubs.

At the far end of the bridge, on the corner of the street, was an old Mission-style church. The lights were on and there were people inside. It was Sunday night. Cars were parked under the trees along the curb. A pair of glass doors were propped open at the entrance. On weary legs L.T. crossed over the bridge toward the lighted doorway and as he climbed the front steps he caught the somber tune of a piano and a chorus of voices. He stood at the threshold and surveyed the crowded room. Three faces turned to greet him. They were singing the words to a song, an old hymn about water and bloodshed. He felt weak in the head, liquid thin, a hollow-eyed starveling with nowhere else to go.

～

He did not remember falling asleep. He had come into the church while they were still singing and sidled into the back row. He tried to listen to the music and later to the preacher's sermon, but he was weary, worn-out, drained, and his mind kept drifting back to the highway where the road unraveled under daytime skies, skies stretched white with clouds, and he felt his chin dropping. His eyelids were closed. He heard sound without meaning. In his mind he was still walking. His chin dropped and immediately he came awake. He heard the hum of the microphone, the timbre of the spoken word, and his chin dropped again.

He slept for an hour and when the preacher woke him L.T. was lying on his side, the skin of his face pressed against the cushion of the pew. He sat up with difficulty, embarrassed and confused. His left arm had gotten pinned under his body. It would take a moment to get the feeling back. Numbness followed by pins and needles. The room had cleared out except for the preacher.

"I didn't hear anyone," L.T. said.

He coughed and lowered his head.

"My sermons have that legendary effect." The preacher laughed and put out his hand. "You can call me Pastor Phil."

He was a young man, early thirties, dressed in brown slacks, wearing a pale-yellow shirt tucked into his belt. His hair was clipped short and parted neatly on one side. He was clean-shaven. His ears stood out.

L.T. shook the man's hand.

"Travis," he told him. L.T. surprised himself. Travis was the name he never used. It was his father's name and the name on the attendance roster at school. He was ashamed of it. To answer to that name always made him feel oddly criminal.

"Well, Travis, I'm glad you came tonight."

L.T. felt a pain in his lower back, a twisting pain. His head felt wobbly and unsteady and his neck muscles were stiff from sleeping crooked.

"I like to see new faces. Do you live here in town?"

L.T. did not meet the preacher's eyes. He tried to slide out of the pew.

"Can I get you anything?"

L.T. shook his head.

"We keep food in the back pantry. Are you hungry?"

L.T. felt the room turn. This was the dominant sensation at the moment, the toppling effect of standing up.

"Stay here a minute. Will you do that?"

L.T. nodded. His mouth was dry, his head whirling. He sat again and waited in the silence. The church was empty now and the stage up front was dark. It was different when it was empty. It reminded him of school and sitting in the classroom alone when the other kids went outdoors for recess. This was his punishment for not turning in the homework page. His teacher, Mrs. Tuckloff, was out on yard duty with her whistle and her black fox eyes. He hated being left behind in the wooden silence of the empty room, hated the straight rows of desks, the chalk powder on the blackboard.

The preacher returned carrying a grocery bag. He came right up the center aisle striding broadly. He seemed to enjoy it. He set the bag down and picked through it.

"Now, let's see," he said. "Look here, Travis." And he began to describe what was inside the bag.

"Say, Travis, I'd like to pray for you. Are you a Christian?"

L.T. had fallen asleep during the church sermon and that was the one thing you were not supposed to do. Now he felt like he owed the man something. If he said he was a Christian the preacher might test him to see if he was lying. And if he said no—well, that would raise more questions, create a new set of complications.

His time was up.

"I guess so," L.T. said, but he regretted the lie.

"You can't say for sure?"

It seemed like a trick question. The preacher sat down on the pew in front of him and turned around. Resting his forearm on the seatback, one friend to another, he said, "Would you like to know?"

L.T. shook his head. He knew enough already.

"All right," the preacher said, "that's fine. I understand, Travis, I do. Listen, I know you're hungry and tired. It's late and I don't want to keep you. But I'd like you to come back. Do you live in town? I know I asked you that already."

"No."

"I see," he said. "You're just passing through then."

L.T. nodded.

"On your way to better places?"

L.T. kept nodding. He felt like a fool.

"You're probably looking for work. Is that it? You're on the road looking for work? I can understand that. A man's got to have work. Some would say it's a basic right. What kind of work do you do, Travis? What sort of experience?"

"All kinds."

"You know something about automobiles?"

"I've worked on cars."

"What else can you do?"

He shrugged. It was an open-ended question. A hard question to answer in specific terms.

"A lot of things," he said.

"Yard work? Painting?"

"Whatever needs it."

"Sort of a jack-of-all-trades is what I'm hearing. I admire that. Are you clean? Use drugs? You don't have to tell me."

L.T. shook his head.

"No drugs, you say. Not on your person."

"Not anymore."

"You gave it up, is that it? You just want to work now. Honest pay for an honest day."

L.T. nodded. He glanced at the preacher, otherwise he kept his eyes low. He wanted to leave but his body refused to move.

"Suppose I had something for you," the preacher finally said. "Piecework, a few odds and ends. Would that interest you, Travis? You think you'd be interested in sticking around for a while? I could use the help."

"I don't know."

"Basically, it's like this. You see, what I've got here—my situation—is general maintenance needs on the one hand and a number of side projects on the other. We have a Sunday school room out back. Three rooms if you're counting. We'd like to fix them up for the kids. One of our members, Mrs. Wilshire, donated her old Buick. It runs, I'm told, but not very well. We'd like to fix that car up and sell it and use the money to finish the Sunday school building. How does that sound?"

The preacher paused and waited. Then he said, "Does that sound like it might interest you? Does it accord with your skills and talents? I can't pay much. And I understand if that's a problem. I believe in fair pay, Travis. A worker is worthy of his wages. But I can't pay much, not what you'd earn elsewhere. What I could pay is maybe fifty dollars a week, plus meals."

L.T. coughed into his fist. The next town if he kept walking was thirty or forty miles north. It would take a day or two to cover that distance on foot. And for what? To pick through a backlot dumpster and huddle against some hard corner of Merced?

"You'll sleep here, of course," said the preacher. "And we'll set a chair at the dinner table."

L.T. didn't know much about Merced. He knew they had an Air Force base with bomber jets, but apart from that it was just another highway town on the map with fuel pumps and cut-rate motels. As far as L.T. was concerned, that was all anybody needed to know.

~

Unlike Wayne Scott, Philip Bigelow did not preach on television to large captive audiences. He was neither rich nor prominent. He was thirty-five and for several years he and his wife had traveled the southwest in a Winnebago preaching revivalist sermons in all the little country churches from here to East Texas. Eventually they landed in Madera, California, a community of farm laborers and fieldhands, an unheard-of place to most. But Philip did not think of his calling, or his people, as small or insignificant. He belonged to an ancient apostolic tradition, he told L.T., to that lineage of men called by Jesus Christ to voyage into the far country preaching the gospel of salvation.

His wife, Vivian, played the piano on Sundays. She was small and pretty, natural in appearance, but sure of herself and unafraid. She regarded a person directly, stared straight into his eyes, and countered any hint of hypocrisy with worthy contempt. Their only child, Virginia, who was in the second grade, looked much like her father, had his dark hair and eyes, but had unmistakably inherited her mother's quick temperament. Her curiosity shifted impulsively between people and objects, between frustration and delight.

The family lived behind the church, across the parking lot, in a small kitchen-studio, a space formerly reserved for Bible studies and women's gatherings and other social events. It was converted, with little trouble, into living quarters for the new pastor and his family. Vivian had arranged three privacy dividers to accommodate two beds and a clawfoot bathtub.

L.T. slept on an army cot in a separate building that housed the classrooms. The room had electrical outlets, overhead lamps, a toilet and sink. During those first weeks it was cold at night and he ran an electric heater to keep the room warm. The windows had no curtains and he rose early with the sun and washed his face. There were lists of things to do. He vacuumed the church, dusted its polished surfaces, cleaned the commodes, mopped floors, washed windows, emptied trash cans, mowed a strip of grass out front, swept clippings and twigs and fallen leaves into plastic bags.

Fifty dollars a week, plus meals. Attendance at the mid-week Bible study for men was expected. They were studying the Proverbs of Solomon, one of which said, *I will laugh at your calamity; I will mock when your terror comes*.

In the classrooms he replaced crumbling drywall and painted the surfaces white, he stripped floors, sanded and finished them. He put new trim around the doorways and installed a new countertop and mirror in one of the bathrooms and replaced the rubber washers in all the leaky faucets. He drove the pastor's car to the hardware store for nails, caulking, and wood trim.

Church on Sunday morning was expected, and again on Sunday evening. Moses and Pharaoh. Plagues of frogs and wild locust and a great cloud of darkness.

L.T. sprayed for bugs. He set out traps for mice and cockroaches, and ate his meals with the family. Evenings he bathed in the pastor's house while Phil and Vivian and Virginia went into the sanctuary to pray. L.T. soaked in the tub while they prayed for every sickness and reported injury, for all the married couples and their money troubles, for the children who played outside on Sundays, and for generations not yet born. They prayed for the born-again, for new believers who were still carnally minded. L.T. was carnally minded. He thought often of Vivian. He wanted to take her somewhere and gently remove her clothing. In the sanctuary they sought forgiveness for sins innumerable, prayed for miracles and manifestations of grace. They prayed for a revival of old faith and for ancient displays of power and might.

At the hardware store, L.T. bought cans of white paint and new vinyl brushes. At the end of the day he hung the brushes upside down to drip. He swept up the mess and threw scraps into the garbage bin. Whenever L.T. needed help he was to call on Philip, or else Vivian. Philip took the tithes and offerings to the bank every Monday and he made house calls three days a week. Pastoral visits, he called them. Those were the days L.T. required help.

After Virginia went off to school one day he called on Vivian to help him mount the baseboards in one of the classrooms and raise a new set of window blinds.

"I'll need you to hold this end," he said to her.

She stepped onto the folding chair and L.T. went to work fastening the hardware to the wall.

"Here's a question," he said. "I'll put it to you, Vivian. Isn't it unfair of God to harden Pharaoh's heart?"

"You're talking about the sermon on Sunday."

"He tells Pharaoh, that's right, to free the slaves and then he hardens Pharaoh's heart against it. Does that sound fair to you? To make a man act evil and then turn around and punish him for it?"

"What's fair?" said Vivian. "Anyway, whoever said God was fair? Where do people get this notion?"

She had smooth arms, small wrists, pretty hands. Her hair was in pins except where certain strands fell down around her face and captured the sunlight.

"So he's not fair then is what you're saying."

He glanced at her. The weather was perfect for a woman in a skirt and a sleeveless blouse. He thought it would be nice to take a walk together outside.

"I'm surprised to hear you say that, Vivian."

L.T. turned the screws slowly.

"Someone define fair," she said.

"What I mean by fair is giving somebody a chance."

"To do what exactly?"

"To make a choice."

"To make a choice. What kind of choice? How can a person make the right choice without knowing the outcome?"

"Knowing comes later," he said. "After the fact."

"Not in my experience."

"Not in your experience? What's your experience?"

"No, because even when you look back on it you never know if you made the right choice."

"You made the right choice, didn't you?"

"Did I?"

"Sure you did."

She would not say. L.T. finished the screws on his side.

"Let's switch," he said. They both stepped down and Vivian moved his folding chair toward the center of the window. L.T. stepped up onto her chair and put a screw through the hole in the bracket on that side. He worked slowly.

"What about you?" she asked.

"What about me?"

"Look at your situation," she said. "Did you make the right choice?"

"That hurts, Vivian."

"It's not a criticism," she laughed.

"I'm a bum. Bums make bad choices."

"You're not a bum. That's not what I meant."

"What am I then?"

"I haven't figured it out yet."

"You haven't figured it out yet. I didn't know you were trying."

"Don't be flattered."

"I'm not."

"Meaning what exactly?"

L.T. put the bottom screw in. The wall crumbled where the screw entered. He had to press hard while turning the driver. Once the threads grabbed, the screw went in firmly and the wall held it tight.

"Why am I holding this?" said Vivian.

"It keeps the center level."

She let go. "I don't see the difference."

"It makes a difference. Trust me."

"Trust you. Why should I trust you?"

She raised her hand to support the frame again.

"Your husband trusts me. Let's me drive his car all around town."

"My husband trusts everyone."

"But you don't."

"Of course not," she said. "I wouldn't lend you the keys. But that's every pastor's wife. Our job is to keep others from taking advantage. It's why nobody likes us."

"Poor Vivian," he said.

"Thanks for saying."

"Don't be flattered."

"And what's wrong with being flattered?"

"Nothing wrong with it. *Always make a woman feel flattered* is what my mother used to say."

"So you *do* have a mother."

"She trusts me very much."

"I highly doubt it."

They stepped down from the chairs. L.T. pulled the cord and lowered the blinds slowly. He raised them up again, and slowly let them down. The action was smooth. The pulley did not squeak and the string did not catch.

"What's next?" Vivian said. The light slanted across her face and neck.

"A cigarette."

They went outside and stood under the eaves of the building in the shade. It was early spring, a warm day, and there were birds in the sky.

"May I?" asked Vivian.

"I didn't know you smoked."

"Not often," she said. "Not for many years in fact."

She leaned toward him as he held the match. It was understood she was breaking a rule. The pastor's wife out back with the hired hand sharing a smoke.

"Did you always want to be a pastor's wife?"

"It's not what you plan," she said. "I didn't get my college degree for it."

"You're a college girl?"

"Junior college."

"What'd you study at junior college?"

"Music."

"That explains your talent."

"That's not my music. Those are just hymns. I play those songs for the church."

"And what's your preference? Saloon music? Ragtime?"

She laughed.

"Hardly."

"Maybe you'll play for me sometime, show me your chops."

She shook her head.

"Why not?"

"Take this," she said, offering him the remainder of her cigarette. "I don't want it."

L.T. dropped his cigarette and stepped on it. He put Vivian's cigarette between his lips. He pressed the tip of his tongue against the filter.

"Why not?"

"You wouldn't like it. I don't play for anyone."

"No one? Not even Philip? Oh, sorry," he said. "All apologies. I meant, *Pastor* Phil. I want to get that right. *Pastor* Phil. I stand corrected."

"Oh stop."

"What?" he laughed.

"Don't be a fool."

"This is something I'm trying to figure out, Vivian. Why does everyone call him *Pastor* Phil all the time? He's a pastor, I get that."

"They prefer it," she said. "And he likes it, I guess. I don't know."

"It's always *Pastor* Phil. As if God's up there in heaven waiting to clobber you if you don't say *Pastor* first."

Vivian laughed.

"It's like a cult if you ask me," he said.

"It's not like a cult," she said. "You're making it up."

"I called him Phil on Sunday and what's-her-name, Mrs. Farquhar, glared at me as though I'd cursed in church."

Vivian laughed loudly.

"You're making it up," she said. "There is no Mrs. Farquhar."

"I'm not making it up, Vivian. She glared at me and then frowned. It's like Jonestown around here."

They laughed and he smoked the cigarette.

"You don't call him that, do you?"

"Of course not."

"In the throes of passion."

"Travis!"

"What?"

"Give me that," she said.

L.T. gave her the cigarette and she took a quick drag and fanned the smoke. She gave it back. L.T. stamped it out on the blacktop.

"You'll have to pick those up," she said.

"I thought I'd let the kids collect them on Sunday. Make it a contest of winners and losers."

"You know what you are, Travis?"

"What?"

Vivian's eyes were large and sharp.

"I don't have to say it."

"Say it."

"You already know."

"I want to hear it, Vivian." He stared at that mouth of hers. "I want to hear you say it."

~

Down along the river, where there was a clearing of sand, they put out chairs and umbrellas and a pair of long tables covered in cloth from end to end. On the tables were bags of potato chips and numerous homemade pies and large bowls of Jell-O and fruit salad. Mothers fixed plates for their children while their husbands stood in circles telling stories and talking politics. Boys and girls chased each other in and out of the reeds, scrambled up the embankment and raced down again, and babies waddled in the sand and cried.

L.T. had volunteered to barbecue. He flipped meat patties and turned hot dogs, stacking the cooked meat on foiled trays for the ladies to put out on the tables. He heard peals of laughter. The young mothers sat together with their babies between their arms and knees. And the men sat in lawn chairs or stood with their hands in their pockets. By now L.T. knew many of their names but he preferred to busy himself at the grill. He wiped his fingers on a borrowed apron and looked for Vivian, but it was Philip who approached him.

"You are a blessing, Travis. I mean it."

Philip touched him on the shoulder.

"God is working in you," he said. "I can see that."

"Is he?"

"You have a gift for serving others. This is how we serve the Lord, with our hands and feet."

"I'm just trying to stay out of the way," L.T. said. "Are you hungry?"

"No, I'm not. Have you seen Vivian?"

"I haven't."

"She'll be down soon then. We're baptizing Virginia today."

"I didn't know."

"She's seven now. She understands things well enough. We have to make sure they're ready."

L.T. nodded. He liked Philip, or thought he did. But he wanted him to go away. Whenever they were together L.T. felt pressed upon and could not explain why. Philip was kind to everyone, a committed man, a man who encouraged confession and honesty. Philip often said that God did not play games, and by this he meant it was okay to be straight with God, and with one another, and to pretend at anything was a great mistake.

"What about it, Travis?"

L.T. used a long fork to turn the meat. He leaned back to avoid getting smoke in his eyes.

"Would you let me baptize you today? There's about twenty who already signed up. You understand what it means, don't you? And why we do it?"

"I heard you explain it this morning in church."

"It's all about death and rebirth. Symbolic of these things. But that doesn't mean it's unimportant. It *is* important. Jesus tells us to do it."

"Well, I didn't really plan on getting wet today."

"You see, that was my point about the eunuch. Do you remember what he said to the evangelist in the book of Acts? After hearing the gospel, the man wanted to be baptized. He said, *what hinders me?* That's all. Three simple words: *What hinders me?* He had an eagerness, you see?"

The two men stared at one another. Then Philip said, "I hope you'll pray about it, Travis. Will you do that?"

"I will," he said.

"And listen. If you see Vivian, tell her to find me."

"I'll look for her."

Philip walked down to the river's edge, rolling up his white sleeves. He reached down and felt the water. L.T. watched him shake the water off his hand. The river smelled brown and muddy. L.T. did not want to get wet. He finished grilling the last of the meat, stacked it on a tray, and carried the tray to the table. Everyone was eating now and some were in line for dessert and others were shooing away flies. He saw two birds wheeling low above the ground. They were darting after a black dog who was nosing around a nest buried in the reeds.

L.T. took off the apron and rolled it into a ball. To keep the heavy cloth from coming loose he wrapped the apron strings around the bundle and tied it in a thick knot. The sky was blue and clear, except for a column of white clouds to the north, and the air was warm enough to make the sweat on his forehead run. On the other side of the paved road the maples in front of the sanctuary were tall and green. He would go up to his room, change into a dry T-shirt, and grab a cigarette before heading back down.

The front door of the pastor's house was wide open and the windows were raised to catch the breeze. He could hear Virginia crying inside the house. L.T. poked his head in the doorway. He saw Vivian and her daughter sitting together on the bed. The child was wearing a yellow swimsuit.

"Sorry to interrupt you girls," L.T. said. "Phil's looking for you. He says Virginia is getting baptized today."

He intoned this last part with enthusiasm, but at the word *baptized* Virginia began to cry again and her mother breathed a sigh of exasperation. L.T. stepped inside where it was dark and cool. It took a moment before he could see anything.

"What's wrong?" L.T. said.

"She doesn't want to get baptized."

"Why not?"

"She won't say."

"You won't say?"

The little girl shook her head and moaned. Her face was contorted with distress, her eyes wet and swollen. A pair of flip-flops lay on the floor beneath her dangling feet.

"I see. Well, you can't blame her, Vivian."

Vivian shot him a look.

"I don't want to get baptized either," L.T. said. "It's that dirty river. It smells like mud and frogs." The child refused to laugh or even smile. "The other thing is that everyone's looking at you. Which I don't particularly like. And I don't like it when water goes up my nose either. That's the third reason. I'll bet Virginia feels the same way."

"Is that true?" her mother said.

Virginia shook her head.

"Then why?" said Vivian.

"Because," Virginia said, and started to cry again.

Vivian stood up.

"Do what you want," she said. "But you'll have to tell Daddy. Not me. You're big enough now."

Virginia cried harder.

"She was fine last night. Now the moment we get her swimsuit on she changes her mind." Vivian turned to her daughter. "Stop crying, Virginia!"

"I can't!"

"What do I care?" Vivian said to L.T. "If she doesn't want to get baptized, why should she get baptized? It shouldn't be forced upon her."

"Who's forcing her?"

"No one. Phil decided she was ready, that's all."

"Then why all the trouble?"

"Why all the trouble, exactly."

They were silent. Together they stared at Virginia.

"He asked me to do it too," said L.T. "He told me to pray about it."

Vivian rolled her eyes.

"And I've decided to do it," he said loudly. "Do you know why, Virginia?"

The child looked up at him. She sniffled and wiped her nose on a fistful of sheet.

"Because," he said. "If I do it now, then I won't ever have to do it again. I can get it over with. Otherwise, I'll have to decide again at the next baptism, and the next one and the next one."

The child was unmoved.

"It's easy, anyway. You just plug your nose like this. It goes really quick is what I'm told. You can go right after me, if you want. Then they won't bother us about it anymore."

Vivian asked her, "You want to go after Travis?" But Virginia looked down and shook her head.

"Suit yourself," L.T. said. "I have to go change my shirt. A person can see right through a white T-shirt when it's wet."

He left them alone to work it out. Virginia was a stubborn child and L.T. admired her will. He liked stubborn women although he did not know why. Vivian was stubborn and he knew this was something he liked about her. He imagined the three of them off together somewhere. Vivian was from Reno, and he saw himself driving up to Nevada, in the middle of the day, with the woman and her daughter.

Both were waiting for him when he came outside. The little girl in the yellow swimsuit holding her mother's hand. She carried a bath towel under her other arm.

"She wants to get it over with," Vivian said.

L.T. cupped his hands and lit a cigarette. "Good reason," he said.

Philip wanted to do all the kids first, then the women, and lastly the men. Vivian took him aside and argued with him. Philip seemed confused, then annoyed. In the end he agreed to let people come according to preference.

One by one they entered the water. Each person was given a minute or two to tell a personal story of how God had intervened in his or her life. A woman named Crystal, who was twenty-eight, spoke of heroin addiction and losing her child to the system. Philip dunked her and pulled her up. Another woman talked about her abusive husband, a man she called Royce, and how he once tried to drive her off a cliff. She plugged her nose and leaned back and when she came up out of the water everyone clapped. People talked about anger and loneliness, and how life never worked out as planned, about love affairs and funerals. They all went under, making white eddies in the current, and when they came up they wiped their eyes and did something to fix their hair. They were greeted on dry land with hugs and applause, and there were dry towels going around, and certain women along the shore were moved to tears.

The line inched forward.

"Come on, Travis," Philip said. "You're up."

L.T. regretted his ploy. He only wanted to persuade Virginia, and not for her own benefit, but to make her mother happy. Now he was committed. He had to do this thing. He was doing it for Vivian, and Vivian, he knew, was doing it for Phil. And Virginia was doing it to get it over with.

L.T. pulled off his boots and socks. He remembered with great clarity jumping barefoot one summer into a shallow canal to grab a dead fish floating on the surface. The boys were arguing whether it was a bass or a yellow perch. Jeff had failed to reach it with a stick. They tried hitting it with rocks to push it toward the bank of the canal. Finally, to prove his courage, and to snatch the fish before it floated into the spillway, L.T. jumped into the canal and went after it. The water came up above his knees and he did not remember it being cold. He took three or four steps toward the fish when he landed on a broken bottle which sliced open the bottom of his foot. It was Johnny who dragged him out of the water and carried him on his back for a mile. At the house they set L.T. in the tub with his foot bleeding into the moldy drain. When Morris came in he took a bottle of rubbing alcohol from the medicine cabinet. "It'll sting," he said, and then he poured half the bottle on L.T.'s foot. Afterward, he called Darlene to come pick up her son. In the car, his mother bitched at him all the way to the emergency room.

Now, slowly, with caution, LT. slogged into the cold water wearing blue jeans and a green T-shirt bearing the name of the Irish pub where Terri Avalon worked. The river current whirled tightly around his calves and knees, up to his thighs, and higher still to the most critical regions. The T-shirt was a gift from Terri. You could buy them at the bar for ten dollars apiece, and Terri either bought it with her tips or else stole it after a closing shift. Sometimes he thought about Terri, although it never ended well. He did not want to get back together with her again in Venice Beach. He imagined her watching him right now from a certain distance with that glare of superiority. *You're going by Travis now?* It was the kind of thing Terri would say. As far as L.T. was concerned, this was all Terri's fault. Which is why it did not end well whenever he thought of Terri Avalon.

"Can you praise Him?" Philip said. It was something he often said to members of the congregation when he greeted them on Sunday mornings.

"All right," L.T. said. "Let's do it." He was careful not to let the sting of cold water show on his face.

Many who were standing on the dry sand applauded. Philip stood waist deep in the river, braced against the current.

"Travis, would you like to say something?"

"I don't have much to say."

Phillip addressed the shore.

"Travis has been with us, what about three months now?"

"Almost," said L.T. He wanted to hurry things along.

"Our kids will have their own classrooms because of this man."

A group of women cheered at this announcement and offered a light applause. People were tired of clapping by now.

"Tell us what God has done for you, Travis. How he's changed you."

"He brought me here and took me in. With you guys. Pastor Phil and everyone. And I'm drug free now, and completely sober. I'm getting my life back."

Philip took a position slightly behind L.T. and gripped his hand. He became very serious now and spoke only to L.T.

"Travis, you are a new man. The old man has died. Do you understand? Walk in the newness of Christ. I now baptize you in the name of the Father, the Son, and the Holy Ghost."

L.T. pinched his nose with his free hand and fell backward into the icy current. His blood drained from his head as the cold iron force of nature barreled over the top of him. He was submerged in the noise and tumult of Sierra mountain runoff. The river was louder and heavier than a freight train. L.T. lay between the rails. His chest tightened. He felt a rush of fear. The heart of a man was a very small thing. The river dragged his hair and shoulders. It pulled at his clothing. His whole body was wrapped in twisted vines. A thousand pair of hands dragging him down, drowning him in darkness. The roots of the earth, the muddy grave, the cold black watery night.

And then, suddenly, against the thick weight of the current, the preacher heaved him upright and L.T. was on his feet again, standing firm in the severe light, breathing the daylight air. He heard cheering and clapping as he wiped his face and eyes. Philip embraced him. Then L.T. slogged toward the shore.

Vivian stood ready with his towel. L.T. pressed the heavy cloth to his face and held it there. It was warm and smelled like midsummer.

"Are there any more?" Philip said. "Where's my daughter?"

L.T. did not see Virginia. He looked for a yellow swimsuit.

"She went up to the house," Vivian said.

"Is she coming back?"

"She changed her mind, Phil."

Philip was still standing waist deep in the river. He nodded vaguely at his wife's words and let his shoulders drop. He looked baffled as though some weariness had befallen him.

"Tell her it's okay," he said. Then he said, in a low voice, "I'll tell her."

Chapter 7

At home, grading papers, her mind wandering off the page, she marked certain errors and ignored others. Occasionally she wrote a comment in the margin, something about content, a question, a critical suggestion. But she did this too hastily, or too haphazardly, misspelling words or scribbling some unintelligible phrase and then crossing it out. At the end of each paper she wrote a short paragraph, a final evaluative statement, a note of encouragement. Rereading these passages she wondered what she had meant to say.

Afterward, she put together a plate of crackers, green olives, white cheese. She mixed a vodka martini in a regular glass. Early afternoon at the kitchen table, sunlight and slow time as she turned the pages of her library book.

The book included numerous black and white photographs printed on dull acid-free paper. Eyebrows, forehead, mouth. Diptychs and four-paneled images of bulging eyes and dilated nostrils. There was a man with a scar on his upper lip and a woman with blond hair and buckteeth. They were not professional models. A father and daughter perhaps, friends of the author? They were shown close-up, faces expressing emotion. The difference between anger and disgust with arrows noting the most prominent features. A wrinkling of the nose, a narrowing of the eyes. The difference between fear and astonishment with figures, numbers, and diagrams.

She remembered playing with Amanda, years ago, nights when their mother went out dancing with Ed West, and Virginia stayed home to baby-sit. Her sister was six or seven at the time, blond and blue-eyed. And how, before bedtime, the two girls would make faces in the mirror. How they frothed at the mouth and growled and played a game of who can make the ugliest face, the scariest face, with toothpaste dribbling down their chins.

Virginia had tried making faces with her son. It was an exercise, a tactic really, to corral his attention, to help him recognize the face as language.

But her strategy abruptly failed. The problem lay in Timothy's inability to meet her gaze halfway, his powerlessness to mimic, his utter indifference. *Watch me*, she would say. *Timothy, look.* But he never offered more than a glance. His thoughts darted elsewhere and soon the body followed.

As a child, Amanda was the opposite, always desperate for attention, always clinging. Amanda hated it when her older sister read books, detested the silence it required, resented being ignored. To gain her sister's attention, Amanda often faked an injury or caused a spill in the kitchen or came clopping into the room wearing their mother's heels. When Virginia ignored these obvious maneuvers, Amanda sulked and nagged, invading Virginia's mental space with petty requests. Even in the bathroom, even on the toilet, Virginia had no privacy. Amanda always wanted in, always felt left out, abandoned. She sat in the hallway slipping paper cutouts of hearts and stars under the door, or ink drawings of misshapen figures with long squiggly hair and spidery hands. She knocked on the door and Virginia told her to go away. She kept knocking, pestering, provoking until Virginia cursed at her and threatened to tell. And sometimes she did tell on her sister, ratted the brat out, although Vivian offered little in the way of punishment. On the contrary, her mother made it clear that Amanda was Virginia's problem to solve. *She's the child*, her mother would say. *You be the adult.* It was Virginia's duty, her obligation as older sister, to babysit, pick up the rooms, fix dinner on the stove and keep the scamp amused.

That was in Reno, Nevada, where they lived in a yellow house on Elko Avenue. The house with the green shag carpet in the bedrooms, the dusty floor heater, the running toilet you fixed by plunging your whole arm into a cold grimy tank. The routine before bed was lifting the covers and shaking out the blankets. Spiders in the sheets, spiders on the walls, spiders under the porch.

They shared a bedroom in the small house. One room, two separate sides, a clear delineation of space. On Virginia's wall *Joy Division* and *The Cure*, photographs of her boyfriend, ribbons of gothic lace dangling from a secondhand mirror. On Amanda's side, crayon drawings and artless sketches, her obsession with colts and foals. Of the two dressers, the taller one belonged to Virginia. It held a portable stereo with an assortment of mix tapes, a jewelry box, a stack of paperbacks. The other rested between the twin beds, beneath the windowsill, and supported an alarm clock and a reading lamp. Its three drawers, always partially open, were stuffed with

Amanda's clothes. The girls fought over keeping the drawers shut. They fought over the radio and who controlled the lamp. They fought over corners and closet spaces, over neat and jumbled zones, dolls scattered along the floor, coloring books and ink pens, a herd of plastic animals. They threw stuff at each other from across the room. Articles of clothing, a balled sock, a dangling bra. *She's the child*, her mother said. *You be the adult*. Sometimes Virginia pushed her sister into the hallway and locked the bedroom door. Other times she surrendered the room, leaving Amanda in the house with their mother and Ed West, and grabbing her coat from the hallway closet she set off down the road where she caught a bus to the shopping mall or the roller rink, or else walked to the 7-Eleven which had a payphone in the parking lot. She'd sit on the painted curb beside the telephone booth, sometimes for hours, waiting for a friend to call her back.

Snow-cold Reno, white winter skies.

At night, when Amanda would wake up, she crawled into Virginia's bed. It was an intrusive habit. That familiar pocket of cold air followed by her sister's nestling body. The twisted nightgown, the hair and bare feet. Too tired to resist, Virginia would roll over and face the wall, inching away, shoulder and hip, adding distance between them. But Amanda, pressing nearer and tighter, squirmed and burrowed until their figures conformed.

Nothing like Neil, who always slept with his back to her, even after rigorous lovemaking, who removed himself and scooted away. If there was a hand on his hip or an arm around his waist he could never sleep. During colder months when Virginia moved closer to get warm, Neil often woke with a start, tossed the covers aside in protest, and marched naked to the bathroom. Without flushing he would return, not saying a word, pulling the blankets hard in his favor while rolling sharply onto his side of the mattress.

There were nights of insomnia, even now, recent nights when the bed offered no comfort, when her pillow felt weirdly flat and the blankets got tangled. Nights when a song was stuck in her head, the repeating chorus a kind of madness, when all she could think about were problematic students and unpaid bills, fragments of dialogue, disputes and grievances. The song on a loop, the chorus, and the gloominess of six in the morning after a night of zero sleep.

Sometimes she got up and went into Timothy's room. Sheets in disarray, pale in his underwear, the boy slept uncovered on his back. Virginia lay facing him on her side, hands folded, knees and elbows drawn together. In the golden glow of the nightlight, she stared at cheeks and eyelids, at blond hair and mouth. His features were mostly Neil's, but she also saw traces of her father, a generational resemblance. She often wondered about Timothy's mental disorder, his inward retreat, and whether this too was something inherited, inborn. There were studies floating around, reputable models, suggesting that certain formative experiences, like personal tragedies, were passed down from one generation to the next.

Her own inheritance was confined to a small canvas suitcase containing her father's things. Virginia rarely brought it out of the closet, almost never opened it. Years passed, major life events, yet the suitcase remained hidden under spare pillows, towels, folded blankets. She always knew where it was, so she never had to think about it except when she packed up and moved, which was often enough, even with Neil. Three apartments in four years, then one more after the separation and divorce. The suitcase was a thing she stored in closets. The last time she opened it was after she married Neil. He kept referring to the things inside as *mementos* which finally led to an argument.

Virginia cleared the kitchen table to make room for the suitcase. It was an overnight bag really, a valise. It seemed smaller every time she handled it. The plastic grip was molded to fit a woman's hand. Why her father's belongings were put inside it she didn't know. It was not a man's suitcase. The rose-colored paisleys were faded in color and there was a hole in the canvas large enough to poke a finger through. She remembered scolding Amanda once for peeking through the hole, for trying to discover what was inside. Virginia did not want its contents revealed, not to anyone, not even her sister, especially not her sister, who was incapable of appreciating the value of past things, who would snatch items and lose them. It was *her* suitcase, Virginia's, it belonged to her and nobody else, and she felt a certain duty to protect what little she had, to guard her secret possession, as though her father's memory was hers alone to preserve. In part, this was a reaction to her mother, who never talked about her dad, as if their years at the church never existed, and partly a reaction to her sister who never knew their father and therefore had no claim on his love.

Virginia released the clasps and flipped open the case. The contents were in disarray. A few photographs, her father's Bible, a cassette tape, a heaped assortment of loose items. The Bible was bound in heavy black leather, massive and intimidating. Virginia thumbed through it examining her father's handwriting, the neat capital letters, like a boy in drafting class whose lines went straight across. It was the same Bible he used when preaching. The one she always saw him with. Her mother carried a purse, her father a Bible. She set it on the table and picked up the cassette tape. The word *Agape* was written in felt tip on both sides. Her father's first sermon, recorded in 1971, at age twenty-two. A sermon on brotherly love. His voice was preserved on the tape. Virginia had forgotten what it sounded like, had not listened to it since graduating high school when it made her cry so hard she swore never to play it again, never to listen.

She found the shoehorn and a pair of red dice, the set of novelty ice cubes with flies and wires trapped inside, love letters her mother had written when they were dating, a funeral notification, cash register receipts, guitar picks and rubber bands, a tin of Miracle Nylon pushpins, a hunting knife, faded pictures of her father fishing at a lake in the mountains, one with her mother in a photo booth at the county fair, and another of him preaching under a circus tent with the words *Texas, 1977* written on the back. Virginia found a leather shoestring tied in knots, a wooden cigar box containing a toy elephant riding a red bicycle, buttons and cufflinks, Mexican coins, a mini screwdriver, a paper tract illustrating the way of salvation.

With few exceptions the objects were universally meaningless. Only the Bible of course with her father's reference notes, his bracketing and underlining, his marginal comments on nearly every page, and the tape recording of his voice, obviously, and the photographs. But everything else. Why couldn't she keep the few items of importance and dispose of the rest? It was the question she asked herself every time. Maybe they were fragments of some underlying narrative. Or pieces to be fitted together. Only they did not fit together, or didn't seem to, which is why she had criticized Neil for calling them mementos. Her whole line of reasoning was based on the apparent randomness of things. Objects without meaning by definition could not be called mementos. It was a stupid argument she later regretted. It was not Neil's fault. Her attachment to the suitcase and its contents was oddly amusing to him. He could not understand her frustration. What she was trying to explain, and could never make clear, was the troubling insignificance of everything inside.

Even so, Virginia could never throw anything away, not even the sales receipts. She found one dated November 17, 1983. The timestamp showed

11:48 A.M. in purple ink. Her father had purchased a book in Fresno on his final birthday, paid thirty dollars cash, and was given six dollars and twenty cents in change. He had treated himself to a book that day and maybe ate lunch afterward at the hamburger stand on the edge of town. A sunny white building where people ordered food through a small window and waited for their number to be called. *Mel's* or *Mac's*, she couldn't remember the name. She looked up the date and discovered it was a Thursday. She did not remember any celebration, although there must have been a cake with candles to blow out. That was the year they bought her the toy oven for Christmas. The oven that baked edible food under a hot lamp. Virginia made a chocolate cake, or a brownie, whatever it was, and served it to her father on a plate. It was a box mix you added water to and then you poured the batter into a metal pan and watched the cake rise in the oven through a real glass widow.

By the time Amanda inherited the oven, the glass was cracked and the lamp no longer worked. In fact, most of Amanda's toys were hand-me-downs, mangy stuffed animals, a broken doll house, the bicycle with its stiff rusty chain and squeaky wheels. Every August, before the school year commenced, Vivian hauled cardboard boxes in from the garage and made Amanda sort through her sister's old clothes.

Later, Virginia realized how unfair it was and apologized to her sister one Christmas Eve for not caring enough. They were alone in the kitchen scraping dinner plates over the sink and loading the dishwasher. Virginia's apology, stirred by too much wine, was sweeping and vague, overstated. The paisley suitcase, the broken toys and outdated clothing remained unnamed. Anyway, it seemed trivial to point out specifics, to offer particulars, and by then it didn't seem to matter. Amanda, who was newly pregnant and cautiously sober, laughed it off, blamed her older sister's behavior on hormones and teenage angst, and changed the topic with ease. They were adults by then, married women, and they were not close, not really, not since Virginia went away to college. Or maybe they were never close. How else to explain a decade of disinterest? Amanda's early adolescence, her teenage years, were featureless in Virginia's mind. Aside from seeing each other on holidays and saying hello on the telephone they hardly related. Virginia was involved in her own studies, working off campus, dating a guy. Meanwhile, her sister got her period and her driver's permit, played on the volleyball team, cycled through part-time jobs and boyfriends.

Apart from major life events, a graduation ceremony, a wedding, the birth of a child, they rarely met in person. They exchanged birthday cards and saw each other annually, on Thanksgiving or Christmas, depending on the year. There were in-laws to consider, total number of miles traveled, and other factors of love and work. It was only after the twins were born that they started chatting occasionally, mostly through text messages and shared photo albums. Even so, their exchanges were typically brief, curtailed to avoid disclosure.

She never told Amanda, for example, that her life was divided into two halves. The first ended at age seven, the second was all the rest. If she was ever nostalgic it was always for the first half of her life, the part she couldn't share with Amanda or anyone else. The blue hydrangeas, the gray alleyway, the store on the corner with the candy machines and the broken pony. At home, behind the church, she rode her bicycle around the parking lot and then around the block past the evil dogs barking behind the fence. Mostly she played alone, gathering jacks on the blacktop with a red rubber ball, or playing teacher in the classroom to a stuffed rabbit and a faction of disobedient ragdolls.

Her memories were not like photographs. More like short video clips on playback, brief gestures infinitely repeated, the details never varying.

Like the woman with clamshell toenails, homeless and obese, who arrived one afternoon with a carload of blankets and hangers, portable appliances, things stuffed in plastic bags. And how the cockroaches came scrambling out of the hot engine, out of the tailpipe, in multitudes.

Or shards of glass from the Coca Cola bottle that slipped from Virginia's hand while standing in line at the corner store, how it broke on the floor, shattered and spilled everywhere, and how she fled the store without paying.

She remembered getting lost in Kmart while loafing in the aisles, her mother nowhere to be found, on her own now among hated strangers, tricksters and kidnappers, and the shame of hearing her own personal name announced on the store's loudspeaker.

And the day she got locked inside the church alone for two hours while doing her dusting chores. Some miscommunication between her parents— her mother shopping, her father napping in the house. Virginia thought the holy rapture had come in the blink of an eye or like a thief in the night, exactly how they said it would happen. Her parents caught up in an invisible cloud, her grandparents gone, everyone in the church vanished, leaving her all alone. Because she knew, she was convinced, that when the rapture happened she would get left behind with all the bad people in the world. She could not say why. Maybe the cigarettes in the bushes, or the meanness she sometimes felt inside herself, a natural cruelty, or the curses she uttered when no one else was around. She remembered talking to Travis about it. He said he was one of the bad people, but Virginia did not believe him.

Chapter 8

The spring rains turned the surrounding countryside mossy green. The clouds were dark and the roads were wet-black. On every avenue the leaves of the trees dripped rainwater and the wind blew the branches together. Across from the church the river was running high and fast along the embankment and there were no more baptisms.

L.T. studied the rain. He loitered under the eaves and smoked cigarettes as puddles formed on the asphalt. Philip had gone alone up to Sacramento to speak at a pastors' conference and would not return until Saturday. Except for plunging a toilet in the men's room, L.T. did almost no work at all. He neglected his list of weekly chores. Instead, he sipped on a tall can of beer wrapped in a brown paper bag and when the rain let up he took a long walk under cloudy skies to figure out his next move. He felt an urge to leave this place and find a real job. He considered all the things he knew how to do, and which skills earned him the most money and which did not. He could try out Stockton and Sacramento if he went north. Or perhaps a better direction was west, out toward Paso Robles and San Ardo, where the oil fields were. He had a little money, enough for a bus ticket and maybe a week in a hotel.

When it started raining again he walked back to the church where he met a delivery driver and signed for a box of communion cups. These were the small plastic thimbles he often found scattered around the sanctuary on Monday mornings when he dusted the pews and vacuumed the carpets. L.T. carried the box into the church to keep the rain off it.

Inside the sanctuary he heard music. It was Vivian, of course, at the piano. The music rose and fell softly, Vivian's small hands, he imagined, meandering right and left along the keys. Until now he had never heard her play anything but the old hymns. Even when she practiced, which was not often, she played the songs she would perform on Sunday morning.

L.T. stood in the dark hallway and listened. The sound filled the empty building. There were no lights on anywhere. Outside it continued to rain and masses of iron-gray clouds were visible through the cold windows. L.T. leaned against the wall and did not make a sound. If Vivian heard him she would quit playing. Music was her secret, although he did not understand why. It was not for lack of confidence. It was something she purposely guarded, almost selfishly, he thought. Just then she made a slight mistake, paused a moment, repeated the same part over again, and continued. He liked it where he was, alone in the hallway, with Vivian.

She played for several minutes without making another mistake. The piano sounded moodier than it usually did. On Sunday mornings she played only songs with simple lyrics and the congregation often engaged in cheerful clapping. Now as she played she gave no thought to words, or so it seemed, and she was not playing for anyone but herself. And what she was playing was not simple. Or if it was simple, it was also difficult and complicated. L.T. knew almost nothing about classical music. He had never learned to read music or play it. He could not describe what he was hearing, he could only listen.

When her playing finally ended he waited quietly in the hallway. He did not want to be found listening. He waited for Vivian to make a noise. He did not hear the bench move or the sound of things being closed or put away. After a minute L.T. reversed his steps, quiet as a bread thief, opened the back door of the church and let it close again. Then he made a fair amount of noise, opening the supply closet, arranging items on the shelf to accommodate the new box. He half expected Vivian to appear in the doorway. When she didn't he grabbed a stack of paper napkins and passed through the sanctuary ignoring the stage as he walked directly up the aisle toward the front doors of the church. The restrooms were in the foyer. He went into the men's room, used the special key to unlock the metal box by the sink, and stacked the napkins inside. Then he came out and reentered the sanctuary where Vivian was still sitting at the piano.

"Oh, I didn't see you there," he said. "Am I interrupting?"

"It's all right."

"The lights were off." His voice echoed. "I'm sorry if I startled you."

"You didn't," she said.

"You're practicing."

"Not exactly."

L.T. walked down the aisle self-consciously. His shirt was damp and the rain had flattened his hair.

"It smells a little musty in here," he said. "Does it smell musty in here to you?"

"Yes, a little."

"I wonder if there's a water leak somewhere."

"It smells like this whenever it rains. I like it."

"You do? Why?"

"Because it doesn't often rain."

Three steps led up to the carpeted stage where the musical instruments were kept. There were three guitars propped on metal stands and a drum kit behind a plastic sound barrier. The pulpit stood in the center of the stage near the front edge of the steps. On a table in front of the pulpit a large ceramic vase was filled with flowers and dried stems. To the right was the piano. It was black with gold lettering and its finish was glossy. The lid was raised at an angle. Vivian was sitting on the red velvet bench in front of the keys.

L.T. went up the steps slowly and rested his hand on the polished wood.

"What are you playing?"

"You shouldn't lean on it."

L.T. did not take his hand away.

Vivian was wearing blue jeans and a green knitted sweater and her hands were folded in her lap. Her hair was down, brushed in a sort of way, but not styled.

"It's nice in here," he said. "I like when it's empty."

Vivian had not yet bathed. If she was wearing makeup it did not show on her face in the pale light. He liked seeing her without it. He had wanted to see her like this, just as she was, sitting privately at her piano.

"But I'm interrupting," he said. "I'll leave you."

"I said you're not interrupting. There's nothing to interrupt."

He thought of her sleeping alone in a large bed under a fold of soft white blankets.

"Did you hear the thunder last night?"

"I counted two seconds," she said, "after the flash."

"That means two miles, doesn't it?"

"I don't think so."

"Two miles away."

"No, it's something else. I can't remember. You have to divide it by ten. Or by half. I used to know it."

He wondered if she wore anything, a nightgown, under the sheets. He preferred to think of her in bed without so much as a nightgown on.

"I couldn't sleep last night," he said. "The wind made everything clatter."

"What are you doing now?"

"Restocking the closet. But it can wait. You should keep playing."

"Why?"

"Because it's important."

"What is?"

"Keeping up your talent."

She responded with a laugh, as though she despised compliments.

"I stopped progressing a long time ago," she said. "I would've been much farther along."

"I'd like to hear you play."

She shook her head.

"It's quite a piano," he said.

"My parents bought it for me when I was a teenager."

"It's beautiful," he said, rubbing its surface.

"They took out a second mortgage on the house. When I married I had to leave it behind."

"Why?"

"Phil and I lived on the road for eight years. When we finally settled here my dad shipped it to me in a Mayflower truck. That wasn't cheap either."

"Eight years. That's a long time. Did you enjoy it?"

"At first I did. Although the best part was driving away. We'd stay a few days or a week and then say goodbye to our hosts, usually pastors and their wives, sweet and eager people. I loved leaving them behind. Isn't that funny? It sounds like a thing you shouldn't admit."

"How did you know where to go?"

"We knew people all over the map. It's really Phil who knows everyone. He's very good with names and faces. He made all the arrangements by telephone. Someone put him in contact with someone else. Then we'd go there and Phil would preach on Sunday. He loved it. Entering a new town, like two strangers on a white horse. He couldn't wait to preach."

"And they paid you how much? How did you make enough money?"

"They'd take up an offering. Sometimes it was nothing, forty or fifty dollars maybe. Other times it was in the hundreds."

"And you did this for eight years."

She nodded.

"The best part was leaving town," she said, "and finding myself in the middle of nowhere, and feeling lost to everyone but myself."

"In a motor home, a Winnebago."

"It's like crossing oceans."

"And you were never lonely?"

"I was alone, always. Even in company. That's how I lived. But I wouldn't call it loneliness."

"Just you and Phil."

"We spent hours staring out of windows. Arizona, Utah, Nevada. We've been all over. And then I would drive and he would sleep."

"Eight years will take you places."

Vivian struck a key on the piano and a sharp little note rang out.

"Do you miss it?" he asked.

"I miss leaving. There's a certain feeling you get. I can't explain it. Some people spend their whole lives trying to arrive. I could never wait to leave."

"And then you came to this place. How'd that happen?"

"I got pregnant," she said. "I knew things were going to change, but I didn't know what to expect. When Virginia was born I felt like my life was over. It wasn't true, of course, but that's what I felt at the time. It's a terrible thing to say. You probably think what about me?"

"A crying baby in a motor home is what comes to mind."

"It's not even that. Or it is that but it's also more. Before Virginia I had a knack for slipping away. I knew how to exit a room, abandon a conversation, without leaving a trace. Now, with the baby, I couldn't go anywhere. I couldn't get away from people. I had to account for everything all the time. Suddenly I belonged to the young mothers' club in every town in America. And all they talk about is babies. Their own babies, other women's babies, sick babies, fussy babies, colicky babies."

"So much for silence," he said.

"Changing babies, burping babies, dressing babies."

"What happened to personal space?"

"You're a man, a single man, you have no idea."

"And then what?" said L.T. "You landed here."

"The church needed a new pastor. Someone contacted Phil about it. So we drove out and stayed a few weeks and everybody thought it was the right thing to do. That was five years ago."

Five years. Who could believe it? Vivian dismissed the reality of it.

"Play something," he said.

"I thought we had an understanding."

"What, we're here, why not play something? If you don't want me to watch I'll sit over there."

She hung her head for a moment. Her hair fell over her face. Then she pulled it back and looked up again. She slid over to make room on the bench.

"Sit down," she said.

The bench was small. His leg pressed against hers. He felt her arm on his. The sanctuary was nearly dark. He could hear the rain outside.

"Hands," she said, and positioned her fingers on the keys. "I'll play. I don't know what. Don't speak."

When Vivian began to play he listened respectfully without making a sound. Compliments were out of the question. She did not need his approval or admiration. He watched her hands and fingers. She wore a gold wedding band and a single gold bracelet on her left wrist. Her fingers seemed to lengthen as she played various chords and configurations. Sitting this close he could smell whatever scent she was wearing, something floral and delicate and lighter than air. It was something she put on the day before and today it lingered faintly on her neck.

The music she played sounded familiar to him, although he could not name it. It filled the room like wind and leaves. It circulated like a rush of cold air. What do you call it when you recognize something you cannot name? Vivian's hands played different parts of the song simultaneously, at different paces, and occasionally ran together, right hand over left. A resounding chord, a pulse, a flutter. He could not understand how a person could manage so deftly the separation of compound tasks. He felt her leg move as she depressed one of the brass pedals.

He watched her as she played. He was no longer interested in her hands. He considered her face in profile. Her brow and the shape of her nose. Her lips slightly parted. The way the lines of her face curved downward to her chin. The way her hair lay draped behind her ear.

Even if his approval or admiration was not something she required, she was playing for him, most assuredly. He was the audience and the artist plays to her audience. She knew he admired her, of course. She was too skilled, too aware of her own talent, to believe otherwise. This was her secret. She played better than anyone, even Philip, knew or suspected. She kept it hidden because there was nowhere to take it, nowhere else to go with it. It was better then to withhold it, to make it her own private thing, preferring the witness of an empty room. Nevertheless, here she was playing for L.T., breaking her own hard rule, with her husband out of town.

Why else would she allow him to stay? He knew he was right about this. It was something they both wanted. The opportunity had arrived, it was passing, and L.T. knew it would not come again if he failed to act on it. So he slowly leaned over and kissed Vivian below the ear as softly as he could. She finished two notes with her right hand and the music stopped abruptly. Vivian stiffened. L.T. kissed her again. If he paused, if he showed any hesitancy at all, she might well rebuke him. That was the word that came to mind. He felt her veer away from him, but she was only reasoning with herself. She had no intention of rebuking him.

~

When it was over they fell quiet and lay close together on the red carpet. Vivian did not reach for her clothes immediately. L.T.'s hand lay on her chest and he could feel the pulse below her breast. The tree outside was blowing against the windowpane. He could hear the branches tapping against the glass. Above them the big piano loomed darkly. In the calm he started to drift, to fall into a dream state. If they were in bed together, in some remote place, he could sleep. But they could not sleep here. He forced his eyes open.

"Are you tired?" he asked.

Vivian shook her head. They stayed together a while longer until Vivian finally moved his arm, sat upright, and began to dress. L.T. put on his shirt and pants. Sitting on the piano bench he watched as Vivian put on her sweater.

"What now?" he said.

"Virginia will be home soon," she replied. "I'll have to make lunch. Do you want a sandwich?"

~

What followed was a week of grievous heat that came up hard from the southwest, a high-pressure buildup with cloudless skies and record-breaking temperatures and a dreadful plague of grasshoppers and flies.

At the parts store L.T. bought new sparkplugs, new wires, a set of ignition points and a new distributor cap. After replacing these on the Buick he started the engine and listened carefully. He pumped the accelerator and the whole car wobbled and died. He thought about the problem. He started the car, listened, and let it die. A hundred and two degrees outside. L.T. dragged the hot tools into the shade.

The tools belonged to Knut Webster. Knut owned and operated a large vineyard south of town. He was a member of the church in good standing. At Philip's request, he brought two large toolboxes to the church, a pair of jackstands, a wooden creeper on caster wheels. It did not please the man to loan out his tools. Tools were expensive and they were personal. A man acquired them over time, the way a woman obtained jewels. L.T. understood the man's concerns. He had lost his own tools to thieves. He told that story to Knut Webster who remained indifferent to L.T.'s loss. Knut demanded assurances. First that L.T. would not leave Knut's tools outside or mix Knut's tools with anyone else's tools. And second that the toolboxes would be kept orderly and secured in a locked environment when not in use. L.T said that was fine, it was common sense. Knut said it was not personal, he simply did not trust other men. Philip gave his word, but the fat son-of-a-bitch kept on about it. Men were incompetent, Knut said, generally speaking, and he could tell a thousand and one stories of inept field workers and worthless farmhands.

~

At lunch, inside the house, a dozen black flies defiled a wedge of pink watermelon set out on the table. Vivian had fixed sandwiches and opened a bag of potato chips.

"What's your expert opinion?" Philip asked.

L.T. was careful not to stare at Vivian. The woman was in a crabby mood. He'd overheard her quarreling with Philip last night, although it was unclear what they were fighting about. Anyway, she would not even look at L.T., not since her husband had come back from Sacramento.

"You want my opinion," said L.T., "I think the carburetor needs to be rebuilt."

"You know how to do that," Philip said, with a full mouth.

"It's not a question of whether I can do it."

"But you don't have to do it in the heat of the day."

"I'm not bothered by the heat," he lied. "The heat doesn't affect me."

"Do whatever's best for yourself," Philip said. "I'd give you a hand but I've got two people to visit this afternoon."

~

L.T. worked under the hot sun with the hood of the car raised at an angle. He draped a floor mat over the front fender to keep from burning his hands on the searing metal. Around mid-afternoon an ice cream truck cruised past the church. L.T. signaled to the driver who circled around the block and pulled into the alley. Mariachi blared from the loudspeakers mounted above the windshield. The old man wore a dirty cowboy hat and a bolo tie with a turquoise stone. L.T. yelled at the house as he wiped his hands. His forearms were black with grease. The grease had worked into his hands and up under his fingernails. There were three or four cuts and scrapes on either hand, little stingers that did not bleed.

"Vivian! Send out Virginia!"

The house was closed up. A swamp cooler was running at full capacity. Virginia was inside the house most likely sitting in front of the fan making the *wah wah* noise. Yesterday she begged L.T. to come over and make the noise with her, but Vivian said no and ordered Virginia to finish her math homework instead.

L.T. called again, "Vivian!"

When the door finally opened Virginia came running out in her summer dress wearing white sandals.

"Pick the one you want," he told her.

"Which one?" she said. She couldn't decide. The truck carried every kind of ice cream. Snow cones, Screwballs, Bomb Pops.

Vivian stood in the doorway.

L.T. paid the old man and let him keep the change. Virginia scampered over to her mother to show her which ice cream she had chosen.

"Virginia, what do you say?"

"Thank you."

"Don't say it to me, say it to Travis."

"Thank you, Travis."

"Next time you can try something else," he told her.

"Like what?"

"I don't know, something different. You know what I mean?"

"What's that one?"

"Mine's a fudge bar."

"Can I try it?"

"No, Virginia," her mother said. "Go back inside the house. It's too hot out here. I'm coming in too."

"What about Travis?"

"Travis is busy."

Virginia went inside licking her ice cream.

"What do you say we get out of here? The three of us. You, me, and Virginia."

"You know we can't do that, Travis."

"Who says we can't?"

"That's not a real question."

"Come off it, Vivian. You hate it here as much as I do. Probably more so."

"You can't take people away."

"Of course you can. People do it all the time."

"I'm going inside," she said.

"Wait a second, will you?"

"What?"

"I heard you arguing last night. What was that all about?"

"It's none of your business."

"Was it about us?"

"No, I don't think so."

"You don't want to talk about it."

"There's nothing to say."

"And you don't ever think about it? About what we did?"

"Your ice cream is melting."

"I do, I think about it. All the time, Vivian. I can't stop thinking about it."

"Try to think about something else."

"Like what, for instance?"

"I don't know, Travis, but you're dripping on the steps."

"I'd like to get the heck out of here. That's something I think about."

"I think that would be a good idea," she said.

"For me but not for you. Is that what you're saying?"

"Yes, and would you please lower your voice."

"You know, I don't get you. You aren't bound, Vivian, you're a free woman. Not everything is decided. You have options. Quit acting like some prisoner in chains. It's defeating."

"Running off with you is not an option."

"Then what is? You tell me."

"Look, Travis, I'm sorry."

"Save it, Vivian. Save your apology."

"It was a stupid mistake."

"Don't apologize to me. If you feel guilty, apologize to your husband. And when he tells you to go to hell, which is exactly what he should do, we'll run straight after it."

"I can't apologize to him. Do you understand? I won't do it. I'm not going to do it. And you and I aren't going anywhere together."

"You know what I think?"

"No, but your ice cream, Travis, would you please?"

"All this," he said, gesturing broadly with his free hand, "I don't think you believe in any of it."

"You don't know what I believe."

"A pastor's wife!"

Just then the ice cream he was holding slid off the stick and splattered on the hot steps.

"Shit!"

"Who cares, Vivian," he said. "It's ice cream. I'll clean it for Christ's sake. Leave it alone!"

He fell into a squat and shoveled up the ice cream. He offered it up to her, half melted, cupped in his greasy hands.

"What do I have to do," he said, "eat it?"

And then, as if to prove a point, L.T. began to suck the melted ice cream out of his grimy hands. Vivian stepped back into the house and slammed the door. She turned the deadbolt locking him outside.

"Vivian!" he said.

~

That night at the men's gathering Knut Webster had a heart attack. The folding chairs were arranged in the usual circle out in the courtyard. The pink summer sky was warm and expansive. L.T. made a point to sit across from Knut. He wanted to keep his distance. He had heard enough out of Knut. Earlier Knut had asked to see the car L.T. was working on. Reluctantly, L.T. lifted the hood and set the prop. He listened to Knut tell him everything about carburetors. Knut could rebuild a carburetor in the dark. He could fix diesel engines, tractors, motorbikes, refrigerators, typewriters, wristwatches.

Knut was a goddamn blowhard, and L.T. was this close to telling him about it. He resolved to work twice as hard to rebuild the carburetor so that he could rid himself finally of Knut Webster and his precious tools.

Tonight the men were sitting on metal folding chairs eating doughnuts and drinking coffee out of Styrofoam cups. L.T. had arranged the chairs beforehand, as expected, and at the end of the hour it was assumed he would fold all the chairs and stack them in an empty closet. Somehow the chairs had become his responsibility, along with the coffee and doughnuts.

The men were reading Proverbs, each man taking a verse and reading it aloud, going around the circle. From time to time Philip would offer up some stale bit of advice, some overworked nonsense. Since his turn to read had not yet come, L.T. was neither following along in the text nor paying attention to what anybody said about it. He was looking up, contemplating where to go and what to do, when he saw Knut wincing. It was a twitch that turned into a sharp spasm. Knut dropped his doughnut and accidentally kicked over his coffee. Then he reached violently for his chest, groaned in agony, and toppled off his chair.

Everyone knew it was a heart attack. They rushed on him, a dozen men, seizing Knut Webster with their hands. L.T. hurried to the ground with them. Philip told one of the younger men to go phone for an ambulance. The hospital was out by the highway on the southern edge of town. The kid ran into the church while the others laid hands on Knut and prayed. Every man put a hand somewhere on Knut's large body. He was lying on his side, half-conscious, the victim of gluttonous living. Philip covered Knut's head with his hands and prayed. L.T. put his hand on the boot of Knut's left foot. He had to put it somewhere. The others had got there first, their hands covering most of the man's frame. It was a large brown cowboy boot, well worn, scuffed with mud.

Knut was dying and they were speaking words over him. Three or four were praying aloud simultaneously and the others were agreeing. L.T. did not say anything. He was touching the man's lifeless boot. Whatever he felt toward Knut, call it bitter disgust, diminished in that moment. He did not care personally whether Knut lived or died. Knut was just a senseless fool like everybody else, born of the dust, ignorant, prideful and deluded. What did Proverbs say? It said, *a rod for the backs of fools.*

It was not long before Knut regained consciousness, rolled over onto his back, and let his shoulders rest. The heart was still beating inside his chest.

"I'm all right," Knut said. "I'll be okay."

They sat him up now.

"Jesus, I'm all right. Thank you, Jesus. Thank you, Lord."

The others began to praise God. Here was a miracle. Here was a man raised to life.

"I feel all right now," Knut said.

Somebody said, "Give him space, give him a little air."

"You want a drink of water, Knut?"

"I don't feel no pain," he said.

"Praise the Lord!"

"Let's get him up," Philip said. "Roger, pull that chair up."

Philip had one arm and Marlon Scruggs took the other. They tried to pick Knut up by the arms. He was a big man and hard to raise.

"I can do it on my own," Knut said. "I'm okay."

"Take it easy, Knut."

He sat up and braced himself.

"Lord, I can't believe it."

"Believe it, Knut."

"I think he healed me," he said, moving up to the chair.

"You better believe he healed you. We're all witnesses."

"I do. I *do* believe it."

Knut sat big and heavy on his folding chair. The kid came back and said the ambulance was on its way.

"I can't tell you what I'm feeling," Knut said. "I mean it, fellas. I can't describe it."

"It's a miracle."

"I've never felt so good in all my life. You can cancel that ambulance as far as I'm concerned."

"That's the power of God."

"I really do feel better, Marlon. I feel twenty years younger."

"Better let them come, Knut."

Knut stood up.

"No, I want to stand," he said, when they tried to stop him.

He shook hands with several men. He hugged others. He did a little dance and laughed. His boots were restless. He could not stop moving his arms. He bounced in place.

"Glory to God!" he shouted. "I think I can leap over a wall."

"Easy now. Take it easy, Knut."

"Huh? What do you think?"

"Praise God," someone said.

"It's a miracle if I ever saw one."

Knut Webster bounced in place, performed a little dance step, like a man testing a new pair of athletic shoes. The others stepped back to give him room to dance. They stood with arms folded, marveling at the sight, now grinning and chuckling at one another. L.T. did not know what to think. He stood back and watched. He heard a siren approaching from some distance.

"Here they come," the kid said.

"They're too late," Knut said and laughed. "God already showed up."

"He's here among us."

"I can't even tell you fellas."

"We'd better call Lynne," Philip said.

"Sure, we'll call her. She'll want to hear about it."

Knut jogged in place, laughing, high-stepping.

"I gotta run," he said. "I feel it in me. God's telling me to run. He's telling me to get out there and run."

Knut began to jog in the courtyard, first in a wide circle, then toward the front gate. The men cheered him on. L.T. felt it, the desire to run. Maybe everyone felt it. They all followed Knut out through the open gate. The siren was getting closer, the ambulance was coming to take Knut to the hospital.

"Wait till they see this!"

"Praise God!" someone shouted.

And it was like the pop of a starter pistol that sent Knut running down the middle of the road in a full gallop. The sandy riverbank lay to the left and a row of clapboard houses lined the opposite side of the street. The men formed a crowd to cheer him on. They all wanted to run after him.

And that's when it happened. Right as the ambulance crossed the bridge Knut Webster tumbled hard against the pavement. Everybody felt it. Each man let out a groan of disgust or a cry of disappointment. They thought he must have tripped in bumbling fashion on the uneven surface of the road. A big man, unaccustomed to running, falling hard like that on a darkening street. It was a fall reminiscent of their boyhood days and they fully expected Knut to get up, any moment now, and brush himself off.

When the ambulance rounded the corner and stopped, all the men crowded up to the window. The lights were flashing red and blue as the medic rolled down the glass.

"That's him up there," Marlon pointed, "that's Knut."

~

Outside the open window the crickets were ratcheting in the dark. L.T. could not sleep, not on any stripped-down sweltering mattress, and certainly not on this oppressive feather pillow which made his head pour with sweat.

Finally, he got up and stood at the window in his underwear and smoked. He kept seeing it all over again, the whole thing from start to finish. Knut running up the street and then hitting the pavement. That ignorant fool. They were all fools. The whole thing was a game, a contest of rules and strategies and golden rewards, not devised by any god but invented by men who played it against themselves, only nobody could see it was utterly make believe. And even on a night like this one, when the vanity and senselessness of it were revealed, they all continued to play on.

L.T. was over it. He'd had enough of the happy-clappy music and the infuriating sermons, the smell of hairspray and breath mints, and the grotesque blubber of the Sunday crowd. He had kept up certain pretenses because he had nowhere else to go. And then he only stayed because of Vivian. A week ago they'd had sex and now she wanted him gone, not out of guilt, never for an instant was the woman persecuted by guilt, as far as he could tell. In her mind what happened between them was merely a mistake, an example of poor judgment, and she did not want to face up to it every night sitting across from L.T. at the dinner table. He had offered her a way out but she was too afraid to take it. That was Vivian. Miserable Vivian.

What L.T. needed was a plan, one that involved transportation. Now that Knut was dead it was only a matter of time before Lynne sent a farmhand over to collect his tools. No doubt one of the Mexicans Knut did not trust. If he could fix the car, L.T. thought, he could drive it off in the night. That would leave ten or twelve hours before Philip figured out he was gone and not coming back. The tools he could pawn in another town when it was safe to do so. There was plenty of food in the church pantry. He could pack a box in advance and lock it in the trunk of the car. With a tank full of gasoline he could drive all night. He would only need to decide where to go.

But for the next several days L.T. was forced to delay the car repairs. The funeral was set for Saturday and there was too much work to do around the church. Fixing the car had been his priority and he had neglected his other duties. The sanctuary needed dusting and vacuuming, the toilets needed bleaching, and the grass perimeter needed mowing and raking. He did these chores and several others, accomplishing each task quietly and efficiently to avoid drawing attention to himself.

Friday evening he was sitting on the back steps smoking cigarettes. All his work was done in preparation for the funeral. Tomorrow he would have to clean up and get things ready for Sunday. Virginia was on her bicycle pedaling around the blacktop. She made several wide circles and then a series of figure eights. After a few minutes she rode up close and stopped.

"Did you hear?" she said.

"Hear what?"

"That man died."

"I was there, wasn't I?"

"It's sad," she said.

"Yes, very sad. I'm all broken up."

L.T. pulled on the cigarette.

Virginia said, "Think he went to heaven or hell?"

L.T. shrugged. "What do you think?"

Virginia was standing in front of the bicycle seat with both feet on the ground, inching her wheels forward and back.

"Probably heaven," she said.

"Then why's everyone so sad? If he's in heaven."

"Because they can't go."

"They could if they wanted to," said L.T.

"No, they can't."

"You've got it all figured out, don't you? But suppose everybody died at the same time."

"That's the rapture."

"The what?"

"When God comes and takes us up to heaven."

"Oh really? When's this supposed to happen?"

Virginia sighed.

"All the other people have to go to hell first," she said.

"What other people?"

"The bad people."

"You mean like the people who start nuclear wars?"

She nodded.

"What about me? I'm bad. Do I have to go to hell first?"

She shook her head and scowled. L.T. took a drag and blew the smoke to one side and laughed.

"What's hell anyway?" he said, glancing at the car. "Can't be worse than all this."

"Fire and the devil."

"You watch too many cartoons."

"It says so in the Bible."

"You haven't read the Bible."

She nodded.

"The whole thing?"

She nodded.

"You have not," he said. "That's a lie. Don't you know what happens to liars?"

"I've read *my* Bible."

"*Your* Bible? What's your Bible? You have a different Bible than the rest of us?"

"It's a children's Bible."

"That's just pictures."

"Not all of it. It's mostly words."

"Alright, if you say so. I stand corrected then. Virginia has read the whole Bible."

"Have you read it?"

"Of course not."

"Why?"

"It's too long. I don't have time for it."

"My dad has read it."

"Well, your dad has more time than me. Look at all this work I have to do around here."

Virginia glanced at the broken car parked nearby.

"Go ask your mom," he said. "I'll bet she hasn't read the Bible."

"She has too."

"Bet she hasn't."

"How much?"

"A thousand dollars."

"Be serious."

"All right, make it a dollar."

"Shake," she said.

"You'd better go wash your hand now," he told her. "It'll smell like cigarettes. Your mom will think you've been smoking."

"That's gross."

"Yes, it is."

"Why do you smoke then?"

"Because I like it. I like the taste. And because I'm gross."

Virginia smiled.

"And because I'm bad," he added. "Someday I might even start a nuclear war with Russia or China."

"You can't."

"Why not?"

"Because you're not in the army."

"Maybe I'll join the army."

Virginia growled under her breath.

"You're impossible," she said.

"Why?"

"Because you say weird things."

"You don't believe me."

"I do, but still . . ."

"All right, you can go now. I'll quit bothering you."

She sat up on her seat and began to ride away, unsteady at first, pedaling hard to correct a slow precarious wobble.

"See you at the rapture," L.T. said.

Virginia cut her eyes at him in disapproval, an expression she had learned from observing her mother.

~

The pews were full on the day of Knut's funeral. The ushers sat together in a row of folding chairs L.T. had set up near the back of the sanctuary. Everyone who belonged to the church was there along with a few of Knut's lifelong friends, a group of poor farmhands, some family and in-laws who had driven in from other towns. The man's body lay in a polished wood casket surrounded by wreaths and flowers. Half of the lid was raised and L.T. could see a portion of Knut's pale face and the pink satin lining of the coffin.

"We can grieve without losing hope," Philip said. "We can mourn without despairing."

It was mostly quiet in the sanctuary. L.T. was sitting on the aisle in the very back row near the wall. He heard only coughing, sniffling. Now and then someone's baby made a noise. Vivian was sitting in the front row wearing black. Her hair was up and L.T. could see the back of her neck. She had played the piano as the guests were being seated. When Philip went up to the pulpit to say the prayer, Vivian stepped down quietly and sat with Virginia in the front row. L.T. had not taken his eyes off her. It might as well be *her* funeral, he thought.

"We were never meant for death," Philip continued. "It wasn't part of God's original plan for us. Death entered at the hour of our disobedience."

L.T. didn't buy it. Wasn't God supposed to be omnipotent and omniscient? Did he not see beforehand the unraveling of time and human history? And if so, if he knew Adam would fall and did not stop it from happening, then wasn't God to blame? It didn't make sense. After all, it was God who had allowed the serpent to enter the garden in the first place. He knew what would happen. So it did not seem fair to blame mankind. The whole thing looked like a setup from the start.

"On days like this," Phillip said, "when we're struck by confusion, when we are overwhelmed by sadness and the experience of loss, when you and I in this room experience separation from our departed loved ones, we begin to understand the penalty of our sin."

Sunlight slanted in through the tall windows. The air conditioning unit was not powerful enough to keep the room from heating up. People were clearing their throats and blowing their noses.

"Perhaps God put grief in our hearts to bring us near to him."

L.T. felt no grief. He experienced no feeling of loss, no urge to mourn. He felt separate, apart from all this, distant from it. Soon he would strike out from this place and he did not expect to remember much of what had gone on. Maybe he would remember Vivian, but probably not. The sex would be there, the outline of her body, but little else. She would stay here with Philip and dissolve like powdered creamer in a cup of black coffee.

"It's hard, friends," he continued. "But we must remember, this earthly body is all that ever dies. The curse of sin, which is death, is lifted from everyone who believes in the cross of Jesus Christ. It really is that simple. We receive forgiveness and we forgive others in return. 'Mark the blameless man,' we say with the Psalmist, 'and observe the upright; for the future of that man is peace.' Let's live peaceably among ourselves. Let us find our peace today in the one who made us blameless before God our father. And let's remember our dear brother, Knut Webster, who has gone on to perfection."

On cue the ushers stood up and walked down the center aisle. Meanwhile Vivian returned to the piano. In the silent interval L.T. slipped quietly into the foyer and out the front doors of the church. He lit a cigarette and went around the side of the building to smoke. He was not interested in hearing more about the life of Knut Webster and he most certainly did not intend to view the corpse. Live peaceably, Philip had said, live simply and forgive. And what would happen if he found out about Vivian? Would he simply forgive her and move on?

L.T. stood in the alleyway between the church and the fenced houses. The air smelled putrid. About a hundred yards north, behind the market where he bought his cigarettes, were two battered dumpsters with locking metal lids. One of the lids had been left open and there were five or six crows flapping in and out of the dumpster, picking though the garbage and beating their wings. This explained the rancid smell. It was meat of some kind, spoiled chickens maybe, or scraps of butchered beef. It was Saturday and the garbage truck would not come around until Tuesday morning.

He would have to walk up there and close the lid. A pair of dogs began to bark at him as he walked beside the fence. They chased after his footsteps furiously until they could run no further, and then all they could do was bark and scratch the fence. When he came up to the dumpster the crows scattered. L.T. looked inside and saw a dead coyote, its head crushed, its lower jaw broken and jagged. One of its eyes was missing. L.T. held his breath and pushed away the flies. Someone in a car had hit the animal, probably at night, dragged the carcass off the asphalt and dumped it in the bin. These coyotes were more than a nuisance. On hot nights they wandered in from the country to hunt the neighborhood cats and to drink whatever water they could find in bowls. Here was one of the culprits. Its forelegs were crushed, its neck smashed, its stomach blood-soaked and deflated. You could tell by its legs it was a coyote and not a dog.

~

On Sunday evening he cleaned the sanctuary for the last time. He collected the plastic communion cups, dusted the pews, vacuumed the red carpet. In the bathrooms he brushed the toilets with powdered cleanser, restocked the paper rolls, emptied the small metal wastebaskets into one large bag, and dragged a wet mop over the tiles. He rattled the front doors to ensure they were locked and made sure the windows were clasped shut. He wanted everything to look right.

In the storeroom he stacked food into an empty grocery bag, dry goods mostly, things he could eat while driving. He thought in terms of handfuls, or things he could eat out of the wrapper, and he filled up the bag. When it was dark outside he quietly placed the bag into the trunk of the car.

The next morning, after a sore night of unrest, he lugged Knut's toolboxes outside and raised the hood of the car. He tried to remember where he had left off before old Knut died. He laid out the remaining parts according to the diagram in the repair manual. He retraced every step from the beginning, trying hard to focus on small but significant details. In his mind he was already gone, out on the highway somewhere.

He kept dropping things. Tools, clips, screws. He searched the dark crevices of the engine compartment or else went down onto his knees and elbows to scan the hot asphalt beneath the car.

He worked on the float valve and installed new jets. He cut a finger on a sharp piece of metal and it dripped blood. He squeezed the finger with a dirty rag, held it for one minute exactly, and then continued to work with the grease rag wrapped around the finger.

He removed the throttle plate from the shaft and cleaned it, replaced the power valve and its gasket, and the idle mixture screws. He dropped one of the screws and searched the ground beneath the car.

The shade was gone and he worked under the sun. He heard Virginia come off the school bus and go inside the house. Later she came out to ride her bike and then went inside because it was too hot. L.T. wiped his brow and studied the pages in the repair manual, examining the same diagrams over and over because they were impossible to follow. The diagram was a flat illustration and the real thing was a large hunk of metal with a thousand necessary parts.

He followed the steps in the manual, reading and rereading the same sentences, double-checking the placement of each part. Philip came out and said hello on his way into the chapel. L.T. did not acknowledge him. His head under the hood, he pretended not to hear. By now everything was its own frustration. The obscure instructions, the fact of so many parts left to assemble, the heat rising from the asphalt, the harsh clarity of the sky, the sweat dribbling into his eyes, his throbbing finger, the primal crouch he had to assume whenever he dropped an object.

His forehead ached and there seemed to be a direct connection between his throbbing forehead and his finger. He was becoming confused. He knew the gaskets were key. You had to place them just right to secure the fit. But he could not figure out which gasket went where. He rotated each gasket, flipped it, rotated it, tried another. The holes did not line up. There were certain gaskets included in the kit that did not belong. And then there were all the vacuum lines, an assortment of narrow-gauge hoses of various lengths connecting the valves. Delay valve. Diverter valve.

The glare of the sun left spots in his vision, the tools burned his hands, his finger bled into the rag. Maybe he had drunk too much water too quickly because now he felt sick in his stomach. But he had to finish this. He couldn't stay here, not another day. He studied the diagram and plugged in the hoses. *To fuel tank. To air cleaner.* He checked for missing parts. There were items in the kit that did not belong.

He put the key into the ignition and started the car. He kept his foot on the pedal and let the engine temperature climb. When he left his foot off the pedal the engine died. He adjusted the idle screw and the mixture screws and started it again. He did this multiple times, a quarter turn, a half turn more, but the engine would not idle. He wedged a hammer against the gas pedal to keep the engine running while he examined the carburetor. He checked the hoses and adjusted the mixture. When he removed the hammer the engine died. He started the car again and let it die. His stomach turned. Maybe because he had not eaten anything. His whole body hurt. He felt the urge to heave. His eyes began to burn and then water, maybe because of the sweat, but why could he not fix this god-damn car?

There was a catch in his throat. He convulsed and held it back and wiped his face with the sleeve of his shirt. He was sick and dizzy and there was no one around to help him. He had put the carburetor back together and nothing was fixed. If it was not the carburetor, then it had to be the timing. He would have to examine the entire ignition system to find out. Or maybe it *was* the carburetor and he had done something wrong or forgot some important step, and now he would have to pull it apart again and start over. Or else it was neither the carburetor nor the timing. It was the fuel line, a crimp or a clog, or some corrosion in the gas tank sending particles into the line.

L.T. picked up the hammer. He had a mind to smash the Buick into pieces. There were tools scattered all over the asphalt. He knew he must move them out of the sun. He felt a stomach cramp followed by a wave of nausea, and bending at the waist he heaved violently three times. In a wild tearless fit of despair he started crying. He groaned. He spit bitterly. He clinched his jaw and tightened the muscles in his gut.

And then he saw him. He saw Philip coming out of the chapel carrying the blue bank bag in his right hand. His shirt was tucked smartly into his belt. His hair was trimmed and parted sharply on one side. He was off to the bank because it was Monday. That was the day Philip drove to the bank with the tithes and offerings. And here he was, striding across the parking lot toward his own car, whistling on his way to the bank.

Until now, everything had rested on fixing that car, but the car was no longer a viable option. There was food inside the trunk and the idea had been to drive away in the night. Eat the food while driving. But now it was clear to L.T. that he could not wait for the car just as he could no longer wait for Vivian. There was no time to work out another plan. He would simply take the bag and run.

He certainly did not expect the man to put up a fight. Philip would protest, he would plead with L.T., beg him to reason, and then try to counsel him out of this misguided scheme. Maybe he would call the police. Or maybe he would just pray.

But none of those things happened. When L.T. reached for the money bag, Philip got startled and would not let go. L.T. tried to wrestle it out of his hand. Philip shouted, "Hold on, hold on!" He knew it was L.T. but he did not seem to recognize him in that instant. There had to be a misunderstanding. These were the tithes and offerings and he was on his way to the bank. He said, "Now, hold on!"

L.T. tried to break the man's trance. No doubt he was the stronger of the two. He did not want to hurt Philip. With his free hand he tried unsuccessfully to jerk the bag loose, but Philip's hold on the bag was unconscious. He was like a man protecting his child in a crowd. Stunned and baffled, unaffected by reason, Philip had made it impossible to let go.

L.T. panicked. He would have to use the hammer. The hammer was meant to threaten and intimidate, but Philip was forcing him to use it. He would use it to break Philip's hold on the bag. He would break the man's arm if he had to. As a last resort. He did not want to hurt him, but Philip had left him no other choice. Because he could not leave without the bag. He could not stay here any longer, and he could not leave empty-handed. Hit the arm, break the grip, then run away with the bag.

But in bringing down the hammer he inadvertently hit Philip on the head. The hammer struck the crown of the head and the man released the bag and fell to the ground. His skull was busted open and blood was draining out of the hole. L.T. looked at the man's head, at the brain matter. The blood at L.T.'s feet was as thick as motor oil.

He heard screams. Vivian was screaming. He saw the look of horror in her eyes, coming out of the house, her hand over her mouth, her body folding in on itself.

L.T. dropped the hammer. He had the blue bag, it was in his possession, and backing away he started to run. Although his legs were moving he did not feel like he was running. Or if he was running, he was running against water, or against an impenetrable wind.

He ran down the steep riverbank where he tracked out across the dry sand through the lanky reeds and bush thicket. He was heading upriver, he knew that. And he knew that while he must stay low and keep moving they would find him soon enough. They would surround him with rifles and dogs and close in upon him. They would bind him in irons and carry him where he did not wish to go.

Chapter 9

She was making room in the closet for the suitcase when the phone rang. Her first thought was Neil, but it wasn't him, it was Amanda calling.

"Am I bothering?" her sister said.

"My house is a mess. I'm getting ready to clean. What's up?"

"I want to ask you about Dad," she said. "I was awake last night thinking about it."

Amanda's timing was peculiar, oddly coincidental, but Virginia didn't mention the suitcase. Anyway, there was work to do around the apartment, things to clean.

"What actually happened back then? No one ever told me."

She wanted to work unimpeded, without interruption, and half-regretted answering the phone.

"I don't know the whole story," said Virginia. "Mom never talked about it, and I never felt comfortable asking. I tried to research it on my own once, but all I found were some newspaper articles and an obituary."

At Berkeley, sophomore year, upstairs in a library for undergraduates, she had searched the archives on microfiche. *Parishioner Kills Pastor*. Travis Lee Hilliard, his mugshot, his drifter's bio.

"What'd they say?"

"Not much, really. He tried to rob us at the church. Dad tried to stop him."

Knight-Ridder, *Associated Press*. Her father's life story told in brief. At the end, robbed of tithes and offerings, he was killed with an ordinary claw hammer, a single violent blow to the head. In every article Virginia was the daughter, always unnamed, who survived her father's death.

"That's all I really know," she said.

"But you were there, weren't you?"

She felt an urge to clean, to pick up the rooms and really scrub the place, but intuition compelled her to put it off. Travis Lee Hilliard was out of prison and Amanda was probing for answers. And why not talk about it? Her sister had a right to know, she deserved to hear at least one version of the story. Their mother never spoke of the matter, either because the memory was too painful or because it was too private, and even Virginia, who was there when it happened, who heard the screams and saw the blood, was afraid to ask about it, frightened by the story her mother might tell, or worse, refuse to tell. And maybe her sister felt it, too. The fear of reproach.

Virginia walked over to the sofa and sat down, cross-legged, with a pillow on her lap. She told Amanda what she remembered. She described the small studio behind the church sanctuary, the parking lot, the school rooms under repair. How Travis came along one day and started working at the church, like a janitor or handyman, and ate meals with the family.

The day their father was killed, Virginia was sitting on the floor watching cartoons. It was too hot outside to ride her bike on the blacktop. Virginia had tried it, circling the lot three times, passing Travis on each blazing lap. He was leaning under the hood of a car, working on the engine, tools scattered everywhere. Virginia pedaled straight for the car as if to crash into it and then veered away at the last moment. But Travis would not look up, would not acknowledge her. He cursed and threw a tool on the ground. Virginia circled past but he paid her no attention. His arms were greasy, T-shirt wet with sweat, his jeans saggy at the waist. She wanted to ride up alongside him to find out why he was so angry, but instead she circled around watchfully, completed a third and final lap, and laid her bicycle at the doorstep. On her way inside the house, she opened the front door and hesitated, glancing at Travis one last time. But her mother said, "Virginia, the flies!" And so she entered the house quickly and closed the door behind her.

For years, even after college, she wondered what might have happened had she stopped to talk with Travis. Maybe he would've told her to go away, or joked like always, or offered to buy her an ice cream, or sent her into the kitchen for a glass of water. A simple request. She could've gotten it on her own. Her father called it *taking initiative*. When you did something without being asked simply because it needed to be done. Virginia remembered thinking *ice water* but then not getting it for Travis, not taking initiative.

When the yelling started, Virginia looked over at her mother on the telephone. She could see Vivian was listening to two things at once, concentrating on hearing both the voice on the phone and the shouting outside. Alarmed, her mother stood up from the dinette table and looked out the window. What she saw startled her, jolted her whole body. She dropped the telephone to cover her mouth, screamed into her cupped hands, then immediately rushed out the front door. Virginia jumped up to follow, but what she heard next, the raw sound of terror that came from her own mother's guts, held her motionless inside the house. She knew there must've been an accident, something awful, Travis pinned under the weight of the car, or his hand cut off, or worse.

At the doorway, craning to look outside, Virginia saw a man lying on the ground, but it was not Travis. It was her father. Her mother was leaning over her dad, on her knees, leaning over his chest, and there was blood on the ground where his head lay. Travis was nowhere around, not beside her mother, not working under the hood of the car. When her mother turned sharply and yelled at Virginia to go inside, go back inside, it finally hit her. Her mother's horrified reaction. Her father lying on the ground bleeding. Virginia was certain he would not get up.

She retreated into the living room and started to cry. Alone in the house, she fell on her knees and prayed. *Don't let him be dead, don't let him be dead, don't let him be dead. Oh God please don't let him be dead. Jesus not dead. Oh Jesus please don't let him be. Oh God forgive my sins, don't let him be my sins, oh Jesus not dead, don't let him be dead God.*

Her prayer was interrupted when her mother came running inside the house. There was blood all over her hands, blood smeared on the tops of her thighs, on her waist and blouse. Crying, hysterical, she dialed the rotary telephone and pleaded for help.

The ambulance, the police officers, lights and blaring sirens, her mother's loud cries. Virginia tried to describe these things to her sister. How they came that night and prayed with their hands, all the grownups, how they crowded around her with their hands and prayed. Her eyes closed, her inward parts full of ache and waste.

And the funeral, the lonely drive out to the graveyard, with her mother beside her in the backseat of the car. How they forced Virginia to hug everyone who walked past the flowering casket, hundreds of mourners gathered on the green cemetery lawn. People eating afterward, people talking and laughing, kids running outside with cake in their hands.

It's anguish, they said of her vomit.

It's grief, her mother said.

Days later they loaded the car and drove out of town. Drove north to live with Virginia's grandparents in Reno, Nevada. That was the summer Vivian missed her period and discovered she was pregnant. The year Virginia started third grade. The new kid at school, no real friends of her own, the only girl with a pregnant mother and a dead father.

When Amanda was born they put a wooden crib in Virginia's room with musical toys and an electric humidifier, and there were new routines to learn, like how to change diapers and feed a crying baby and how to close the door without making a sound.

The next year, around the time Ed West came along, they moved into the house on Elko Avenue. By then Vivian was working at a casino, first as a waitress, then as a dealer at the blackjack tables. Wearing a red vest to work, wearing a man's black bow tie.

Sometimes Virginia thought about Travis but nobody ever mentioned his name or said where he'd gone or what finally happened to him. Eventually, she understood Travis was to blame for her father's death, although no one said as much, and she wasn't entirely certain when or how she figured this out. It wasn't until years later, in college, that she read about the trial, learned that Travis Lee Hilliard was found guilty of murder and sentenced to life in prison.

~

Virginia didn't know what else to say. The pillow on her lap, a thrift-store find, was coming apart at the seams, and she could hear the twins crying in the background.

"I hear babies," said Virginia, pulling on a loose thread. "Should I let you go?"

"It's only fussiness. A minute ago they were napping."

"But they're sick with a cold, I should probably let you go."

"Folsom Prison," said Amanda. "Don't you think it's odd? That's like twenty minutes from my house."

"I know," said Virginia, "I said this to Mom. The man could be anywhere. Not that you should worry, I don't mean that. You're nobody to him. But it's beside the point. The point is why hand down a life sentence if parole is an option? This makes no sense to me. The man doesn't deserve freedom, he deserves death."

"I guess," her sister said. "But it's been how long, like thirty years? That's longer than I've been alive. It's a long time behind bars."

"Not long enough," Virginia said. "Not for bludgeoning a man to death. They should've executed him. Not gas, not lethal injection. The electric chair. Hooded terror, death convulsions, eternal darkness."

Amanda let out a laugh.

"God, Virginia, tell me what you really think."

"You're the Republican," Virginia said. "I'm simply agreeing, for once. Relish the occasion."

"Thirty years ago, absolutely, I get it. Line up the firing squad. But now? After all this time? It doesn't seem right to me."

"That figures," Virginia said. "The one time I thought we'd agree, and you take the other side."

"I'm just saying. He's probably a completely different person now, don't you think?"

"No, Amanda! I don't think," she said. "But it doesn't matter, we don't have to agree. I don't expect you to understand. You weren't there. You didn't live through it."

"Virginia, I do understand. Like I said, I get it. What you and Mom went through?"

"But it's not just that," Virginia said. "Don't you see? It's everything else. It's my entire life. Altered, defined, even determined by what this man did. And not only my life, but yours and Mom's. And who knows? Now they're saying trauma can be passed down from one person to the next. On the genes, or whatever. So I don't know. My point is it's unfair to let him walk free. It's not fair to us."

"And I get it," said Amanda. "Everything you're saying. I totally understand."

But it wasn't true. She did not understand, was incapable of understanding, even if she meant well. It wasn't her fault, of course. Amanda had no memories of her father, no reminders, and no one to tell her who he really was.

"Anyway," said Amanda, "the girls are still crying, I'd better go. But I'm glad we talked. I mean, I sort of knew what happened, but not really, if that makes sense."

"We should've told you a long time ago," Virginia said. "One of us, anyway. Obviously, she knows more than I do."

~

Wearing rubber gloves and a faded cotton blouse, she piled her hair up and started throwing out old jars she found in the refrigerator. Expired mayonnaise, oily artichoke hearts, empty bottles of salad dressing. There were things hidden in the back, items neglected or forgotten. A gristly piece of meat covered in aluminum foil. Fuzzy strawberries in a green plastic basket. There were egg rolls from last week in a small Styrofoam box. Checking expiration dates, lifting the lids and smelling, she threw out containers of cottage cheese and half-eaten yogurt.

In Reno, on Elko Avenue, is where her mother changed. For the first time Virginia began to think of her as someone else, someone other than her mother, or someone in addition to the mother she knew. She began to think of her as a person with a name. Vivian smoking cigarettes, first in secret, now openly. At night fixing her hair before the mirror, Vivian in the bathroom, a cocktail in her hand, a completely different person, unknown.

Virginia unloaded the refrigerator onto the countertop, plastic tubs, glass jars, cartons of juice and milk, and sprayed glass cleaner on all three shelves. If there were stains she let them soak and then scrubbed them with a sponge. She wiped the rubber molding around the door along the edge and between the folds.

They slept in separate rooms, her mother's at the end of the long hallway, the door always closed. Virginia and Amanda down at the other end. She remembered the men who came to the house smelling of this or that cologne. Men who did not resemble one another, who did not look anything like Virginia's father.

She cleaned out the crisper. The wrinkled limes had to go, the squashy cucumber, the alfalfa sprouts unopened. She stuffed things into the garbage can, a twist of spinach, a dry scattering of onion skins, a wet bag of black cilantro. With her fingernail she picked at the red vegetable mess stuck to the plastic drawer.

It worried her. The belief, a childhood fear, that her mother would die soon. Her father gone, now her mother. A strange man would choke her to death, or else she'd die in a car accident, a head-on collision, or a light pole on the frozen motorway. Nights when her mother went dancing Virginia watched the eleven o'clock news, waiting for the live report from the accident scene.

She used scouring powder on the kitchen sink. Next she removed the burner grates to clean the stove. Pancake batter, bacon grease, spaghetti sauce. In the oven she chipped away at something black and cancerous. She polished countertops and cabinets using citrus spray on a damp cloth.

Then she unloaded the dishwasher, glasses, plates, and silverware. She stacked the cereal bowls on the shelf with the plates. She put the plastic cups and the big plastic bowls down in Timothy's cupboard. It was his cupboard because she allowed him to play in it when she fixed dinner, stacking the cups and bowls, placing the smaller bowls inside the larger, then separating them, repeating the sequence, and finding lids to match. Sometimes he removed the cups and bowls, every plastic lid, and crawled into the empty cupboard where he remained until Virginia pulled him out for dinner. She watched him do this and took notes for the psychiatrist. The cupboard was a hole, according to Bremmer, and holes were always dangerous. The only way to fix a hole was to plug it. Think of the cupboard as a mouth, he told her, a mouth with teeth. Any sharp edge, any object inside the cupboard. Timothy removes the objects, makes the inside smooth, the dark space inhabitable, then plugs the hole with his body, which is safe. Think of the body as a hard tongue in a soft mouth. The tongue plugs the hole, he said, producing a sense of safety and well-being. The cupboard is a refuge, a veritable sanctuary. "Otherwise, what?" she asked. Bremmer didn't hesitate. "Otherwise, he'll be eaten."

The facts were irrevocable but the ramifications remained unseen, the many black unravelings, how a single event determines all the rest, down to the third or fourth generation. It was plausible, even likely, that Timothy was marked in the womb, his genes tagged with calamity. And whose fault was that?

Broom in hand she swept bits into a pile, crumbs of wheat toast and flakes of bran cereal, a plastic bread clip, a raisin, a dead housefly. The kitchen floor was mottled with splatter stains. Virginia went over it twice with hot water and bleach.

In court he pled not guilty. He confessed to the robbery but claimed the killing was an accident. As though chance or fate had anything to do with it. The jury sided with the prosecutor. The crime premeditated, committed with malice aforethought, a heinous act, merciless, evil.

When the verdict was read the defendant showed no remorse.

In the bathroom she wiped pee stains off the toilet, the gross cavity behind the seat, and a smattering of her own menstrual blood off the linoleum floor. She poured bleach into the toilet and stirred the sides with a brush. She scrubbed a disgusting ring of filth and scum off the walls of the tub. The shower curtain would have to be pitched. She tossed an empty bottle of conditioner into the trash. She used a toothbrush on the moldy grout, on the caulking. Was it mold or mildew and why didn't she know the difference? She cleaned the hard water stains off the knobs and faucets. On the walls she sprayed foamy tile cleanser. Then with a pair of tweezers she extracted thick wads of hair from the shower drain.

She picked up and vacuumed, first in the living room, then in the bedrooms. In Timothy's room she gathered up cars and trucks, the wooden blocks, the toppled stacks. The blocks were hard and smooth. Squares, rectangles, and arches. They varied in shape and size but he stacked them indiscriminately. Large blocks resting on smaller ones, for example, stacking them higher and higher until the whole structure collapsed.

And the action figures with plastic legs and arms, what Brenner called the *sticking-out parts,* the parts Timothy removed and reattached obsessively. Virginia recorded this on her phone. Video of how he pulled off the limbs, covered the holes, the hollow joints, with his own fingers and thumbs, then reattached the arms and legs methodically. Bremmer said the plastic figures posed a dilemma: how to remove the vulnerable parts without opening new holes?

Virginia carried the garbage to the big dumpster downstairs and called her mother.

"I don't remember you complaining," her mother said.

"You're missing my point," Virginia said. "It's not about whether I wanted to go to church. That's not the issue. It's a question of *why.* Why did we stop going? Our whole life was church. Then Dad died and you never brought it up again, not once. Did we pray before dinner or at bedtime? I don't remember ever doing that in Reno."

"After thirty years you're curious?"

"Yes, is that odd? Is it difficult for you? You don't want to talk about it."

"I don't know what you want me to say, Virginia. I don't know the answer to your question or why you're even asking it. Maybe I'd had enough church for one lifetime. I needed something else, something different. I suppose I should've gotten you involved somewhere. I didn't think you were particularly interested. Now I'm hearing the opposite."

"The point is we didn't talk about it. Don't you see? You never told me anything."

"Virginia, you were a child. What can a person say to an eight-year-old?"

"I wasn't completely oblivious. You could've said something."

"We had to keep living. I didn't know how best to do that, I'm sorry. I was a widow, I was pregnant, I had you to look after. I was making it up along the way."

"I'm not asking for an apology," said Virginia. "I just wonder sometimes why everything had to change."

"Everything did change. Neither of us were ready for it, I know that. But this is what happens. And no one can tell you what to do or feel about anything. You simply make it up as you go."

They were both silent. Ten seconds of silence on the telephone. She imagined Timothy wandering in and out of rooms. She looked at the box of photos on the kitchen table.

Her mother said, "I probably shouldn't have mentioned anything."

"About what?"

"About Travis. I shouldn't have said anything to you or your sister. It doesn't matter. It's not useful to anyone."

"Of course you should've told me. Why would you say that? Of course it matters, it matters a lot. I wish you'd told me about the hearing. I don't know why you didn't. You see, this is what I'm talking about. You never tell me anything. I would've gone to the hearing. I would've said something."

"What would you have said?"

"I don't know. Something."

"So he's out of prison. It doesn't change anything. You don't come out of prison after so many years and simply pick up where you left off. The man's life is finished."

"What did you know about him?"

"When?"

"When he first showed up, what happened? He just showed up, some stranger?"

"Your father was eager to help people. He thought it was his duty, his calling in life. He didn't believe in chance or coincidence. In his mind if a person came to the church it was by the *sovereign will of God.* Your father's words. He trusted people, complete strangers. People like Travis who wandered in."

"What about you? Did you trust him? I can't imagine you trusting anyone."

"Travis wasn't the first person we helped. Or the only person. People came and went. Vagrants, destitute families, drug addicts, single mothers. You were too young, you don't remember, but your father would take them in for a few days or a week at a time. He would see a family sleeping in a car or a homeless person on the street and he would invite them to stay for several days, feed them hot meals, bring them into the church, give them Bibles. I cooked meals for many of them. Some even used our tub to bathe in. So, yes. We tried to help people. Others did too, people from the church, but your dad especially. He was very well-meaning."

"And you didn't think anything was wrong with him? With Travis. You didn't get a sense."

"The two of you played games together. Bouncing the ball outside or playing board games on the floor. He would tease you in a funny way. Do you remember Candy Land? How he used to call you Queen Frostine?"

"No."

"You used to get mad at him for it, but that was only an act. He thought the world of you and you enjoyed all the attention. Queen Frostine. I guess I should've been worried about you. About Travis being around you. Although he didn't strike me as a pervert, not to my thinking. But, who knows, maybe he was. We were too trusting. I imagine you had a crush on him."

"I never had a crush on him. What a horrible thing to say."

"It's true. You liked him. You always did."

"Not after what happened. I've always hated him, all my life. I still do."

"I never thought he was capable of violence. Your father didn't either. Travis was good-natured. Or so it seemed. He had a flash of defiance in him but we never guessed he was a dangerous man. I certainly never did."

"That's the problem," said Virginia. "Nobody knows anyone else. We think because we know certain details about a person we know all the rest. We trick ourselves into believing it. With Timothy I've learned this. He makes it explicit. Every gesture says *you don't know me*. I'm still trying to get a grip on this. I carried his body in my womb, which is as close as anyone can get. But do I know him? Does he know me?"

"We expect too much of one another. I've always thought that was true."

"*Blessed is he who expects nothing, for he shall never be disappointed.* That's Pope in case you're wondering."

"The Pope said that?"

"Not *the* Pope. Alexander Pope, the poet."

"He sounds like a very charming man. I'll have to tell Ed about him. Speaking of which, are you dating?"

"Hardly."

"You should be dating."

"It's not that easy. Someone handsome, intelligent? Someone not preoccupied with all the wrong things? I met one last night, briefly. Super cute guy, clever, good looking. His name is Matthias. Isn't that nice? I thought so. He invited me to sit with his friends. I was alone, mind you. That's who I've become, the woman who sits alone in the bar. Anyway, I say okay. But I've got to pee first. So I go to the bathroom and wait in line, and when I get into the stall I find out I'm bleeding. And I don't have anything on me, of course, because it's way too early. Like two weeks early. I have no idea what that's all about. Stress? I don't know. And I'm thinking why, why is this happening to me?"

"Well, did you get his number, at least?"

"No. Are you kidding? I left right away, practically ran from the place, totally humiliated."

"You're too hard on yourself, Virginia."

"I probably overreacted. I'm thinking now, in hindsight. It was dumb to run out like that. I should've taken his number. Instead, I came home and cried."

～

She folded the last basket of laundry in front of the TV. The regular newscast was interrupted by live footage of a car chase on the Santa Monica

Freeway. Helicopters drifted overhead, news choppers and LAPD. The reporter on scene provided commentary from the air, his squelchy voice altered by static and rotor noise.

A parade of cop cars with sirens and flashing lights chased the fugitive up and down the freeway. He led them in a circuit, Western to Overland, Overland to Western. A man with outstanding warrants, drug charges, weapons. He kept taking the same exits, crossing over the bridges, entering the on-ramps again at high speeds. According to reports, he was driving an old Honda Prelude with shiny wheels and an obnoxious muffler, an auction vehicle, fully restored, slammed and modified. The type of car Virginia often heard outside her window at three in the morning. But high above the freeway, from this altitude, the vehicle resembled one of Timothy's cars, a toy he clutched in his fist, the sort of thing that left a mark on his hand, that signified a lack of trust.

The pursuit continued well after dark. The driver swerving dangerously between lanes, braking and accelerating, slowing at the exits. There was nowhere to go, no way of escape, but the man refused to pull over. Western to Overland, Overland to Western.

Chapter 10

The bus driver let him out in Thousand Palms on the corner of Varner and Ramon where there was no Greyhound station.

"Which way to Palm Springs?" L.T. said.

The man pointed a finger.

"How far?"

"'Bout nine-ten miles."

"How am I supposed to get there?"

The driver shook his head. "Best to call a cab or some other," he said. Then he closed the door and the bus moved on.

The night was warm and windy. L.T. was in the high desert now without so much as a wristwatch to tell the time. He knew only that it was late at night. He could feel the highway unraveling in his bones. From a vending machine at the station in Fresno he had eaten a cold sandwich with sliced cheese and mayonnaise. On the bus peanuts and a chocolate bar. But that was several hours ago. Now he was hungry again.

He would have to find a telephone. The muscles in his legs were stiff. He pushed into a convenience store and asked the clerk where to find a pay-phone. The kid said the only one he knew of was behind the gas station across the street. L.T. bought a pack of cigarettes and a lighter. He withdrew cash and asked the kid to break it into smaller bills and coins. In the booth across the street he paged through the phone book and dialed for a cab.

He rubbed the back of his neck and peered into the dark. The driver had pointed his finger in that direction. Nine or ten miles was too far to walk. L.T. opened the pack of cigarettes carefully and slowly. His back was sore and while he waited for the cab he started thinking about the prostitute who had robbed him the night before. He wondered how many cigarettes were left in the pack she stole. Then he told himself to forget about it. *Blessed are the merciful, for they shall obtain mercy.*

He was about to light a cigarette when the cab pulled up alongside him. The driver wore glasses with black plastic frames and needed a haircut and shave. The interior of the car smelled like corn chips or corn nuts, something in a snack package. L.T. tucked the cigarettes into his shirt pocket. He tried to make pleasant conversation but the radio was too loud. A talk show of some kind. The host was irate and kept using the word *incensed*. In Palm Springs they parked outside a two-story building on a dark leafy street.

"This is it," the driver said.

L.T. read the sign on the wall, *Darren P. Williams, Attorney at Law*.

"Darren P. Williams. You heard of him?"

The man offered no reply. L.T. watched his eyes in the rearview mirror.

"I assume there are hotels nearby. Can you take me to one?"

"I've got to know which one."

"Any hotel is fine. Nothing too expensive."

"See what I mean? What's expensive? I don't know."

"What do they run around here? What are the rates?"

"Two or three hundred a night. It all depends."

"Nothing cheaper?"

"Not around here. Listen, I have to let you out. I've got another call waiting for me."

"Alright," said L.T. "What do I owe you?"

People were out walking along both sides of Palm Canyon Drive. They were gathered outside of bars smoking and laughing. Young women in skirts and heels. Club music, crowded patios. It was after one in the morning when he found a motel on a side street. There were no rooms available. The innkeeper mentioned the names of two hotels and pointed vaguely in opposite directions. L.T. forgot their names immediately. Anyway, the night was reaching a point of diminishing returns. In other words, you rented an expensive room for a toilet and a shower and five or six hours of rest. Then again, what were the options? He retrieved the cigarette, the loose one from his shirt pocket. He would walk until he found a decent place to stay, regardless of the cost.

Up ahead several men were arguing. L.T. thought it was laughter at first. But no, they were arguing, a group of young men, three on one side and two on the other. L.T. could not hear what was said. The three were military types, all ears and shoulders. There was a Marine base out here somewhere. Camp something-or-other. He could not remember the name. The other two wore shorts and collared shirts. They wore shoes without socks.

They were gay, or one of them was. L.T. could tell by the voice he was hearing. Maybe they were a couple. In prison they were known as *galboys*. These flamboyant types who painted their lips and eyes and waggled around the cellblock. L.T. tried not to despise them. It was wrong to do that. The *galboys* were the feeble ones, the weakest among the prisoners, the most terrified and therefore the most desperate. You would help them if you could, if your own personal safety was not at risk. But that's not how it worked inside. Inside you were always at risk. L.T. had learned not to interfere.

He stopped short with the thought of turning around or finding another route toward the hotels. It was the smart thing to do. He did not want to get caught up in some drunken scrum. He was considering his options when one of the Marines pushed one of the *galboys* against the wall and held him by the throat. And the other one tried to help his friend, or his lover, or whoever he was. But the two Marines grabbed him, too.

L.T. called out, "Hey! Cut it off!"

The sound startled him and he felt a rush of anxiety and dread. The words were all impulse. He had meant to say *cut it out* or *knock it off*. In any case, he was involved in the argument now. He had involved himself by issuing a command without considering the consequences. The five men were watching as L.T. started toward them with all the swagger he could muster. He walked tall, shoulders square, trying to make himself look like a bigger man, a man with some authority. He could feel the adrenaline ramping up. It made him feel stronger and more fierce than he really was. He was not a fierce man. Yet the thought came to mind that he was a hardened ex-con and these were only boys. He tossed the unlit cigarette and hollered again. "Knock it off, damnit!"

It was three on three now. L.T. had taken sides in the matter on a mere assumption of the facts. Three against two. The stronger against the weaker. He did not want to fight. The idea was to break it up peacefully. If they were Marines, as he suspected, then they were men who followed orders. Exert a high level of command and they will obey.

But when he came near, one of the Marines threw a swift right hand at him, more like a jab than a cross. The kid was drunk and off balance and it was not a very good punch. L.T. ducked out of the way and felt the boy's fist graze the side of his head. A scrape or a burn is what it felt like. L.T. stumbled against the wall of the building and dropped the bag he was carrying. He was in the fight now. From a crouch he came up hard with his own right hand, a wild swing that caught the kid under the jaw. And then the other two Marines were up against him and he took blows to his face and his left ear. They had him jammed up against the wall and it felt like his left ear had been ripped hotly away. He felt several quick hard blows to his kidney. Pinned to the wall, he tried to tighten his stomach and protect his head.

The two gay men were yelling and he figured they were fighting to pull the Marines off him. He knew it would all be over soon. Fights never lasted very long. But first he had to get off the wall. Against the wall he was an open target. With his head lowered he lunged outwardly and tackled somebody around the waist. He drove hard with his legs until they were on the ground together. The fight had whirled off the curb onto an empty street. L.T. dragged the guy down to the pavement and was trying to hit him with short arms. He was trying to find the guy's face in order to hit it. Then another Marine grabbed L.T. around the neck and corkscrewed him off the other one. L.T. hit the ground hard and rolled, hitting his head on the pavement. He tried to scramble to his feet but fell over sideways.

He braced himself for another barrage but no one rushed after him. Looking up he saw the Marines running off and heard their laughter. He was glad it was over. The Marines were gone and he assumed the police were on their way. Things like this did not happen without police. The other two men were trying to pick him up off the ground. They were lifting him by his arms. They were speaking words but L.T. could not understand them. All of his adrenaline was gone, used up like rocket fuel, and he felt great pain, which was louder than whatever they were saying, clearer than any spoken word. They were trying to help, but L.T. waved them off. He made a sudden heaving motion and sat upright. He felt soreness in his ribs and back. His face hurt. The left cheekbone and ear. He made sure his ear was intact and not bleeding. His left forearm was scraped raw but he assured the two men it was nothing. It took some polite arguing before they allowed him to stagger away.

It was a mild night, rather serene now that the fight was over, and the cool wind was quite soothing against his skin. He could see things very clearly, the sharp outline of the town with its storefront windows and windy palms. But his head felt drunk and unsteady and taking up the duffle bag he wandered into a nearby park and found rest on wooden bench. When he came awake it was Sunday morning. The light was gray, the grass wet with dew.

Chapter 11

The heavy bleeding was over. Maybe. It was hard to be certain. She unwrapped a tampon and inserted it. Then in T-shirt and underwear she walked through the house, no lights, quiet rooms, unimagined stillness. In the kitchen she poured water into a glass. Outside, over the rooftops and ragged palms, the light was violet gray. She opened the slider to the balcony and walked out on her bare feet to feel the air. Sunday morning, the hour of dark windows and obscure doorways. The air smelled damp, earthy, floating up from the soil. Out on the freeway, in the grim distance, a handful of cars were traveling into the dismal city. She thought of her son, still in bed dreaming, if indeed he dreamed.

She went into the bedroom to find a pair of shorts. It was too early to be awake but here she was, an hour before sunrise. She started a pot of coffee and opened her laptop on the kitchen table. In time his name might appear on social networking sites or in the public records. Or else he would find a job and his name would come up on a company's website. No one was invisible these days. Everybody was exposed. Out of curiosity she searched her own name and found an accurate chronology of residential addresses, phone numbers, faculty lists, direct links to three articles she had published after grad school, each of the twenty-eight women across the nation who shared Virginia's exact name. If Travis Lee Hilliard wanted to find her, he could do it easily, unannounced. But then what reason would he have? What motive? No, she thought, any such appearance was extraordinarily unlikely. And, anyway, what she said to her mother was more frightening and true. If Travis showed up at her door she'd kill him.

In dreams it was always her father appearing unexpectedly. He was the murderer let out of prison with whiskered jowl and woolen hat. Or the man arriving home from a faraway place, his wife remarried, his daughter fretful and restless. The scenarios changed, the particulars, but never the baffling circumstances surrounding her father's long absence. Where had he gone, and why, and what happens now? In every dream his manner was distant and evasive, never contrite, never apologetic. He was there, but always difficult to approach.

Virginia sipped her coffee and listened to the sparrows outside her window. Somewhere a dog was barking. She pulled two photographs out of the box she'd bought. The first picture was of a man driving an automobile. A passenger in the front seat had pointed a camera at him. What Virginia saw was the driver's fleshy profile, his wiry sideburns, the dead weight of his chin. He was staring at the road ahead, but his thoughts belonged to the past. Or so it seemed. The other photograph showed an old woman in a convalescent hospital. She was sitting in a green armchair, gripping a tissue in her right hand, the fabric of her hospital gown pulled tight across her humped stomach. The woman was not aware of the camera, or the tube in her nose, or the way her skin smelled of crystallized urine. Her eyes were flat. Hard as marbles. Her family was gone, the room, everything.

~

Later that morning Virginia drove up to the shooting range. It was crowded with men. There were women also, wives and girlfriends, but it was mostly men, bearded and clean-shaven, mountain types, military types, Harley types. Men wearing white T-shirts and leather vests, others wearing all camouflage. Men who drove four-wheel-drive pickups with extra shocks or springs, or whatever it was that made pickups stand tall on their wheels. Men in blue jeans and cowboy boots, men wearing combat pants and black tactical gear. Men with tattoos: the flaming skulls and medieval blades, the iron crosses, the implements of epic torture. Tattoos of women, angelic full-breasted women, blue whores and seductresses. The names of first wives, the names of the combat dead. There were motorcycle tattoos, military insignia, American flags and screaming eagles, bull horns and buck antlers.

They carried holstered revolvers, semi-automatic pistols, assault rifles with scopes and laser pointers. They hauled crates of ammunition to the firing line, hundreds of rounds, thousands. Bullets designed to fragment and expand. Rounds measured in millimeters and grains.

Virginia found her assigned station at the far end of the firing line under the corrugated awning. A long table covered in soft green felt ran end to end. The rule was to shoot from behind the table. The targets were posted downrange under the sun. They sold them inside the office, the classic bull's-eye targets, the competition grids, the human silhouettes. Virginia purchased a three-pack of paper targets, black silhouettes of the male head and torso, and two boxes of full metal jacket cartridges. She brought her own pistol, clear plastic eyewear, yellow earplugs.

It was not her first time on the firing line. She knew what to do. Listen to the line officer, follow instructions. She could feel the wallop of gunfire in her chest as she loaded multiple cartridges into the magazine, the spring mechanism stiffening with pressure as she pressed down each bullet with her thumb. She liked cradling the bullets in the palm of her hand, the gravity of multiple rounds, the weight and substance of copper and lead, the brassy smell. The bullets seemed heavy but the pistol felt light in her grip even when it was fully loaded. She did not understand the laws of physics, the transfer of mass or the termination of opposing forces. What she understood was how perfectly the gun fit inside her hand. It was devised for her hand, or else her hand was devised for the gun, an adaptive strand of evolutionary logic. It was a simple design, ingenious. Made of matte black polymer, the gun appeared toy-like. And she had decided, after her first experience at the range, that there was definitely something infantile about target shooting, the puerile astonishment of discharge and penetration.

Her son never played with toy guns. One, because she didn't buy them for him. Two, because Timothy wouldn't know how to play with it, how to pretend, so the gun, as a concept, made no sense. In his mind the world was all shape and surface. The point of objects was to tap them for pleasure, the point of a hole was to plug it. Anyway, Virginia had an opinion on the subject of boys playing with guns. Perhaps if they were to grow out of it by age ten or twelve, okay. But that's not how it worked. Men grew into their guns.

After buying her own handgun she realized why it was true. There was a reason why men never gave up their guns. Or no, it was not reason in the truest sense, it was not rational. It had nothing to do with fear or protection or Constitutional rights. It was intuitional, it was a visceral experience formerly unknown to her. The perfect symmetry of palm and pistol, the trigger pull, an explosive shock that rattled the root-ends of her teeth.

Virginia owed this latest fascination to a former student, Kyle Knox, a guy in her Composition class last fall who always wrote KKX on the sign-in roster. She knew from the first week of school he would be problematic. The way he looked, always a sneer on his face, a smart-ass remark to every question. All semester he mocked the reading assignments and made strange noises in class. He argued with Virginia, he belittled other students in conversation, he commandeered discussions with his extremist tirades. Kyle Knox. She gave him warnings and then told him to leave class. When he balked she threatened to call campus police. Then she did call campus police. They got involved. The Dean got involved. Her colleagues on campus were incensed. Nevertheless, teaching had always been a lonely profession, particularly for the adjunct instructors who rarely spoke to anyone outside of class. In the morning, standing at the copy machine, her colleagues were sympathetic, but that was all. She even told Neil, the ex-husband, but what could he do? Nothing. She was alone in this.

Kyle Knox disappeared for a week and then returned wearing his black trench coat. The racist comments, the vulgar gestures. When he called her a cunt she kicked him out of class again. Finally, middle of November, she had him permanently removed. Over the next two weeks he sent her threatening emails. One day she saw him on campus watching her leave class.

Thanksgiving week, a day before the break, she found her front tires slashed. She called campus police to report the incident but there was little they could do. They would look into it, of course, review the security footage, and they would provide an escort anytime she needed one. They were committed to her protection, they said. Virginia felt sick. What if Kyle Knox brought a gun into the classroom and killed everyone inside? He matched the type.

So she bought a gun of her own. Black Friday, found it on sale, a Glock 9mm with a box of Blazer hollow points. She told her story to the salesman behind the counter who was genuinely sympathetic, full of understanding. He wore his pistol on his hip, and not just during business hours. "Don't try to wound him," he said to Virginia. "Never try to wound anyone."

The message was clear. Kill the son-of-a-bitch. But it had to be an act of self-defense, an open and shut case of defending your life. "Think of the typical jury," he said. "Do you wear glasses, contact lenses?" Virginia didn't wear either. "I was about to tell you to wear them at all times. What they're looking for are technicalities. She wasn't wearing her glasses at the time of the shooting. Or she didn't mean to pull the trigger, she panicked and shot.

Something like that. You'd be surprised. Try to pin you for negligence. I've seen it happen." He shook his head gravely. "Tell them you knew exactly what you were doing. Tell them you feared for your life, and stick to it."

She nodded. It was good advice. She was grateful to this man and was in no hurry to leave his shop.

"I'd even take a defensive shooting class if I was you," he said. "Defensive skills. You can apply for a concealed weapons permit, log some hours on the range. Go all the way with it is what I'd do. Then they'll take you seriously."

There was an application to complete, a federal background check. She waited ten days before she could pick up the gun. Then she brought it to campus fully loaded for the remainder of the term. She hid it in the zippered pocket of her book bag. No one had a clue. At home she practiced reaching into the bag. At school, during the final week of instruction, when there were no students in the room, she would drop behind the computer desk, unzip the middle pocket, and reach inside. She practiced the crouch in her skirt, wearing heels. In the event of Kyle Knox she would do it like this. She would use the desk as cover. From behind the desk she would fire across the room.

He never appeared, never entered her classroom armed. He slashed her tires and maybe he was satisfied. During winter break Virginia was off campus and did not think much about it. But in January, when classes resumed, she did not forget to bring the gun that first month. She waited for Kyle Knox to step out into the open, in the parking lot, on the main quad, inside the dining hall. She searched for his face in every crowd.

On the overhead speaker the line officer gave instructions to cease-fire, to clear all weapons. Guns on the table open and unloaded, chambers empty, magazines on the bench, muzzles pointed downrange. They all marched out together, a cohort of twenty or thirty shooters advancing toward the targets. Between firing sessions the shooters had several minutes to examine their performance and to remove or attach targets to the frames as necessary. Virginia went out with them to clip her silhouettes in place twenty-five feet away. It was hot under the sun. The dry hills surrounding the range were treeless and white. On another section of the range where they shot high-powered rifles she could see, two or three hundred feet in the distance, puffs of dry white smoke, little whiffs of cloudy dirt, where bullets penetrated the embankments.

She returned to her station and waited until the line officer gave the order to commence firing. Then the air exploded with sound and power, the percussive force of war marching through her vital organs, vibrating bone and brain matter. Virginia raised her pistol, aimed at the shadow-target downrange, fired once, then fired a few more times, three quick knocks against the target. She fired at the chest and at the head. She had heard this phrase repeated in a movie, "Two in the chest, one in the head." She couldn't remember which movie, didn't know the context, didn't care to know. What she liked was the rhythm of eight perfect syllables. Two in the chest, one in the head. She aimed the gun and fired a series of three rounds. Two in the chest, brief pause, one in the head. She did it again, repeating the three-shot sequence until the magazine was empty.

The pistol lay flat on the green felt as she reloaded the magazine. She would have to pace herself. There was no category on her budget sheet for whiskey and bullets. Money would be tight for the remainder of the month. Summers were the worst. They were the leanest months and this summer she was scheduled to teach only one course. She would need more money, more financial support. She would have to talk to Neil about that. Her opportunities were diminishing.

During the next sequence she aimed with careful precision before firing. The goal was to identify an area on the target, the heart for example, or the middle forehead, and create a tight grouping of six or seven bullet holes within a two-inch diameter. If she pulled the trigger too hard or too fast she was off the mark. But when the trigger gave on its own, unexpectedly, her shot was more accurate. She could do it when she focused, when she relaxed. Breathing in and out she held her aim until the gun fired. She learned this about accuracy, that it required the steady flow of oxygen and precise visual acuity. If she held her breath, or if she stared too long at the target without blinking, her aim was off. The thing to do was relax, breathe easy, let the gun do all the work. After a hundred rounds it was over. She picked up the brass casings by the handful and tossed them into an orange bucket. She trashed the empty ammunition cartons, the paper silhouettes ravaged with holes, shoulders torn away, eyes ripped through, head and heart massacred.

~

She had to ask about their weekend together because Neil was never forthcoming. That was one issue they had between them. Neil would hurry through the transfer, *here are his things I've got to go,* and he wasn't inclined like any normal person to share a funny thing that might have happened, an endearing moment, an incident, and so she made a point of asking.

"He kept putting quarters in his mouth," Neil said. "Every time I turned around he was sucking on a quarter."

"Where did he get the quarters?"

"I don't know. He finds things."

Neil put an envelope on the kitchen table with money in it. It wasn't his table anymore and he seemed aware of this fact. They sat on opposite sides.

"Coins," he said. "Does he do this with you?"

"No," she said. "He does everything else with me. What about the wetsuit?"

"We took off the wetsuit in the middle of the night," Neil said. "He slept right through it. We pushed and pulled. I took this arm, she took that one. He slept right through it, the little wishbone. We're calling him Wishbone now."

"Don't give him a nickname," she said. "I hate nicknames. Especially *Wishbone.* Whose idea was that?"

Timothy came in and circled the room. Her son was home and she felt safer now.

Neil said, "Show Mom your new airplane."

"A new airplane? Let me see it. I want to see."

He circled past. She was not hurt or offended when he ignored her. He could not be held responsible for certain things. He was simply unable. As long as he was present, that's what mattered. As long as she said whatever came to mind and he was present to hear it.

"Airplane," she said, and he circled past. "Clouds, sky, flying." Always a note of desperation in this, no way to hide it, not even from herself.

Timothy left the room and she said to Neil, "Does he get along with the girl?"

"The girl?"

"Yeah, the girl, what's-her-name."

"Don't call her the girl."

"I don't remember her name, Neil."

"It's Kendal."

"Fine, whatever. Do they get along? Which is what I asked."

"Like two peas in a pod," he said.

"Oh, right. Two peas."

"He totally loves her," Neil said.

"I'm sure."

The envelope was unmarked. Inside there was a check for alimony, for child support. The amicable sum. Neil insisted on sealing the envelope.

"Did we have good sex, Neil? When we were married?"

"I don't know. What kind of question is that?"

"It was great, wasn't it? Sometimes?"

"I don't really remember."

"Not even vaguely?"

"It's hazy," he said. "Why are you asking? Is this what you wanted to talk about? In your text you said you wanted to talk."

"We have to talk about money," she said.

"Did I tell you I bought him an ice cream?"

"I'm only teaching one class this summer. That's all they had."

"He got all pissed off. It was his own fault. He was eating it way too slowly. Or let me rephrase. He wasn't eating it at all. I told him, hurry up or it'll melt."

"I'll need about a thousand extra, maybe eight hundred a month, but that's cutting it."

"He was holding it against his lips but not eating. So of course it started melting everywhere, dripping all over. He didn't like that. He started throwing a fit, flapping his hands, making guttural sounds."

"Maybe we can work something out. A payment plan. I can pay you back in the fall. A few hundred every month."

"So I tried taking it from him," Neil said. "Give me the ice cream! But no, he wouldn't give it. He would not give it to me. I said, you won't enjoy this. I said, *sticky*. You know how he gets with sticky things. I said, *sticky*. I said, look at you. You're all sticky now. He didn't like it. His fingers stuck together, chocolate all over his face. But he wouldn't give me the ice cream. He's stubborn. What's the word? Obstinate. He's very obstinate."

"A thousand extra a month for three months," she said. "Make it four. Let's do four. As soon as October rolls around I can start paying you back. A few hundred every month. Starting around Halloween. I'll keep close accounts."

"And he's squinting like this. Like he's on the toilet only nothing's coming out. Or like he's trying to cry, trying to force himself to make tears but the tears won't come. And he's so pissed off, you know, pure rage. I didn't know what to do. There's nothing you can do in that situation. I'm looking at Kendal, she's looking at me."

"So what happened?"

"So what happened was I finally reached down and grabbed the ice cream with my bare hand, not the cone, just the cold scoop of chocolate ice cream on top. Or what was left of it. And suddenly he stops screaming and looks at the mound of ice cream in my hand. And we're both kind of shocked standing there looking at it, all three of us, and then I squeeze my hand and the ice cream curls up through my fingers and out both sides of my fist. And were all just staring at it, like it means something."

Neil went silent. His face changing from bewilderment to something else. His smile was gone and the inner corners of his eyebrows were slightly raised, just like the book said, and she recognized what is called the sadness brow. It lasted only a moment, then Neil sort of laughed and raised his eyebrows to clear whatever was there.

"And then what?"

"He was fine afterward. He ate his cone and tagged along. We found a public restroom and I cleaned his face and hands."

When Timothy came into the room again Virginia caught him and gave him a tight squeeze. He smelled like his pillow.

"There you are," she said. "Where's your airplane? I want to see Timothy's new airplane."

She let go when he pulled away. She looked at Neil in shorts and T-shirt, wearing sandals. He was handsome when dressed down. She knew what he looked like underneath, the stride and flow of his body, and of course it came to her, the thought of how good it felt whenever they were together and the weight of him on top of her. You can be completely over it and still have moments of longing.

"You want anything?" she said. "A beer or anything?"

And then Timothy came into the room and she said, "Here he comes," and they both watched as he felt his way along the circular path, touching every object. When he turned the corner for the hallway she said, "There he goes," so that he might think of coming and going as opposite emotions, as opposing states of mind.

"Speaking of going."

"I have beer," she said.

He did the thing with the wristwatch.

"Are you sure?" she asked him.

Neil made his way to the front door. He offered her the simple version of why there was no more money. He explained the devaluation of the investment portfolio, the empty bank accounts. He said he could show her the financial statements as proof he wasn't a liar.

"I don't know what to do," she said.

"Find another job."

"Another job doing what?"

"Whatever people do, people without PhDs."

He said this on his way out the door. Virginia stopped him.

"Hey, I forgot to tell you," she said.

Neil turned around.

"Tell me what?"

"They let him out."

"Let who out?"

"Travis Lee Hilliard."

Chapter 12

L.T. waited in the lobby while the lawyer finished a call. It was a small office in an older building with leather chairs and leafy plants and magazines. Architectural photographs hung in silver frames on the walls. The receptionist, a freckle-chested woman with blond hair and red cheeks, was rubbing lotion into her hands.

"Coffee?" she asked.

"No, thank you. I've dragged you in on a Sunday. My apologies."

She smiled, staring a moment at his wounded face, his scuffed clothing. She glanced at the black bag at his feet and then got up to retrieve his file from a cabinet. L.T. looked at the pictures on the walls. Photographs of houses built in the 1950s. Desert homes with sweeping interiors and large rectangular windows and bean-shaped swimming pools.

After a time the lawyer came out of his office. He was a tall dark-skinned man wearing tan slacks and cowboy boots. He wore a light blue shirt and a bolo tie. L.T. rose up gingerly to greet him.

"What happened to you, Tex?"

They shook hands.

"Lost my balance."

"Darren P. Williams."

"L.T. Hilliard."

"Hear that, Glenda? The man say he lost his balance. How many days he been out of prison?"

"Two days," said the receptionist.

"Uh-huh. Come on back then, Mr. Hilliard."

L.T. gripped his bag and followed Williams into a private room with floor-to-ceiling bookshelves. In the center of the room was an oval table with chairs. The window faced a row of trees in the parking lot.

"Have a seat at the table. Coffee? Water?"

"I'm fine, thanks."

"You don't look fine."

"It's just a little swelling."

"Swelling, huh? Well, let's look at what we got."

He opened the file.

"Title transfer," he said. "What we call a gift deed: 'with no consideration other than love and affection.' How's that for legalese?"

"And this makes me the owner."

"Makes you the title holder. More important. Anybody can claim ownership. Title holder owns the property. Be surprised who comes in here claiming this or that. Which is why we don't say *owner*. We say *title holder*. Title holder owns the property, simple as that."

"Where is it?"

"We'll get to the *where*. First you got some marks to make. Your uncle did his part, now it's your turn. Sign everywhere you see the X."

L.T. took the ink pen and flipped through the pages.

"Old Morris," Williams said, and laughed.

"You knew him."

"Bought a horse from me is how I knew him. Then I put him to work for me, on occasion you might say. Glenda and I handle some real estate sales on the residential side of things. Need handiwork from time to time."

"How'd he die?"

"Got sick."

"Cancer?"

"Don't know what it was. Don't think old Morris knew himself. Came in here one day and said he was sick, and we had us a little talk. Mentioned your name."

"Where'd he die, the hospital?"

"No, wasn't no hospital. Died at home. Wouldn't a found him neither, except it weren't for the Mormons. Couple a boys knocking on doors out in the boonies. Knew it right away when they come up near the front door. Story in *The Desert Sun* is how I heard about it."

L.T. imagined Morris dead in his mobile home. He pictured his body lumped under bedcovers, then slumped in a chair, a record player hissing static.

"This here is the title of the pickup. Write your information in this part and mail it to the DMV."

"Does it run?"

"Been sitting out with the tumbleweeds about two years, so you got to figure."

"I have another favor to ask. Something unrelated. I have to call my parole officer and I can't seem to find a payphone."

"Forget payphones. Payphones are gone. Hardly anyone even has a telephone anymore. Meaning a landline. What you need is a mobile phone. Get yourself set up with a service plan. I got me a Samsung with unlimited data. But we'll ask Glenda to hook you up with that. Something else I got to tell you. About that horse I sold your uncle. Name's Black Joe and he's been eating my grain twice a day. Kept him as a favor to old Morris and don't intend on charging anything for it. But he's your horse now, like it or not. Unless you want to sell him. That's up to you."

"I don't know much about horses."

"Tell you the truth, they don't know much about us either. But somehow it works."

Williams pushed back his chair and stood up.

"I have another obligation this morning. Afterward I'll drive you out to your property so we can take a look. In the meantime you make your phone call and I'll talk to Glenda about the other thing."

L.T. stood with great effort and shook the man's hand again.

"Mr. Williams, I'm grateful. This is all new to me."

"Uh-huh. Call me Darren."

～

Williams drove a newer model Cadillac SUV with gold trim. The windows were blacked out. The seats were made of soft leather and included armrests. Williams put on the cold air and turned the music down low. He wore a cowboy hat and aviator sunglasses.

"Nice truck you've got."

"Palm Springs," he said. "Got to have it. Style is what they live by in the desert. See an ugly mountain, build a pretty house. Can't find no water, dig a swimming pool. No grass anywhere, build a dozen green golf courses and turn on the sprinklers. See what I'm saying?"

"You like it out here."

"Got my Frank Sinatra house and two acres of landscaping. What they call Rat-Pack living. Palm trees, swimming pools, and dry martinis." He smiled. "Come a long way from forty acres and a mule. But let's talk about you."

"Not much to say."

"You ain't telling me what really happened."

"There was a scuffle. I tried to break it up."

"Uh-huh. Peacemaker. Okay then, what are we talking about? Damsel in distress type thing?"

"Not exactly."

"I hope she was pretty."

L.T. laughed. He looked down at his phone. He tried to make it work by touching the screen.

"They show you how to use that thing? You looking like a kid with a loaded gun."

"The girl in the store gave me the rundown. I'm trying to remember how she did it."

"Swipe and tap. That's all you got to remember. Treat it like a lady."

"Treat it like a lady. Funny, I've forgotten how to do that too."

"Yeah, well, they got *pills* now. You know about these pills they got?"

"I've heard of them."

"I guess you had TV in there. So you know what's going on in the world then. I don't have to bring you up to speed on the global chaos."

"I follow the headlines."

"They give you internet access? You know about Google and YouTube and all that?"

"I never used it much."

"That's what you're holding in your hand. The Internet. You want the facts about something, or say you got a how-to question, you swipe and tap. That's how they do it now."

The road out of town passed through a windmill farm, tall pointed turbines with three-bladed propellers, hundreds of them, even thousands. Some were turning slowly and others stood like white sculptures in a garden museum. The sky was clear and the bright distances were ruthless on the eyes. Sun, rock, and wind. It was ancient land. A dry lakebed surrounded by rust-colored mountains. At one time there had been water, but now the water was gone.

"I got a question for you. Something I've always wondered. How's a man survive so long in State Pen?"

"Like a snake under a rock. And if you're fortunate, as I was, God grabs you by the head."

"I see. So you a religious man."

"I don't think of myself as a religious man, not especially."

"So by 'God' what you mean is in the general sense."

"No, I wouldn't say that either. My belief is specific. Jesus saved me is the clearest way I can put it."

"You was a convert is what I'm hearing."

"I thought I was going to die. I mean that literally. Prison is a hard place. And scary as hell. Living in constant fear and paranoia and hopelessness. They gave me a life sentence, you understand, twenty-five years to life."

"I won't ask why."

"I wouldn't tell you."

"I wouldn't even think to ask."

"In prison you learn what it means to be stuck between a rock and a hard place. You don't want to live, but you don't want to die either. The human mind can't imagine death. Before you were born you had no consciousness. And you want to believe that when you die it's like that again. But you can't do it. The mind is incapable of erasing itself. So what you imagine is pure darkness. I used to dream about it. About a darkness so black my whole body had disappeared. I couldn't see it, couldn't feel it. All I could feel, the only sensation, was panic. And there was a sense, an awareness you might say, that everything was final, that it was permanent. As if my soul was locked in an eternal state of dread. So I'd come awake in the dark confinement of my cell—and it's pretty dark in there at night—and I'd sit up and look around and find the light outside the cell door. Then it would take a moment for my heart to settle down and I would lie on my back again, unable to sleep, thinking how lucky I was to be alive, because there were other men, convicted murderers like me, on death row facing execution."

"That's some deep shit, right there."

"I don't know how else to describe it. There aren't any words for it really. You say the word 'God' and people think one thing or another. It's very specific to the individual. Or not, depending on who you ask. But I'm not talking about religion. It's more than that. I know it sounds strange. I don't understand it myself. But when I got saved, death no longer frightened me, not in the same way."

"And now you a free man."

"Now I'm a free man," he said, "so they say."

"You still got some years left in you. What you need is good woman. Get your mojo back."

"I'll need a job first."

"I might have some odd jobs here and there. If you're interested. I can look around."

"I'm not particular."

"Let me think some and get back to you on that. Meantime you got a new cell phone and a service plan. We'll take you out to your new rock, see what's what."

The Cadillac had a GPS screen that looked like a sophisticated weather map on the local news. L.T. glanced at the screen and then stared out the window. A satellite was orbiting somewhere high above them. The truck followed the arrow to Yucca Valley where the highway cut through a row of filling stations, fast-food restaurants, a supermarket and a hardware store. Then on past the roadside motels, the plywood billboards, a Baptist church and a bowling alley. Williams talked about his wife and kids. He talked about playing football at USC and his law practice. The things you say to people you hardly know.

Morris's place lay somewhere between Joshua Tree and Twentynine Palms. There was a dirt road that bisected the highway. L.T. would have to identify a set of landmarks to find the turnoff. Triangulate his position by noting something close to the highway and one or two points in the far distance. The row of mailboxes was one thing to remember.

The dirt road split three times. He could see houses and trailers set off from the main road. The boundaries were vague. Williams followed the map for at least half a mile before the road ended at the foot of a mountain. It formed a circular path in front of the mobile home. A corrugated shed stood beside the house and Morris's old pickup, a blue and white Chevy Silverado, was parked in the weeds between the shed and the corral.

"Old Morris done found some peace and quiet out here, didn't he? What you think, L.T.?"

"I owe you a deluxe carwash. And more for taking up your Sunday."

Williams gave him the house keys on a ring. One key opened the front door, another fit the padlock on the shed, and the third key had the GM stamp on it.

"Take a look around," Williams said. "I have to pick up this call."

It was hot outside the Cadillac. It was the word *heat* repeated in waves. He felt a burning sensation on his arms, little flares of intensity. Nothing moved under the cactus and scrub. Cat claw, saltbush, snake weed. In time he would learn the common names. For now he understood the basic truth. There was rock and no wind. Only a natural oven made of baked sandstone and coarse granite.

L.T. fit his key into the slot. He opened the door of the mobile home but did not enter. The trapped heat had to come out first. He stepped off the small porch to clear the way. With his eyes he followed the horizon. He saw no birds circling in the air. Only Joshua trees scattered across the plain. He saw rooftops in the distance and small cars out on the highway.

He left the front door open and walked around to the pickup. He passed a black oil drum where Morris must have burned his garbage. There was a red wheelbarrow overturned. He saw three bags of powdered cement and some fence posts. In the bed of the truck he found a bale of dry hay, a broken shovel head, an oil rag. He used the rag like a potholder on the door handle. Hotter inside than out. He opened both doors and unlatched the hood. He leaned in and tried the key but the battery was dead. It hurt to lean in, hurt even to breathe.

Behind the seat he found a lug wrench, a pneumatic jack, and a quart of motor oil. He found other things behind the seat. A pair of work gloves and a ballpoint pen, a sales receipt, a few bits of loose change, a set of jumper cables. He pulled out the cables and set them on the seat. He was sweating now, his mind running on shorter wavelengths, his vision razor thin. On the horizon things danced and shimmered. He would need sunglasses and a hat, maybe a bandanna for his neck.

At the shed he turned the key in the padlock and unlatched the handle. With the door open he could smell axle grease and gasoline fumes. Inside were all of Morris's tools, organized and disorganized. Cardboard boxes and five-gallon buckets full of car parts and power tools. Nuts and bolts in a coffee can. Ropes and hoses and heavy chains. An air compressor covered in dust. Two freestanding toolboxes with drawers. A jar full of rusty nails. A pair of sawhorses and a leather saddle. Clamps and drivers. Shovels, rakes, and a felling axe.

L.T. wiped his forehead with the oil rag and walked back to the front door of the mobile home. The scrape on his forearm was stinging with sweat. He went up the steps and looked inside the mobile home. He tried to identify the stench. It was not the smell of a dead thing, a rat or a man. It was the smell of manufactured objects advancing through the stages of decomposition. The air was stained with chemicals, with plastics or solvents, and behind the television the paneling had separated from the wall. Morris's belongings were scattered about the room. A *TV Guide* and some paperback books, a set of drink coasters, a pile of busted ceramic, a reclining chair and a floor lamp, a box of videotapes.

L.T. tried the lights but there was no power. He cranked open the windows. There were cans of beans in one cupboard. Cans of tomato soup, cans of corn and mixed vegetables, cans of pears and peaches. There were several jugs of purified water on the floor. On a higher shelf he found a bottle of Old Crow and a sealed carton of Marlboro cigarettes. He saw dry oats in a twisted bag and a row of unopened boxes of rice and noodles from the grocery aisle. He did not open the refrigerator.

He lifted the handle on the faucet and hot water came out. There was air in the pipes and the water sputtered hard into the sink. Through the kitchen window he could see where a well had been dug and the tanks for propane and septic storage. When the water was cool he rinsed his hands and splashed his face. He turned the knob on the stove and then off again when he smelled the gas. The stove lighter was electric and there was no power to spark the flame.

Outside the air felt cool on his wet skin. He dabbed his face with the oil rag. He liked the smell of it. The arch of his brow was swollen and tender, and he was sweating through his shirt. He walked back to Williams's side of the Cadillac and waited for the window to come down.

"Would you mind pulling around to the back? I want to try jumping the pickup."

"You have you some jumper cables?"

L.T. nodded and waved for Williams to follow him around. He nosed him up to the Chevy. With hoods raised he clamped the cables to both batteries. He turned the key in the ignition, pumped the gas pedal, and held it. The engine started and black smoke poured out of the muffler. L.T. pumped the accelerator. He revved the engine and let the needle fall. He did it three times before allowing the engine to rest at a rough idle. Then he removed the jumper cables and closed the hood of the Cadillac.

"You go on back to town," he said to Williams.

"We need to discuss this, L.T."

"I'm staying."

"You ain't even got no power out here. It won't be till Wednesday the earliest is what Glenda mentioned."

"I'll manage."

"Like I said, we need to discuss this. I'm leaving town tomorrow at daybreak. Can't leave you out in this heat for three days. A man your age, no disrespect. But a man in your condition. It's unethical."

"I have the pickup if it gets too hot."

"*If* my ass! I think this heat done got to you already."

"If it gets too hot I'll find a hotel in town."

"You ain't got no driver's license, L.T."

"I'm working on that."

"Tags is expired."

"I'm working on the tags."

Williams looked at him in disgust.

"There's food and water in the house," said L.T. "There's work to do. I'll be fine."

"You putting me in a hard place with Glenda."

"I have my phone."

"That's what I'm saying. You ain't even figure out how to use it yet. Can you dial out? Say you in an emergency situation. Heat stroke, heart attack, snake bite. I want to know can you call 911 with fangs on your leg."

"I tap this button, then dial. Simple."

"I see how it is. 'Delirious Man Dies in Desert, Lawyer to Blame.' Be seeing me on CNN."

"Enjoy your vacation. I'll just grab my bag."

~

The pickup idled roughly. L.T. found a screwdriver in the shed and used it to adjust the carburetor. He tapped the gas pedal and brought up the RPM's. In time he would change the motor oil and replace the coolant. For now the important thing was to give the battery a full charge. He revved the engine and let it settle. It was necessary to keep the motor running.

Morris was dead. He died alone with only his horse to witness. It was winter and there was probably snow on the ground, the sky blue and sharp for miles. Quite possibly it was a peaceful death, cold sunlight shining through the blinds, the man's life fading into blue. The starved horse, circling the coral, eyeing the house and the worn path, expecting the man.

L.T. returned to the shade of the mobile home. He was a stranger here. On the walls were paintings of wild horses, photographs of Morris's two sons, a Mopar calendar, a clock with AC Delco stamped on the face. An ashtray was turned over on the carpet at the foot of a yellow recliner. The chair faced the television. It was an old TV with rabbit ears and the glass was gray with dust. In the cabinet below, a video cassette player was wired up to the television. L.T. piled the loose videotapes into the box and set it upright. They were plain black tapes without labels. Morris's books, a collection of Western novels, had tumbled out of the cabinet beside his chair. Louis L'Amour, Zane Grey, A.B. Guthrie. L.T. sorted them into columns. He picked up the reading lamp and the *TV Guide*. Across from the television stood a wood-burning stove with a black stovepipe and a set of iron implements. A rack of buckhorns was mounted on the wall above it. Next to the stove was a worn-out couch and a walnut coffee table. These faced the front window. L.T. did not want to sit on the furniture.

The bed in Morris's room was unmade and his cowboy boots lay sideways on the floor. The old man's shirts were hanging in the closet and there was a small dresser in one corner with the top drawer half open. On the far wall a pale blue ribbon. On this side of the room plastic models of semi trucks, Kenworth, Mack, and Peterbilt, parked at an angle on a low bookshelf.

The other bedroom was at the opposite end of the house. There was a filing cabinet in that room and a metal desk with a wooden chair. On the wall above the desk he saw a map of California. Colored thumbtacks marked various locations on the map. L.T. found Folsom on the map and traced his path downward. He located the general area on the map, found the town and the national park, but he did not know where he was exactly. Through the window blinds he saw acres of scrawny brush and drab cactus.

On the floor were two crates of camping equipment and a hunting rifle in a black scabbard. Columns of labeled boxes were stacked along one wall, the bottom row buckling under the weight of billing statements, tax documents, receipts, and requisition forms. It all belonged to L.T. now. The furniture, the books, the clothes, the model trucks, the boxed loads. They were things he did not want.

Walking back to the pickup he felt a grim tenderness in his side where someone had punched him. He had fallen hard against the pavement and skinned his forearm. He had meant to wrestle the Marine to the ground, trap his arms, pin the torso. The idea of grappling was to avoid getting hit. Although he had taken the worst of it, L.T. was certain he'd given one of the Marines a sore chin. The kid would have to answer to his superiors for that. The Marine base was nearby, across the desert heights to the northeast, no more than a dozen miles as the crow flies. Camp Wilson it was called and it was on the map.

L.T. turned the key in the ignition to shut off the engine. This was the necessary test. At a certain point you had to turn off the engine to see if it would start again. It was a risk he had to take. He tried it, not without doubt or apprehension, and was grateful when it started. L.T. pumped the gas and listened to the engine. He was satisfied with the way it sounded. He put the truck in gear, drove forward a short distance and applied the brake. He pulled on the headlights and tried the turn signals. Both the radio and the cigarette lighter worked. He shifted the transmission into reverse and rolled it backward. The pickup was old but mechanically sound. Morris understood the fundamentals of maintenance and repair. He knew motors, transmissions, electrical wiring. There was no engine problem that did not make perfect sense to Morris. Pull it apart and put it back together. Replace the broken element with the new.

L.T. shut off the engine and looked out across the empty corral. The heat was more than an imposition, it was omnipresent, a cosmic force. Here was a plot of arid land. Here lay silence and sweaty exile.

Chapter 13

She took Timothy to Griffith Park where he flopped on the grass. Virginia wore jogging shorts, a tank top, running shoes. She wore the pink baseball cap with her hair pulled through the opening in the back.

It was hot out, upper eighties, everybody in shorts and sunglasses lying face-up or down on blankets or on the grass itself. There were dog walkers and Frisbee throwers and someone trying to fly a kite. Three teenage girls were posing for photographs in front of the trees.

Timothy flopped on the grass. Afterward he got up and walked ahead of her, ten or fifteen steps in front of her, and then suddenly he let his body go slack and fell on the grass. He lay there a moment with his arms and legs bent and twisted as though he had fallen from some great height.

Behavior is communication. The question is, what? What are you saying?

Timothy walked ahead of her and flopped. She understood that a sensory need was encoded in the act. The need to fall or the need to stop falling. The grass was soft. He could fall a hundred times and never hurt himself. The purpose was not to hurt himself.

"Look what happened," she said. "Timothy fell down. He was walking, and then he fell."

She worked at the meaning of this, interpreting his performance as she would a work of art. The fall of man. The fall from grace or innocence. Thinking in universal terms. The unconscious reenactment of human transgression and divine punishment. Bremmer had warned her against this tendency. "You mustn't explain his actions in terms of what they might mean to you," he said. "Timothy doesn't know the symbols."

It was one of those days, Sunday in the park, when everyone is either eating ice cream or drinking bottled water and every conversation is pattered with laughter. There were women with babies in strollers and there were dogs sniffing at people and things. And there were young men with shirts off, shirtless men in their early twenties, playing catch with a football, running pass patterns and sprinting to reach the long throw.

Timothy headed for the shade, under some trees, where he kneeled in the dirt. When she caught up to him she saw what he had discovered, a gopher hole with a mound of fresh dirt piled up around the sides. He was covering the hole with his hand.

"Look what you found," she said. "You found a gopher hole. You found where gophers live."

She kneeled beside him.

"The gophers can't come out to play," she said.

Timothy uncovered the hole and looked inside. Then he covered it again. Virginia guided his free hand to the pile of loose dirt. She touched it with him, the warm dirt, the soft brown earthy smell.

"How did all this dirt get here?" she said. "Who put this dirt here?" She waited a moment. "Timothy put it here," she said, because the goal was to challenge him, to make him think, to provoke a response.

He looked at her. Then he took her hand and used it to cover the hole.

"Now it's dark inside the hole," she said. "How will the gophers see?"

Timothy raked the dirt over her hand. He buried her hand and the hole and pressed the dirt with both of his hands.

"Oh, no!" she said. "Where did Mommy's hand go? Mommy feels sad."

Timothy got up and started walking, keeping in the shade of the trees, touching the trunks as he passed. Virginia brushed the dirt off her hands and followed him. She walked where he walked and touched where he touched.

"These are big trees," she said. "Who lives in trees? Gophers or birds?"

Timothy flopped. He lay on his side in the dirt with his eyes closed. Falling is the prerequisite for stopping, she thought. First falling, then stopping.

"Who lives in holes?" she said. "People or birds?" But what she had meant to say was gophers or birds.

She saw two boys shooting rubber bands at each other. She saw bicycle riders on the path taking evasive action to avoid people on foot. A homeless man was talking to himself, mumbling, using his hands to speak. And someone else was trying to get the attention of an elderly woman who was dragging toilet paper on her shoe. Timothy lay in a crooked position between two trees. In the distance Virginia heard car horns and transit brakes, and then a jet airplane overhead.

"Come on," she said. "Let's go ride the merry-go-round before they close it."

Timothy got up and walked with her. She heard music, the clown-babble of organ play, and smelled popcorn in the air. There was a line of people waiting to ride the carousel and only a little shade. They stood in line and waited in the heat while two groups of riders entered through the safety gates. Virginia and Timothy moved forward in line. She watched the carousel spin and listened to the carnival music and bits of conversation happening around her.

She kept an eye on her son as he drifted out of line, once to follow a pigeon, and then again to walk circles around the homeless man who was busy collecting bottles and cans from the trash bin. She called to him, *Timothy*, whenever she moved forward.

When it was their turn to ride she made a big a deal about choosing the best horse. Which one did he want to ride today? Because each horse was painted differently and they were all uniquely positioned, suspended in mid-stride, so that choosing a horse was like choosing a moment in time.

"Hurry and pick one," she said, but like always Timothy would not choose. She wanted him to pick the horse he most liked, she wanted to see which horse he would go to.

But Timothy would not choose. He stood on the platform and did not appear to see any horses at all.

Virginia had to choose. She had to, finally, because the other riders were claiming horses and she did not want to get stuck on the chariot again. So she lifted her son and set him on the nearest horse, one on the outer edge that looked like a boy's horse, gray-bodied, with blue and gold colors and a masculine gait. She picked up her son and put him on the horse and placed his feet in the stirrups and wrapped the strap around his back to keep him from falling. And then she got up on the next horse, the one beside his, and said *are you ready*, and when the bell rang they started to turn.

The music played and the platform began to turn. Slowly at first, but then the carousel picked up speed and the horses started to rise and fall in a windy cloud-gallop. And the song was something from the cartoon archives, music that evoked images of friendly dwarfs and animated forests.

Timothy held onto the pole with both hands and Virginia saw the muscles in his arms flexing. His face was blank but intense, looking straight head.

She said, "Look, Timothy's riding a horse." But his face was blank and intense.

Two dollars buys you four minutes of spin, and the song was like the old cartoon when horns and drums and organ pipes come alive.

They rode in circles of bright light and dim light and she heard kids shouting above the music and somebody saying, "I love this! I love this!" and she saw parents lined up at the gates recording video on their cell phones, parents who called out the names of their children coming around.

Timothy gripped the pole. Gripped, clutched, grasped. His expression was blank but there was terror in his iron posture. This was new. Or else she had never noticed it before. She called his name but he would not look. He had always loved the carousel, or so she thought. She made festal sounds, happy exclamations of joy to remind him that he loved the carousel, but the terror was unmistakable. His horse was moving up and down opposite her own. They circled past the adults and the old people sitting on benches.

Timothy was all hands. He existed for the sole purpose of knuckles and fingers, hands no one could pry from the pole. And she said, "Timothy," in a tone that sounded like a scolding but was really one of concern.

And then she got off her horse. The ride was still moving, still circling, but she got off to stand beside her son and brace him. And it was a little dizzying at first, standing on the platform after floating along on the horse. It was like the floor coming out from under her, spinning out from under her feet, or like the top of her body moving slower than the bottom half so that she had to make a balancing effort to keep her shoulders over center.

She put her hands around his torso and used his body to establish her footing. The carousel turned and the song was *Popeye the Sailor Man.*

"I've got you," she said.

His body was tense, the stiff muscles in his back, inflexible in every way. "You're okay."

His frame was set hard and rigid against the whirling motion, against the windy flight of up and down. And she saw parents recording it on their phones. They were waiting for their own children to come into view and they were recording the intervals. Later she and Timothy would appear in playback mode, appearing as strangers on the web, uploaded, repeating the circles, replaying the child who comes around counterclockwise who is stiff like the horse he rides, solid as the horse, the boy who carries the terror inside.

She held him until the music stopped and the ride came slowing to a halt. Timothy was not ready to give up his hold on the pole. He held to the pole and it did not matter that the ride had stopped.

"It's okay," she said. "Relax, Timothy. I've got you, relax."

She released the safety strap and let it fall. She patted his hands because they were still locked around the pole. She patted his hands and rubbed them. He stared straight ahead at the pole and did not remove his hands.

"Let go," she said. "I've got you."

People were exiting and others were waiting to get on. The music kept playing and it sounded louder and clearer since the carousel was not moving.

"We'll go to the playground," she said, and gently she worked his hands free by rubbing them lightly, by carefully loosening his grip. She picked him up, lifted him off the horse. His body was stiff and did not mold to her figure. He did not wrap his arms around her neck or his legs around her waist or sit on her hip.

He wanted down. She carried him out of the enclosure and let him walk. He went along the path through a row of green trees and then flopped on a patch of grass. It was like witnessing the birth of an animal, the way a newborn tumbles out of its mother's womb.

When Virginia caught up to him she flopped beside him on the ground, and this caused Timothy to raise himself partially to look at her. She had disrupted the order of Timothy falling and Virginia watching and it surprised him.

She lay twisted, perfectly still, trying not to laugh or smile. She lay on the grass with her eyes wide open. Typically he avoided direct visual contact with others. He avoided eyes and faces, or if these were too close he covered mouth and eyes with his hands. But for now he looked at her eyes. Or it's possible he was looking into them. There is a difference, isn't there, between *at* and *into*? But how exactly do you determine it?

Finally she blinked and this apparently was the thing he was waiting for. He got up then and Virginia smiled at him as he looked the other away.

"Where are you going now?" she said.

It was not easy getting up. Her muscles were sore and she did not know why. It scared her to think that a permanent state of soreness was overtaking her body and that being out of shape had little to do with her appearance in the mirror.

On the diamonds they were playing softball. Coed slow pitch. She followed Timothy to the ball field where he put his fingers through the fencing and gripped the twisted wire.

"Look," she said. *"Umpire. The umpire wears a mask."*

She watched the pitcher toss the ball high into the air and as it came down the batter hit it far into the outfield. They heard the clink of the aluminum bat and the vibration of it when it fell to the ground and they watched the ball land in the outfield and roll. And then they heard voices rising from the dugout as someone crossed home plate.

She said, "Home run," but what she meant was a base runner had come around third base and scored.

They stood at the fence and watched the game for a while. Shapes through the diamond wire. One team switching places with the other. There were more hits. Then she said, "Let's go to the playground," and led Timothy by hand through the trees.

He was not interested in the swings or the seesaw. He was not interested in water play or anything involving other children. What he was interested in was the rock formation, the gray mass of granite that ruptured the softer surfaces of dirt and grass. He liked to touch the rock and climb it with hands and feet. He climbed and came back down, inching along on his bottom, and then climbed again and repeated the process.

After several minutes he was joined by another boy. The boy started matching whatever Timothy was doing. When Timothy climbed, the boy climbed next to him. When Timothy came down on his bottom the boy mimicked his movements.

Virginia saw the boy was trying to talk to Timothy but Timothy would not acknowledge him. When they came down together she said hello to the boy.

"What's your name?" she said.

"Fonso."

"Hi, Fonso. That's Timothy."

Timothy started back up the rock.

"Why he don't talk?" said Fonso.

"I don't know," she said. "He can't. Nobody knows why."

Fonso was older, maybe eight or nine.

"How he say things?"

"He doesn't say things. He just does them."

Fonso folded his arms and watched with curiosity as Timothy climbed the rock. He was a skinny kid with long arms and legs. His sneakers looked too big for his body.

"Could he hear?"

Virginia said he could.

"I'd rather have hearing," he said.

"Me too," said Virginia. They watched Timothy. "Do you have any brothers or sisters?"

Fonso glanced around. Maybe he was a little older, nine or ten.

"My brother," he said. "He somewhere around here. Want me to get him for you?"

"No, that's okay."

"Maybe he don't want to talk."

"Maybe."

"Some kids scared to talk. Don't nobody know why."

"This is true," she said.

"I got me a cousin in a wheelchair."

"I'm sorry to hear that."

"It's all right, he don't mind it none."

Timothy was coming down the rock on his bottom.

"He afraid a falling."

"Your cousin?"

Fonso nodded toward Timothy.

"Him," he said. "He think he about to fall. That's why he slide on his butt. He okay long as he stay low."

They watched Timothy come down the rock and then immediately start climbing up again on all fours.

"There he go again," said Fonso. "Don't he ever get bored?"

Virginia laughed.

"It's different for him," she said. "Every time is like the first time."

"He don't remember?"

"Well, not like you and I remember. His mind works differently."

Fonso showed her his elbow. He had an oval shaped scrape that looked red and wet where the skin was missing.

"Ouch, what happened?"

"Skinned it," he said.

"You should go rinse it off in the bathroom."

"It don't hurt."

"Did you show your mom?"

He shook his head.

"She ain't here," he said.

"You must be pretty tough. It looks like it hurts."

"It just stings a little," he said.

Fonso showed her all his scars from falling and fighting with his older brother, and briefly told the story behind each one. He was not bragging, merely stating facts.

Timothy came down the rock halfway and stopped.

"Why he stop?"

"I think he's resting. He's probably tired."

"Want me to get him for you?"

"No, I'll go up and sit with him."

Fonso looked around the park.

"Where my brother go?" he said.

"Maybe he went home."

"He around here somewhere."

"Well, it was nice talking to you, Fonso. Thanks for keeping me company."

"No charge."

"Don't forget to clean your arm."

"It ain't bad," he said.

"Maybe we'll see you again some time."

"Most definitely," he said.

And he walked out across the grass, slump-shouldered, holding his elbow. Under a warm L.A. sunset the boy's brown body, his lanky frame, shimmered with light.

Behind her the sun had settled below the tree line and the big rock lay in its shadow. It was time to go home. There were things to do to get ready for the week. The meal planning and what to wear and how to manage the work. It hit her on days like this, the heft of a Sunday evening, the funereal dread. But there was something else. She could feel it now, hovering on the edge of awareness, the looming fear of some imminent confrontation, some test of the will.

Virginia ordered her son to come down off the rock and then waited for him. Eventually he would move, out of obedience, or out of boredom. Timothy would inch down on his bottom until his feet touched the grass. Then he would run ahead of her until the distance between them was satisfactory, their separation complete, and in that instant, when his mother was nowhere close, when the space between them was total, he would perform the fall.

Chapter 14

Inside the house, starting in the back, in Morris's room, he began clearing out the garbage. He stripped the bed because the blankets, sheets, and pillows had to go. He would decide later about the mattress. But the clothes had to go. They were dead man's clothes. Things on hooks and hangers. He cleared out the closet and four dresser drawers. T-shirts with yellow armpit stains, boxer shorts, socks with holes. The shame of a man. Boots, slippers, and a pair of nylon running shoes. He carried armfuls outside and dropped them on the ground. He took down the blue ribbon and any pictures he found on the walls until they were bare. The scale models were put together with patience and careful attention, but now they were garbage, a dismal record of insidious loneliness. The outdated calendar, the broken wall clock, the dead family photos, books and unmarked tapes. He carried loads in boxes and dumped them into the great pile accruing in front of the house. He rolled up the rugs and tossed the couch pillows out the door. Everything but the furniture. He opened every cabinet in the kitchen and filled several boxloads of mismatched plates and cups, mixing bowls, a tray of silverware, the entire contents of a junk drawer, and he dumped these onto the pile outside. He cleared out the refrigerator leaving only traces of black mold along the rubber door seal. A coffee maker, a toaster oven, a microwave. He carried the appliances outside.

He worked through the pain and the oppressive heat. He drank jug water and poured it over his head and went back inside the house. He removed the heavy boxes from the second bedroom one at a time. All of Morris's old business records, several decades of paperwork. None of it mattered anymore. A man's entire life is whatever fit into a box.

L.T. built the pile out front. He thought of it now as a thing constructed. The more he worked the more he realized everything must go. As evening came on he would empty the whole house. The lamps and fans. All the food in the cupboards. He dropped the saddle by the corral and hid the rifle in the shed until he could get rid of it permanently. He would talk to Darren Williams about that. Maybe give him the rifle for feeding Morris's horse. Meanwhile, the sun dropped below the far mountains and the sky bled as he worked. He dragged the soft couch through the door by giving it a quarter turn and pulling. He hauled out the yellow recliner and flipped it over the pile. Returning up the steps he stumbled and cursed. His legs were giving out.

He wrestled with the wretched mattress and the box spring. He carried the breakfast table and two chairs out the door. He loaded the bathroom contents into a box. The dandruff shampoo, the stick deodorant, a plastic comb and a hairbrush, a package of disposable razors, a dry bar of soap, metal toenail clippers, three varieties of drugstore cologne and a bottle of cough syrup, a can of shaving cream, tubes of toothpaste and sunscreen, a stiff hand towel and a thin roll of toilet paper.

L.T. had gutted the place. In the driveway lay a miserable heap of manmade waste. The zero sum of human toil. Darkness was settling fast over the desert slope and for the first time all day he felt a draft in the air. He noticed porch lights in the distance. Beyond that he could see headlights appearing and reappearing on the highway. Against the red horizon the Joshua trees reached upward like alien forms.

At night the bugs came out. The flying insects. When he was certain that smoke would not be visible from the highway, L.T. circled the junk heap three times with a full can of kerosene. He splashed the stuff high and low until the can was shaken empty. Then he scratched a stove match and tossed it onto the pile.

He was not prepared for the explosion, for the uproar of flame and fireball. The blast of burning air sent him shambling backward in a fool's step. The fire whipped around the pile and spiraled high into the air. The couch in flames, the chair, the burning bed. As things caught fire and burned a cloud of smoke welled up, a thick column blacker than night. Sparks shot upward into the dark sky. He smelled rubber and plastic in the air and heard glass shattering.

Behind him the mobile home was vacant. Its walls were stripped bare, its drawers, cupboards, and closets were all empty now. He owned no change of clothing, there was no food to eat, nowhere to sit, and nothing to sleep on. Morris's cigarettes were all that remained.

L.T. tore open the carton and unwrapped a single pack of Marlboros. He cupped a match and lit a cigarette, inhaling too eagerly, too desperately. He hacked and groaned, then took another drag. Everything hurt inside. There was no part of his body that did not feel pain. Afraid to sit down, afraid to rest, he paced in front of the fire. Even from here, from this distance, he could feel the skirling heat, the complicated blaze. These things would burn, as they must, and tomorrow would be ashes.

PART II

Chapter 15

She was searching for a particular road, rough and unpaved, a dirt road somewhere off the main highway between Joshua Tree and Twentynine Palms. She was no longer following the map on her cell phone, which placed her in the middle of an incomprehensible void. If only she could give the phone to her son and say, "Here, figure this out for me." But that was something else she would never experience, the pleasures of passing it off to the kid.

Timothy was belted into his booster seat asleep in the back of the car. If the car was in motion he traveled well. The car was a closed container. What he did not like were stops of any kind, doors opening and closing, or any of his mother's demands. In the car he would hold his pee for hours. When she stopped for food he would not go to the bathroom and he would not eat what she offered. On the road he slept like a space traveler in a sealed capsule, outside of time, never aging. Occasionally Virginia might say something to him, a word meant to rouse him from deep sleep, but Timothy would not stir. Whatever people dreamed about before language entered the world, that's what he dreamed. On the road inside the car he had discovered oblivion.

It was August and the summer session had ended. Virginia graded final papers, posted final grades. Then one of her fall classes got cancelled for low enrollment and there was none to replace it. This is what Ellen Parks had told her in the email. But it was clear to Virginia that Ellen had written her out of the schedule. She was left with two classes now, two sections of remedial composition offered on separate campuses for less than eighteen hundred a month after taxes.

"It's impossible," she told Neil.

"Then find another job."

She filed for unemployment and mailed a deferment request to put off her student loans. To save money she and Neil agreed to hold Timothy out of school for another month. Neil said she would have to quit buying things, little things like lattes and nail polish remover. And she would have to stand in line at the food bank every week, if necessary. Neil, for his part, promised five hundred a month extra and for now they were calling it a loan. Virginia combed through the bills cancelling whatever could be cancelled.

She said, "I've already cancelled cable. Even the car insurance, cancelled."

"You can't cancel your car insurance," Neil said. "This is L.A., be reasonable."

"It's cancelled," she said. "The policy lapsed. I'm uninsured now."

"Then you shouldn't drive."

"I have to drive. You can't not drive in this city."

"Then don't get stopped," he said. "That's the first thing they ask for."

"The first thing is always license and registration."

"Smart ass," he said. "What they want is proof of insurance."

"Well, I don't have it."

"Then don't get stopped," he said. "And do not get into an accident, whatever you do."

"There are no accidents, only assholes."

"I have to hang up now."

"I need more money, Neil."

"Five hundred," he said. "That's all I can do."

"I can hardly make rent. We're eating government cheese."

"Then you'll have to move, Virginia. It's not complicated. Move somewhere cheaper and find another job."

"One, I'm on a lease. Two, I can't afford to move. Do you know how much it costs to move?"

"I have to go."

"Go where? Where are you going, Neil? You're at home sitting on your ass. Am I right? On your Eames chair, the Herman Miller?"

"I'm hanging up," he said.

Neil was right. There were too many debts and not enough money. She would have to find another job. On short notice she would pull out of her fall classes to free up her days. Either they would find late replacements, others to teach her courses, or they would cancel both sections leaving her students stranded. So be it. There was no loyalty at stake, no one was loyal.

In the schedule of classes Virginia was not even listed as the instructor of record. It said only *Staff*. And staff members, the part-timers, remained nameless because they were expendable.

But what did it matter? She had never wanted to teach basic writing anyway. Too much resistance, too much bad feeling. What she wanted, or once wanted, was to teach Keats and Coleridge to happy undergraduates in the northeast where the leaves changed color every fall and snow settled quietly over the quad. But where that vision came from, that deceiving dream, where that version of self-fulfillment originated, Virginia could not say. She knew the brick and ivy were backdrop, mere fantasy, an evasion of the facts. Like the snows in Reno that always made her melancholy. Or like waiting for Timothy to speak, waiting for him to utter a single word, as though the word, like a crust of bread, could somehow satisfy a withered appetite.

Unreal desires, impossible demands. They led inexorably to this bizarre moment in time. A woman with a loaded gun, *a raven croaking for revenge.* The pistol lay in the glove compartment with her vehicle registration and an envelope of photographs. And what if she found Travis Lee Hilliard? Then what?

It had taken weeks, months, before his name surfaced on the web. Every morning and evening she opened the bookmarks on her laptop computer, searched the man's name, scrolled through the results. She used different search engines to find him. And what she found, finally, was a real estate transaction with his name on it. A legal notification, a public announcement, buried in a database of fictitious business names and bankruptcies. From there it was not hard to pinpoint his exact location. She typed the address, clicked the satellite view, and hovered over a white rectangular structure, a trailer or a mobile home. All her life she had pictured him a certain way, a man from the past who never changed, never grew older, and now she was determined to see him face to face, to find out what becomes of a man, what three decades of imprisonment looks like. She hoped to find the figure of ruin, the face of wasted days.

But first she had to find the place. There were roads on either side of the highway and many of them were unmarked, perpendicular roads that unraveled like lengths of yellow rope. So they were lost. Or at least Virginia was, being the adult, the driver, the person at the wheel. Timothy was never lost. It was something she envied. To be lost required a destination, and this necessitated a plan. Timothy did not plan. He was wayward, a wayward child, but only because he didn't know there was a way to be found, and so he was free from having to search for it.

She pulled off at the next road, stopping long enough to read the names on all the mailboxes. Then she turned around and drove back the other way. Her feeling was that she had passed the turn some time ago. It was all expanse to her now, these leveled distances, the broken horizon.

Years ago she came out here with Neil. Before the pregnancy, before they were married. Their hotel was in Palm Springs, a kitschy place with Sinatra records in all the rooms and an hour of free martinis served around the pool. They drove to Joshua Tree National Park and hiked up the rocks at sunset. Piles of rocks, enormous boulders piled high, heaped skyward. In college she had driven to Arizona with friends but even the Grand Canyon did not feel as ancient as this place. There was something about it. The trees belonged to another age, fabled and dreamlike.

That was on the other side of the mountains. On this side lay the highway and the plain. Everywhere she looked she saw the same scrawny bushes blowing in the wind, the barren exteriors of land and sky, the shattered fragments of chalk-white rock. There were houses off the main road, broken-down shacks painted in vacant shades of pink and green and boarded up with plywood, spraypainted, gutted, thrashed by the local kids, crusted with glass.

And then she saw it, a road sign, not more than three feet high, nearly hidden on the side of the road like one of those crosses that appear along the highway marking the loss of life.

She slowed onto the dirt road, examined a row of black mailboxes, and found the name spelled out in reflective lettering: T. L. Hilliard.

It was late afternoon. A white dusty road lay ahead. The road to his place. When she touched the back of her hand to the window she could feel the abysmal heat outside the car.

Timothy was awake. Right now, suddenly. She caught him staring at her in the rearview mirror, wide-eyed, gluey lips. He was looking right at her as though he had something important to reveal.

"What is it?" she said. "Whatever you have for me. Tell me, I want to know."

In the car, with the doors locked. Dust blowing, the mailboxes shaking, the car wobbling in the wind.

"If you say it we'll go home," she said. "We'll turn the car around and go home, I promise."

Chapter 16

This was day three of the wind event. It came up from the southwest, out of the lower Great Basin, a strapping wind, ruthless and full of grit. Out in the corral the horse put his rear to the wind. He would hold that pose for hours, like a noble monument tarnished by climate and time. L.T. had gone outside to feed the horse and to fasten the tarpaulin over the wood he had chopped, and then he went back inside the house to escape the wind. He did not like the wind when it battered the walls and windows and threatened to blow down the house. The house was not even a house, properly speaking. It was a mobile home on a raised foundation, an ephemeral thing vulnerable to the elements.

Anyway, this was the last of it, according to the weather report. Tomorrow would bring cooler air and rain. The weather was the first thing that concerned him every morning. It was the one preoccupation even before brushing his teeth. The weather app on his phone showed an accurate picture of what he must endure. Either the searing heat or the maddening wind or the lashing rain with floodwaters. He lived at the center of such extremities and the weather served as the principal indicator of his existence.

He had no television. The old transistor radio played ragged static during the day and talk radio in the evening. And so at night he would listen to the voice on the clearest frequency. What he liked most was hearing the names of the towns where people called from. White River, Junction City, West Plains. He found them on the map in the room and stuck a thumbtack on the name of the town. He had burned Morris's maps. And then, face to face with the bare walls, he decided a map wasn't such a bad thing and he bought a large U.S. map at a drug store in Yucca Valley and tacked it to the wall. On nights when there was static, a common occurrence, he diverted himself by reading the minor prophets. Habakkuk, Micah, Amos,

Malachi. The ancient criers of tragedy and ruin. He was drawn, of late, to visions of destruction, to sackcloth and ash, to the cadences of devastation only God himself understood.

All summer, in the heat of day, he had worked around the property clearing brush out of the corral, chopping a load of wood for the winter, organizing the tool shed, repairing fence posts and door locks, fixing a water leak, and working on the pickup, changing its vital fluids and replacing the brakes. He added to the burn-piles in front of the house and hauled loads of garbage out to the landfill over on Old Woman Springs Road, including all those things he had tried to burn that first night, all of Morris's possessions, the hard objects that would not burn, and the remnants of half-burned things.

On occasion, Darren Williams hired him to clean up overgrown yards or to haul away abandoned furniture or to complete minor repairs on foreclosed properties. Anything requiring a pickup and a pair of gloves. L.T. did not mind the labor. He preferred to keep busy working with post diggers and ropes. It was diverting and it brought him a small income, and the soreness he felt at the end of the day was well earned, so he did not feel disparaged.

In the morning he wrote a letter to Frank Teller, drove it down to the mailbox, and, disappointed that he had missed the carrier, came back up to the house with his mail and cleaned the coffee pot with a vinegar solution and a soapy sponge. Now, some hours later, as he gazed out the front window beyond the withering scrub, he saw a car coming up the road in the dust. It was a small car, light blue, or silvery blue, approaching slowly and tentatively, with caution. The road was uneven and the flooding had made it much worse. There were large stones on that road, now partially exposed, which could puncture a muffler or break a tie rod. To navigate the safest route required some clever maneuvering. L.T. watched the car come up the road dipping and wobbling, flares of white sunlight striking the windshield.

A woman was driving the car and there was nobody in the passenger seat. He watched to see what she would do. She did not drive onto his property where the driveway looped around but turned left at the end of the road and applied the brakes. There she paused a moment with her foot on the brake pedal, and then made a quick three-point turn and parked facing the house.

She was probably lost. It happened from time to time. People relied too heavily on their cellular networks, but what they did not know was how screwy the signals could get out here and how a person could get lost on trails and dirt roads and forget all sense of direction.

He wondered what she was doing out there in the car. Waiting for the map to load or else trying to make a call. He considered what he might do next if she stayed very long. One option was to remain inside the house and wait for her to drive away. The other was to open the front door and step outside, ignoring the parked car, and walk out to the corral non-chalantly just to confirm, if she were wondering, that someone was in fact home and could offer help if necessary. The third option was to approach the car directly and ask the woman if she needed help.

He would give it five minutes. He would leave the window and come back and maybe she would be gone by then and he would not have to decide. In the meantime he would put together a list for the grocery store. Cigarettes. Bread. Peanut butter. What else? A dozen eggs. He tried to think of things he would soon run out of. The basics. He checked the bath-room cabinets for mouthwash and hemorrhoid ointment and opened the refrigerator door in the kitchen. He had resolved to eat more salads and more fruit. He wrote it down. There was plenty of coffee in the cupboard. He thought a slow cooker would be a good thing to have in winter. When it came to food he was sparing and unimaginative. In prison he ate what-ever they served and never had to plan it or prepare it. Everything tasted more or less the same. Age and habit had dulled his senses. L.T. underlined the word Cigarettes so he would not forget to request a carton at the cash register. He put antacids on his list.

Then he walked back to the bright window and saw the dusty Honda parked out front. The woman had driven around the driveway and had parked on the other side of the burnt circle. She must be lost, he thought. Or else, what? Maybe she was from the parole office, come out to perform a surprise inspection, or else a caseworker of some kind, a life counselor, a social worker. He wondered if he should hide the liquor.

L.T. opened the front door and waited for the woman to get out of the car. He hoped she was merely lost in which case he could be of some help. It was hot outside, late afternoon, and because he was running the air con-ditioner inside the house he shut the door behind him and stood on the narrow porch at the top of three wooden steps and waited. Dust blew out across the driveway.

The woman sat in her car and stared at L.T. through the window. He waved at her more awkwardly than he intended, but she offered no acknowledgement, did not smile at him or wave or even roll down the window. Wearing sunglasses she stared at him across the driveway. Finally she opened the car door.

"Any dogs?" she shouted.

"What?"

"Dogs! Do you have any dogs?"

"I don't have a dog."

The woman looked young, late twenties. Her brown hair was piled up in a twist and her neck looked very pale. She got out of the car and pulled up the front seat to gain access to the back. He watched her bend over. There were women all over Palm Springs who had nice figures. It was something he noticed whenever he was there. Women in high heels striding down the sidewalks or else crossing in front of him at the stoplight.

He watched a kid crawl out of the backseat of the car. A young boy, a child with blond hair and red knees. The woman's child, obviously, but what was she doing bringing her kid along? The boy did not like the wind. He stood stiff as a fence post until his mother grabbed his hand and then the two of them started toward the house.

They were leaning into the wind and she was talking to the boy. He thought he heard the woman say two or three words to the boy but L.T. could not make out the sounds. Maybe she wasn't from the State after all, in which case she was merely lost.

L.T. was eager to find out. He called to her, "You must be lost," but the woman ignored him.

She pulled the boy by his wrist. He lagged a half-step behind and the woman pulled his arm taut like a piece of rope. To keep up with her the boy scuttled along awkwardly, his gait crooked, his feet small and clumsy, until he finally stumbled and tripped. But the woman held him upright, kept the boy from falling, kept him from skinning his knees.

"You must be looking for somebody, is that it?"

"My son needs to pee. May we use your bathroom?"

"There's nobody around. He can go right where he's standing."

"He won't do it outside. He has special needs. He'll hold it until we find a toilet. And he's been holding it for hours. It's an emergency."

L.T. did not want the boy to use his personal toilet. The boy might urinate behind the seat where it was hard to clean. And the woman would have to accompany the boy and L.T. did not like the idea of bringing this woman into his house. Her manner made him wary.

But the boy was squirming, he could see that, and the woman was lost and probably aggravated, and it was not an outrageous request.

"Well," he said, "come on up."

L.T. opened the door and let them pass. Near the window in the living room a shaft of light fell upon the bare floor. The rest was shadowy. L.T. waited for his eyes to readjust. He pointed down the hallway.

"That first door," he said.

The woman removed her sunglasses. She led the boy to the bathroom and closed the door.

The wind beat against the house in blistering intervals. In short, freighted bursts. But coming in from the heat made the air inside feel cooler. He could hear the fan turning in the air unit. It squeaked and this worried him. A bearing issue, perhaps. If the air unit went out . . . but he didn't want to think about that. Maybe it was only a loose belt.

He heard the toilet flush. It was not an outrageous request. The Bible warned against turning away strangers. That was the book of James, or else it was Hebrews, one or the other. In any case, he would offer the woman a bottle of cold water for the road and point the way.

When they came out of the bathroom, he spoke to the woman, hoping to send her off quickly.

"It happens all the time," he said, "on these dirt roads. If you'll tell me where you're headed."

"We're not lost," she said.

"You're not?"

"I'm with *The Times*," she said. "A reporter. From Los Angeles."

"A newspaper reporter."

"Yes, with *The Times*."

She put out her hand.

"My name is Valerie," she said.

"L.T.," he said, taking her hand briefly.

"This is my son, Timothy."

L.T. nodded at the boy. He did not understand why the woman had introduced herself or what she wanted. The boy was looking around the room wearing a blank expression. Something odd about his eyes.

"Fine," said L.T. "I guess you'd like to get on your way."

"No, I'm sorry. You don't understand. I'm a reporter from *The Times*. I'd like to talk to you. I came here to talk to you."

"Talk to me. About what?"

"I'm doing a piece, a story, sort of a profile piece. If you're familiar. I'm writing an article for *The Times*."

"I don't understand."

"No, of course," she said. "To be clear. I'm on assignment. I'm writing a piece on former inmates. Men like yourself. Who have served lengthy sentences."

"No, I don't think."

"If I can explain first. My project."

"Your project."

"Yes."

The boy was tugging at her. He wanted the woman to let go of his arm.

"You see, I know who you are," she said. "You're Travis Lee Hilliard. You earned a life sentence for murder. Recently paroled, I believe, if I'm correct. I'd like to speak with you."

"What about?"

"About life on parole."

"I wouldn't be interested."

"I'm conducting interviews. I'm writing a profile of what it's like. Adjusting to life again, to living. After so many years. Living on your own again, out here. To be out of prison. The process of re-establishment, how the system prepares a person, what they offer you in terms of preparation and counseling. And if this is an issue for lawmakers to address. The lack of support. Or whether it's sufficient, if that is the case. And what's currently available."

"I'm sorry, what was your name?"

"Valerie," she said.

"Valerie. I'm not interested in giving interviews. I don't know how you found my name."

"Research," she said. "I'm a reporter. I would've called first. Naturally. But I was unable to track down your phone number. What I have is an address. I realize, yes, that I've. That you weren't expecting me."

"You should've mailed me a letter, saved yourself the trouble. It's a long drive back to L.A."

"I understand. But letters go unanswered. As you might expect. It's important to speak directly, in my line of work, to people in order to. I've learned this, Mr. Hilliard. In order to establish trust. Willingness."

"I'm sorry to disappoint you."

"May I ask why?"

"I don't have anything to say to reporters. I can't help you."

The boy was trying to free himself. His disturbance was mounting. His arm was stuck and he was trying to get unstuck. He was writhing now, struggling to get loose, making bizarre noises, feral sounds, brutal utterances.

"I've driven a long way, Mr. Hilliard. I would very much like to talk to you. Thirty minutes of your time. If you would."

"I don't want my name in the papers," he said.

"We can do it anonymously. Or else I can change your name for the article. People understand these things."

"You brought your boy."

"Yes. Timothy." She looked down at him. Her grip was firm on his arm. "It was unavoidable. I hope you don't mind."

"Why would I mind?"

"You weren't expecting us."

"But here you are."

"Yes, I'm sorry. Perhaps we can reschedule. Is there a better time to do this?"

"Not really."

"I can understand your reluctance. But thirty minutes of your time."

"He won't last thirty minutes."

"I have toys in the car, things to keep him occupied. He's actually very focused."

"He wants you to let go."

The woman did not respond. She tethered the child without scolding him.

L.T. said, "You can let him go. It's alright."

"He'll touch everything. He has to touch things, it's how he learns. He's very tactile."

"There's nothing to hurt him," L.T. said.

When she let go of his arm the boy fell onto his knees and sat remarkably still. L.T. stared at him. The woman looked at L.T., then down at her son.

"Is that all you wanted?" she asked the boy. "You wanted me to let go?"

"He doesn't speak?"

"No," she said.

They stared at the boy. It was not L.T.'s business to ask, but perhaps it was some issue between the woman and her husband, an argument most likely, which would explain why she brought the kid with her. That's usually how it worked. People carried things over. But glancing at her hand he noticed her ring finger was bare. Maybe an ex-husband then, or a quarrel with a new lover. Or maybe it was a problem with the sitter. In truth it could be any number of things, he thought, or some buried thing.

"Could be he's hungry. Does he eat saltine crackers?"

"You don't have to do that."

"It's no trouble," he said.

In the kitchen he opened a cupboard and removed a package of saltine crackers from the carton.

"Does he eat these?"

"Are you hungry?" she asked the boy, but he neither moved nor acknowledged her voice. "You haven't eaten," she said. "He hasn't eaten since breakfast. He won't eat in the car."

"Maybe he'll eat at the table."

He set out the package and turned on the overhead lights. Then he reached for his cigarettes.

"In my house I like to smoke," he said. "If that bothers you."

"Of course not. You can do that. It's your house."

"Do you smoke?"

"No."

"What about a drink?"

"Oh no," she said. "I mean, yes, of course. Whatever you're having."

L.T. lit a cigarette and moved the ashtray to the table. Out of the cabinet he brought down two clean glasses. He added ice cubes, poured whiskey into each glass, and set the bottle on the counter beside the coffee pot.

"I drink mine on the rocks."

"That's fine," she said.

"On hot days," he said. "Windy days."

"Ice is fine."

"It's Canadian," he said. He pulled out a chair from the table. "Sit down then. And let's hope the air doesn't give out. That's the squeak you're hearing. The air conditioner. Hear it? That chirping noise, sounds like a bird?"

"I thought it was a bird."

"A half-eaten bird maybe. A bird with its wing in somebody's jaws," he said with a laugh. "It's an old ground unit outside the window. Air comes in through the floor vents. I don't turn it off, not out here, not recently. I set the thermostat so it's always running. And now it's starting to squeak and that worries me. My electric bill is in that stack of envelopes on the counter. I'm afraid to open it."

"Why did you move out here?" she asked. "After your release in May."

"Is that your first question?"

"Yes, the desert."

The boy shifted his position from sitting to lying on the floor. The woman turned and said to him, "Come get a cracker," but the boy ignored her. He appeared to be staring at the paneled wall. There were no pictures hanging anywhere. The photos belonging to Morris had burned in the fire. L.T. had not replaced them. Williams had given him the furniture, the armchair and matching couch, the two lamps on side tables, an oval rug woven in a ring pattern. There were other things. The dining room table and chairs, a chest of drawers in the bedroom. Someone had foreclosed on a house and left the furniture inside and Williams told L.T. he could take whatever he wanted. So L.T. had loaded these things into the pickup and moved them out here. But he had not decorated the walls. There were no pictures of anyone, no clocks or mirrors anywhere, not even a nail. The wall in the living room was simply a flat paneled surface, completely bare, with a blade of sunlight running slantwise across it, directly above the electrical outlet.

"It belonged to my uncle," he said. "This was his place. And that's his horse out back."

"Horse?"

"You didn't see the horse? Maybe your boy would like to see him. Does he like animals?"

"We don't keep pets."

"I don't either, except for that one horse, although I wouldn't call him a pet. I never saddle him."

"You don't ride the horse."

"No, I throw hay and brush off his backside. And twice a day, every morning and evening, I run a garden hose out to the water trough. He watches me with one eye. I don't know what he thinks of me. We don't talk about it."

She smiled thinly.

"It must be very strange," she said. "Living out here alone."

"Lately I've become aware of my pulse. I've been hearing it in my inner ear. A muffled drumming inside my skull. That is until about three days ago when the wind started blowing. It shakes the place. Yesterday was worse."

He pulled on his cigarette and was careful to blow the smoke to one side. He moved the glass ashtray in front of him and tapped the ash into it.

"It's usually quiet out here. The heat is compressed, the air dead still, no movement, no sound of birds or crawling insects. Although, quiet is not the right word for it. You're a writer. What's a word that means more than quiet? A sort of absolute quiet?"

"Dumbness."

L.T. laughed.

"It's dumb alright," he said. "Anyway, it's different from what I'm used to. Prisons are crowded, full of noise. You hear a lot of voices but nothing makes sense."

He sipped his drink and sucked on a piece of ice. He had found the whiskey glasses and the ashtray in a thrift shop in Palm Springs. They were articles from another era, things that reminded him of his mother.

"You don't have to drink that," he said.

The woman picked up the glass and swirled the ice. She drank the whiskey, all at once, without making a face, and set the glass down on the table. Behind her, the boy lay motionless on the floor with his eyes wide open. Eyes that were fixed on the wall, on a patch of sunlight climbing slowly, almost imperceptibly, toward a stain on the white ceiling.

Chapter 17

She tipped the glass, swallowed hard, and set it down perfectly on the small watery ring that had formed on the table. Whatever he called it, this wasn't whiskey. It was alcohol without taste. The smell of ripe banana was the sole takeaway. It was like stain remover, she thought, or something to treat an infection.

He poured her another one and screwed the lid on the bottle. This time he left it on the table and sat down. His cigarette was burning in the ashtray. She followed his movements as he picked it up. She recognized something about him, or thought she did. What was it? Her memories of a younger man with a moustache were unclear. Travis was clean-shaven now and smelled of drugstore aftershave. His hair was mostly gray. She expected someone taller than her father, only more nimble, and discovered thick fingers and a solid waist.

Her left eyelid was twitching. She wondered if he noticed from across the table. She tried to make it stop by squinting, then she tried holding her eye wide open, and when this failed she tried to relax the lid through an act of will. She was tense all over. Her neck and back, her abdomen. She was trying to remember a phrase from yoga class, a Hindi phrase repeated to affect inner peace.

"Timothy," she said.

She opened the package on the table. She wanted him to hear the plastic sleeve tearing open.

"Come get a cracker," she said to him.

No response. Timothy lay on the floor ignoring her completely. She felt a twitch above her left eye. She put her hand over the eyelid.

"I'm sorry," she said, covering that half of her face. "It's my eye. My eyelid keeps twitching."

"Irritation," he said. "It's the wind. Which reminds me, I should add eye drops to my list."

Out of his shirt pocket he pulled a folded piece of paper and scribbled on it. Virginia tossed back her drink and crunched what remained of the ice. He gave her a look.

"There's more where that came from," he said, "but you'd better slow down. I'll get you a glass of water if you're thirsty."

"I don't mean to keep you."

He stood up and went to the freezer for a tray of ice. He twisted the tray and tilted it over her glass. Two cubes fell into it.

"Where are your notes?" he said.

"Notes?"

"You don't take notes. I thought reporters always took notes."

"I do take notes," she said. "I have a notepad. I should get it so we can continue."

He tipped the bottle over the ice, poured the glass half full, turned his head and coughed.

"Let this one sit a moment," he said.

"I'll run out to my car," she said. She stood up in haste and felt the alcohol go to her head. "Timothy, get up." No response. "Honey, let's go. Give me your hand."

His legs were scissored, one arm draped forward, head at rest on the floor.

"It's okay where he's at. It's no trouble."

"Are you sure? I think he's tired. Anyway, they're in the trunk. My notes. I keep them in boxes. My car doubles as office space. It's the job. It's all freelance now. Nobody pays for anything."

She was standing, looking down on him, watching him light another cigarette. He dropped the match into the ashtray.

"Let me ask you something," she said. "Do you feel? Or how should I put this. I don't know the right words. But are you satisfied?"

"Meaning what?"

"Your conscience. It's something I have to ask."

"My conscience?"

"Do you believe, or to put it another way, would you say that you've paid your debt? That you've paid for your crimes? To society? Or to, whomever?"

"There are two ways of answering your question. The first answer is no. From a societal standpoint, let's say, or a human standpoint. I committed an unforgiveable crime. I took a man's life. The debt is not repayable. No amount of time served is adequate. No form of punishment can change what I've done."

"Some argue for execution," she said. "A life for a life."

"That's an old way of settling it. But what good would it do? Not even my death could set things right again. You can't exchange the living for the dead."

"So why incarcerate then? Why punish?"

"I don't ask why incarcerate or why punish. We punish because the law doesn't work. That's the whole point of punishment. What else is there?"

"You're saying laws are the problem. The justice system."

"No, I'm not saying it's the law. The law itself is not the problem. There must be rules. Problem is the rules don't work. They don't make people good. And if the law can't make people good, then what can?"

"You tell me," she said.

He smoked his cigarette. Virginia pulled out the chair and sat down again. Hard to believe she was sitting across the table from him. Travis Lee Hilliard. For a moment she avoided his eyes. She concentrated on his cigarette, on the burning end, on a thin continuous ribbon of smoke. Outside the wind was blowing hard against the walls of the house. Behind the paneling the lumber creaked and groaned under the stress of each gust.

Travis, she realized, was watching Timothy. When she turned she saw her son emerging from behind her chair.

"Are you hungry?" she said to him.

Virginia shifted the package so Timothy could look inside. It was important to let him reach for a cracker all on his own. It was important to resist the impulse to do it herself. To be patient, to let him reach for it. He stared inside the open package and made a sound. There was no describing the sound, it required no interpretation. It was a sound, or maybe only a noise.

"Take one," she said.

It was important to wait, to let him initiate movement. He stared at the crackers. They were suspect. Everything contained a hidden menace, even saltine crackers, and she did not understand this. To her it was simple. A plain cracker. But to Timothy it involved peril and the decision required prudence. He hesitated.

She glanced at Travis, who was also watching Timothy. Her eyelid twitched. She blinked as Timothy touched a cracker with his fingertip. He touched it gently. With the tip of his finger he would feel a hard rutted surface. He would feel spiky granules of salt. They watched him in silence as he removed a cracker from the package and set it flat on the table. Then he removed another cracker and set it on top of the first. Then another.

"He does this," she said. "This is typical."

"How so?"

"He's stacking."

"Stacking," he repeated. "What for?"

"The stack is hard, it's separate. It feels safe. As the stack gets taller he feels more and more powerful. Only there's no end to it. He'll keep stacking until it falls over. It's an act of self-sabotage, only he doesn't realize it. And he'll keep repeating it, repeating it, until he's diverted. One thing to replace another. But this is only a theory."

"Nobody knows?"

"There are different explanations, various schools of thought, treatments that finally produce negligible results."

They watched him build the stack. Virginia took a cracker from the package and held it up to his mouth. He ignored them, the mother, the cracker, until she touched the cracker to his lips, and then he made an angry noise. It was not anger directed at her. She knew this. He did not like the prickly feeling on his lip.

"Eat it," she said. "You're hungry."

He ignored her. He built the stack slowly, placing each cracker on top of the next. The stack was becoming unsteady. Timothy would keep adding to the stack until it leaned one way and finally toppled over.

"We'll go out to the car," she said.

There were toys in the car, on the floorboard in the backseat, an airplane, a tractor with spinning wheels. Timothy liked to turn the tractor upside down and spin the wheels. He liked the rumble sound and the vibration. She grabbed Timothy's hand and stood up from the table.

"Come on."

He did not want to go. He wanted to stack the crackers. She pulled and he did not like the pulling. He made a loud noise in defiance of her pulling.

"It's okay if he stays."

"He needs a diversion," she said. "It's never easy. We'll go out to the car, he'll be fine."

Timothy let out a cry. He moaned and whimpered and made a grinding noise. She dragged him, picked him up, he stumbled and wailed.

"Stand up," she said. "We'll get you a toy from the car."

She raised him to his feet and he fought against the pulling. It was the defining gesture between them. Her pulling, his resistance.

"Let's get to the car," she said.

Outside he dragged his feet in the dirt. He was clumsy only because he did not want to go to the car. The wind was loaded with sand particles. She felt the bite on her face and bare arms, a stinging sensation, a swarming element.

She moved the seat forward and guided him into the backseat of the quiet car. The hot car with the open door. Inside where it was not so bright, where the light was less intense, Timothy curled up, semi-catatonic, on the empty seat in the back. This was his part of the car, his own familiar space. With his eyes closed, with his jaw locked, he plugged his ears with his fingers.

In a box in the trunk were yellow notepads, pens to write with. The idea had come to her on the spot, sitting here in the driveway with the windows rolled up, staring at the man who killed her father. A newspaper reporter from *The Times*. By taking notes she would sell the act, although it seemed too easy, too obvious.

Virginia opened the glove box. Inside were the photographs and the handgun. She grabbed the envelope and pulled out the photos. They were pictures of her father and mother, and of herself, oblique reminders of early childhood. Years ago she had removed them from her mother's photo albums. She had chosen only the most random or candid photos, nothing posed or prompted. Her mother couldn't remember who had taken them or why and didn't care about losing them.

Virginia put them into her purse and reached for the gun. The magazine was fully loaded and locked into the receiver. By pulling and releasing the slide she chambered a hollow-point round. The action was smooth, effortless. She gripped the handle, held it firmly, gripped and squeezed until it felt like an extension of her own hand. She stuffed the pistol into her purse muzzle-down and closed the zipper.

"Come on," she said.

She could not leave her son in a hot car with the door wide open. She pulled his left finger out of his ear, exposing him to the clamor, and tugged his arm to get him up and out.

"Let's take your airplane," she said. "Wings, windows, wheels. Let's go back inside, hurry."

He would not follow on his own. She crossed her purse over her shoulder and picked him up. He would not wrap arms around her shoulders or legs around her waist. His body was cargo, a load of deadweight.

She kicked the car door behind her and cut through the blowing wind toward the house carrying her son and his airplane, the yellow notepad, the purse.

"I have it," she assured him, meaning the airplane.

Travis was waiting for her at the kitchen table holding a cigarette between his thumb and forefinger. The lamplight was cloudy with smoke. When they entered Travis coughed. She heard the ice rattle in his glass.

Virginia lowered her son to the ground expecting him to collapse on the hard linoleum, where in a state of numb repose he could quietly process their latest ordeal. Instead, he landed on his feet and took the airplane out of her hand. Immediately he began to strut around the house according to the layout of walls and doorways. She tailed him for several steps.

"Should I close the bedrooms?"

"There's nothing to hurt him," he said.

The living room with its spare furnishings felt hollow and uninhabited. A green couch, a pair of side tables with lamps, an armchair. These were moved here from another place. They belonged to someone else. She could not imagine Travis sitting anywhere in this room comfortably. She was convinced that where he was sitting now, at the kitchen table, was where he always sat. At night after eating a plate of food he would work through a pack of cigarettes under the lamplight listening to the radio on the counter. In the bedroom down the hall is where he slept alone.

She stood with the purse over her shoulder watching her son drag his hand along the walls. He carried the airplane in his left hand, but not as an airplane. The wings were never wings. The wheels were for spinning, never for landing. She was starting to doubt herself.

"Tell me about the man you killed," she said.

"Why don't you sit down."

Virginia approached the table. Using her notepad she scraped the salt crackers into a pile and sat down. She picked up her glass and finished the whiskey, ice cold, sugary and bitter. She uncapped a red pen.

"What do you know about it?" he asked her.

"I've read articles, digital archives. I'm familiar with the proceedings," she said. "I looked up the town. The man was a minister, am I correct? A family man."

Travis nodded while he smoked his cigarette. He tapped the ash and let the cigarette rest on the rim of the ashtray.

"And you were there because why? I'm confused."

"It was chance," he said, "bad luck."

"He employed you."

"I was down and out, as they say."

"And he offered to help in order to what? To get you back on your feet? That sort of thing."

"Something like that."

"And you lived there, on the premises, with the family."

He nodded.

"Tell me about the family," she said.

"He had a wife and a little girl. I never saw them after my arrest. Vivian didn't come to the trial. They didn't force her to testify. I thought she might appear at one of my parole hearings, but she never did."

"Did you hope to see her there?"

"Not really," he said, and picked up his cigarette.

"No," Virginia said, "I wouldn't think so. Because if she testified against you, obviously. Or spoke against your release is what I mean. They would've denied your parole."

"There's a good chance of that."

"So you don't know anything about the family. About what happened to them afterward, although you must've wondered."

"From time to time," he said.

"About the man's wife. His daughter. And about their experience, as separate from your own? And more important perhaps."

"Sure," he said. "I've thought about them."

"You have," she said. "About what, may I ask? What does a man in your position think about?"

"A little room of a house out behind the church building. That's the clearest picture I have of them. I can't imagine them growing older or living somewhere else."

He paused, remembering. Then he said, "Nevada."

"Nevada?"

"It's where her parents lived. Reno, Nevada."

She wrote this down and underlined it twice for effect.

"And you never tried to find them?" she asked. "On the Internet?"

"No," he said. "Find them? Why would I do that? She didn't want to be found. Not by me."

"I've heard of meetings, sponsored events, between prisoners and victims' families."

"Reconciliation programs," said L.T. "No, Vivian wouldn't have wanted that."

"You call her Vivian."

"Is that strange?"

"You knew them well," she said. "You speak with a certain, a sort of familiarity. I'm wondering what this indicates, what it reveals."

"I don't follow."

"You were a vagrant. They took you into their home, into their private life, the life belonging to the family. What I mean is, you must've felt, and maybe you still feel it, a sense of treachery, of having betrayed others. I'm interested in knowing what you felt, at the time, and what you may or may not feel even now, as a free man."

"It's hard to say."

"You're ambivalent."

L.T. smoked his cigarette and sipped from his glass. She waited for him to continue.

"It was a long time ago," he said. "The truth is I no longer identify."

"You don't remember."

"No, it isn't I don't remember. It's that I don't identify with what I did. Or with the man."

"The man you killed?"

"I'm talking about myself. Who I was then and who I am now."

"You're saying you've changed."

"Sure."

"How so?"

"I'm as different as you are. How you've changed over so many years. Say twenty or thirty years depending on your age. Are you the same person you were twenty-five years ago?"

"I was a child."

"Well, that's what I mean. You've changed. You get older, your mind, the things you say. You no longer think like a child. At a certain age you begin to see things differently. Certain experiences shift your outlook."

"And there are other experiences that determine your outlook, wouldn't you say? A killing, for example. Or the death of someone."

"Look, you asked if my conscience was clean. If I had paid my debt, and so on. And I said there were two answers to your question."

"Yes."

"The first answer has to do with society. Did I pay my debt to society, and I said no. The second answer is more important, as far as I'm concerned. It's a question of the soul."

"I don't believe in a soul. There's only brain function, or malfunction in some cases. The mind of the individual. But there's no evidence of any soul. People are soulless. Their brains and bodies die. And I find it ironic, if you don't mind my saying, that you're a religious person. You killed a church leader."

"Not until prison did it ever occur to me," he said, "that a killing, a murder, was also a sin. And not only a sin. But an indicator, you might say, of an essential predicament."

"You broke the law," she said.

"Yes, I broke the law. And to pay for my crime society locked me up for life."

"Not for life," said Virginia. "How can you say for life? You're not in prison anymore, they let you out. The parole board."

"They let me out. Okay, why? Because I paid my debt in full?"

"No. You said it yourself. We both agreed."

"That's right," he said. "The only punishment that fits the crime is death. But that's as far as it goes. My death wouldn't redeem the act. It wouldn't reverse the course of time or erase the consequences of my actions. Nor would it satisfy the demand of my soul. Because my guilt, which is what I'm trying to explain—my debt, so to speak—is not for this crime alone. In prison it took many dark nights for me to realize something. That I had been weighed, according to both flesh and spirit, and in both cases I was found lacking. That my condemnation was total. And it had less to do with my crime, less to do with what I did, and more to do, or everything to do, with who I was."

"You're talking about original sin," she said. "You're blaming your actions on a myth."

"Not a myth," he said. "I was a murderer long before I committed the act."

"I don't believe in original sin," she said. "You are whatever you do. If you corrupt yourself, if you corrupt others, then you end up with this, the world as we've made it. People don't have a soul. They have a choice. If you murder someone, then you're a murderer. Your actions define you, not some preexisting condition."

"I'd have to disagree."

"You disagree with philosophers," she said.

He finished his cigarette and rubbed it out. Virginia turned in her chair to find Timothy circling the room, dragging his hand along the wall. He moved like an apparition, pale and hauntingly quiet.

"You can't pass it off by saying people are evil by nature," she said, watching her son. "Timothy doesn't know evil from good. And quite frankly I'm glad."

"You ought to be glad," he said.

She turned to look at Travis.

"But you're saying he's condemned."

"I never said that."

"Well, look at him," she said. "Isn't he condemned?"

Chapter 18

The boy came dragging his hand along the wall. That seemed to be his thing, his obsession, to learn the dimensions of the house by measuring the walls, by changing course at each right angle, letting the vertical surfaces guide his path. Where one wall joined another he occasionally drew to a halt, his toes up against the paneling, his nose touching the wall, eyes wide open.

The woman reached for her glass. She took the liberty of pouring herself another, which was fine, L.T. had set the bottle between them on the table for that purpose. But there was something wrong with this woman, he could see that, and if the third drink hadn't touched upon it, this next one would.

In any case, she was making him nervous. He lit another cigarette. There was something he wanted to come back to, something he needed to clarify.

"Look," he said, "you've been asking about guilt, about remorse, and the answers are complicated. I've been trying to work out the answers to these questions for thirty years. That man I killed, the preacher, I betrayed him. You used the word *treachery* and you're right. But not how they said at the trial. Truth is I never meant to kill him. He was carrying a pouch, a bank bag, with the weekly collection inside. I tried taking it from him and he fought me for it. All I wanted was the money, but he wouldn't let go."

"He wouldn't let go, so you killed him."

"Not exactly."

"Yes, you struck him with a hammer. They said you crushed his skull."

"I only wanted the bag," he said. "I never thought he'd put up a fight. Philip wasn't the type. It was all impulse on my part, and his too, for that matter. Under normal circumstances neither of us would've done anything like that. I panicked, tried to break his grip, but he held on, and he was stronger than I thought, a lot stronger. Which is why I swung the hammer, to break his grip on the bag. And that's how it happened. He ducked right into it."

"You're suggesting it was his fault."

"I'm not saying that at all. I'm telling you it's my fault. I've accepted the blame. I hit him in the head, that's a fact. Broke his skull wide open. But he stooped into it is what I'm saying. At the trial they said it was planned, premeditated, and I'm saying it wasn't like that."

The woman stared at him. He could tell what she was thinking. She didn't believe what he was telling her.

"You think I wanted to kill him? You think I wanted to throw my life away?"

"Did you?"

They stared across the table. The woman's gaze was sharp and accusatory.

"Listen," he said, "what is it with you? I thought you came to hear my side of the story."

"Did you?"

He dismissed her with a shake of his head and got up from the table. Why not tell her to go, he thought. He opened the freezer, cracked a tray of ice over his glass. Some of the ice fell out of the tray, bounced off the counter, and broke against the floor. He reached for the bottle on the table and poured a full glass. The woman watched him with a look of repugnance. He picked up his cigarette and puffed on it as he leaned against the counter.

It was true. He had done an evil thing in robbing the church, but the other part, the vicious aspect, was chance, or fate, or some kind of punishment. He could neither explain nor reconcile it.

"You think there's something else," he said to her. "You think there was some sinister motive, is that it?"

"Tell me," she said. "What exactly did he do to you? What crime?"

"He didn't do anything to me."

"He must've done something."

"I told you, I was desperate. People do senseless things. Terrible mistakes are made."

"You said money, but it couldn't have been money. Money is not all. People aren't violent like that."

"You don't know people."

"Normal people. The average person. You seem like an average man to me. And an average man doesn't act out violently. Not without some reason, not without motivation."

"You want to talk about motivation? Tell you a funny story. Up at San Quentin. Do you want to hear this? They put me in with a shrink. Mandatory counseling. The guy asked me all sorts of questions. Wanted to know everything about me. Twice a week for a couple of months we had to meet. And you know what he said, finally? The one thing I still remember. He said I murdered my father. Meaning psychologically. That I murdered my father was his conclusion."

"You disagree."

"It's horseshit."

"It's an explanation, a theory."

"There are no explanations. You can't explain an accident."

"No, but you can explain a disguise."

"Meaning what?"

"You tell me."

"I just got done telling you. Aren't you listening? I never meant any violence toward him. Snatching the bag out of his hand, that's all."

"That is violence," she said.

"The money was all I wanted. I figured at most he would call the police. And to be honest I didn't think he'd do that. You had to know this guy. He was a preacher. He was *meek*."

"The kind of person who deserved it."

"Those are your words."

"You blame him."

"I don't blame him. I told you I don't blame him."

"For *stooping*. Your word."

"Look, you came here to talk to me. You said you wanted my story. Those were *your* words."

"I don't want your story," she said.

"Then what do you want?"

"The truth."

"The truth? And who are you to come in here demanding the truth? You think because of your job? You think, what, because you're a newspaper reporter you have the right? Listen, lady, you don't know me. I said the man was *meek*. That is the truth. *The meek shall inherit the earth*. What I did was wrong. It was an awful thing. An irreparable deed. You ask me do I feel guilty? Do I feel regret, remorse? Absolutely, all those things."

"Then why accept your parole? If you really believe it's not justified. Are you an honest man, as you claim?"

"You're going to blame me for this? A man locked away for ages?"

"And what of the victims?" she said. "The family. Did you consider the survivors? I'm sure they have a story to tell."

"Then go tell it. Why waste your time with me? Mine isn't the story you want."

"They'll have to live for years knowing you're a free man."

"A free man? What makes you think I'm free? Define free."

"You're alive," she said.

"Alright, I'm alive. Is that all?"

"Is that all? Yes, yes, that's more than enough," she said. "And the irony that you would have the audacity, after killing a minister no less, to take his place behind the pulpit. To claim salvation for yourself."

"You ever heard the one about the thief on the cross?"

"There were two thieves, as I recall, a scoffer and coward. Which one are you?"

"To hell with this," he said, "we're done here."

He slammed his glass on the countertop and pulled back his shoulders.

"This is no interview. You didn't come here to interview me. Are you really a reporter?"

The woman got up and backed away from the table clutching her purse.

"You show up unannounced, you push your way inside my house, drink my whiskey, which I offered. I set out food for your kid. What is it you want? I thought the idea was to help people like me. Or am I mistaken? I thought you came to offer assistance of some kind. Isn't that what you said?"

"You want to know what's in it for you."

"Yes, what's in it for me?"

The woman turned and opened her purse. She reached inside and brought out an envelope and closed the purse again.

"These are pictures," she said. "Photographs of the family. Which I have obtained."

She removed three photographs from the envelope and placed them face up on the table. L.T. glanced at them.

"You don't want to look?" she said.

"I want you to leave."

"You should look first," she said.

"I don't need to look. Go on, get your kid."

"I acquired them from a reliable source."

"What source?"

"Vivian," she said. "She gave them to me. I spoke to her on the telephone. And then in person."

"You didn't tell me you spoke to her. You withheld that. Who are you, anyway? Did Vivian send you? What else are you keeping from me?"

"Listen, I have no intention. Please, if you will. I have no intention of keeping anything from you. I did not come here to argue."

"Is that so?"

"The fact is," she said, "there are two sides to this misfortune. You'll agree. There is no criminal without a victim. I'm giving you a chance to tell your side of the story."

"I never asked for a hearing," he said.

"I'm aware of that."

"Then why did you come here?"

"I came to speak to you," she said. "I have a job to finish."

The counter was wet where his drink had spilled and there was water on the floor where the crumbled ice had melted. L.T. used a hand towel to dry up both spills. Then he drank what was left in his glass and poured another. He went to the table, put a cigarette between his lips, and sat down.

Out of habit he touched his shirt pocket feeling for his reading glasses, but they were in the bedroom under the lamp on the nightstand. L.T. picked up the picture of Vivian and brought it into focus. She was standing in her narrow kitchen in front of the gas stove, arms folded, a wooden spoon visible in one hand. She was a small woman, but never frail or delicate. She kept herself separate is what he remembered. Her discontentment had hardened into obstinacy, into tough-mindedness. The photo was taken in late spring or summer. He assumed this because she was wearing a red tank top with cutoff blue jeans. Her hair, slightly longer than he remembered it, was fastened with barrettes. What he saw was her profile, the shape of her face and neck, the slope of her bare shoulders, the small of her back, her white legs. She was looking at whatever was on the stove, a silver pot without a lid, whatever was in that pot. She was waiting to put the spoon in and stir. The photograph was slightly overexposed. Behind her, through the small window at the end of the kitchen, the raised window above the porcelain sink, the sunlight shone excessively bright. It made what was inside appear more radiant than it was, illuminating the edges of Vivian's slight figure, a brilliant, almost electric light, whiter than Vivian's skin.

He lifted the two remaining photographs by their edges.

"She gave you these?" he said.

He looked at a picture of Philip standing in front of the church wearing a green flannel shirt tucked into tan trousers, his hair well combed and carefully parted. A rake was in his hand but he was not raking. The day was overcast, littered with dry leaves, cold. Philip was looking eastward, or so it appeared, and whatever he was staring at was far off, maybe the mountains, the high Sierras, peaked in white snow. In another moment, without self-regard, Philip would turn to face the camera and smile.

"He wouldn't think of not smiling," L.T. said.

"What?"

He glanced at all three photographs.

"Nobody's smiling," he said. "They don't know their picture is being taken. Was that done on purpose?"

"On purpose—how do you mean?"

"I'm wondering why these particular photographs."

"Does it make a difference?"

"Did she pick these, or did you? Does Vivian know about me? That you're talking to me?"

"No."

"I don't believe you."

"You said your plan was to steal money. Why? Why steal from the people who took you in? It doesn't make sense."

"It fell apart."

"What did?"

"Everything."

"No, please. Explain what you mean."

He was beginning to feel the whiskey. He felt dizzy and there was a bitter taste in his mouth. He concentrated on his cigarette.

Then he said, "You have to understand Philip. He made himself a servant to the church, gave himself to the task. That was his calling, he said, to pour himself out like a drink offering. Maybe he thought he was the Apostle Paul, I don't know. Only Paul didn't have a wife, and Philip, he gave himself to everyone *but* his wife. That was her sacrifice, Vivian's. The congregation, they coveted him, they lauded him with praise and admiration, and then abused him relentlessly with petty complaints. Vivian despised them for it. The way they plucked at both cheeks. She wanted to defend him, that was her nature. And by defending her husband she would also defend herself, and maybe that's what she wanted most of all."

"What?"

"Revenge," he said. "Only Philip wouldn't allow it. He never let her fight back, not in self-defense, and this made her despise him even more than she despised all the women in the church."

"Despise him? Her husband, how? How do you know this?"

"They were a married couple like any other. They bickered and quarreled, shouted at one another. They never let it show, not to anyone in the church, but I heard it more than once. Vivian stored up all sorts of cruelties, which made her vicious and explosive. Like I said, the fight came naturally to her. Philip was the opposite. It cost him everything to work up enough courage to fight back. He took the moral high ground and she broke him at the knees."

"And you remember all this? From so long ago?"

"You wouldn't think so," he said, "but somehow I do. These were my last memories as a free man. When they locked me away, it was all I had left. There are years, whole decades even, which I can't remember. But I can recall those days with clarity. Days I'd rather forget."

"You listened while they argued."

"I had a stake in it."

"A stake? What do you mean?"

"I took her side. I heard what was said between them and always defended her. In my mind, that is. I didn't involve myself directly. But I thought she was right to accuse him of certain things. He was a pushover as far as I was concerned."

"A pushover?"

"You know, the suffering type. The kind of guy who thinks weakness is a moral virtue. He martyred himself, a tortured saint, and came strutting down the mountain glowing like Moses. I'm only telling you what I thought at the time. I had no respect for the man, no feeling toward him except resentment."

"The man who invited you into his own house," she said. "Who gave you a job, a place to live? You had no respect for this man?"

"I'm not defending myself, I'm just telling the truth. Vivian and I hit it off early. We shared a temperament, a streak of meanness. We both felt trapped in our circumstances. Her especially."

"What makes you certain?"

"She told me."

"She told you. What exactly?"

"I wanted her to leave him. Philip didn't deserve her as far as I was concerned."

"But what did her marriage have to do with you? How's this any of your business?"

"You're not understanding me."

"No."

"I was in love with her."

"In love with her, with Vivian? You're joking."

"I'm not," he said. "I thought she felt the same way."

"Why?"

"Listen, who's kidding who? Don't you get what I'm saying?"

The woman fell silent. L.T. watched her. She narrowed her eyes.

"You had an affair with Vivian."

"I take it she didn't tell you this, when you spoke to her?"

"No. No, she did not."

"Don't look so surprised. Not that it's anyone's business. I don't know why I'm telling you. Anyway, it was a one-time thing. It probably didn't matter to her the way it did to me. I got caught up in it, she didn't. I wanted to run off with her, take her daughter with us. But Vivian only wanted to punish her husband."

"Did he know? He must've found out."

"Philip? He never knew anything. But that wasn't the point. It didn't matter if he knew about it or not. The point is it happened. Keeping it a secret was good enough for Vivian. And I had no reason to tell him. What good would it have done? Vivian made it clear she wouldn't leave him. Not for me anyway."

"So you killed him."

"It had nothing to do with that. I had a plan for us but Vivian wouldn't hear it. She wouldn't even talk to me. She got what she wanted and that was the end of it. So I determined to get the hell out of there. Only I was short on money and needed a car."

The woman shook her head in dismay. Then she reached for her glass and took a long drink. The boy, Timothy, came in, circled the room, and drifted down the hallway.

L.T. looked at the girl in the photograph, crouched on her bare knees, drawing shapes on the blacktop using a thick piece of colored chalk. Her bicycle was on the ground beside her. It had a long seat attached to a sissy bar, and there were pink fringes on the handlebars, and the basket up front was crushed on one side where the bike always landed.

"She wouldn't use the kickstand," he said. "She'd ride this bike in a big circle, and when she got tired of pedaling she simply threw the bike down on its side. You can see where the front is banged up. She was always asking me to straighten the handlebars for her."

He stared at the photograph. The child was looking upward, not smiling, a blank look on her face. He stared closely at her, recognized certain familiar features, the shape of her brow and the bridge of her nose, the color of her eyes.

He looked across the table. His eyes shifted from the woman to the photograph and then back again.

It couldn't be, he thought, not after all these years.

And then, of course, he knew it must be her. It all fit together now. Her counterfeit story, her antagonistic demands. She was no reporter and this wasn't any newspaper interview. It was an interrogation. The way she examined him with loaded questions. How she personalized everything. She was a woman now, he could see that, but in those days she was just a kid.

Chapter 19

In the bathroom she ran cold water from the faucet. She rinsed her eye twice, rubbing the eyelid where it twitched. When she finished she dried her face with a roll of tissue paper and sat on the oval lid of the toilet.

The man's bathroom, its mere existence, appalled her. Odors of aftershave and musky hand soap. A white crust on the shower door. There was mold growing in the grout between the tiles and all along the inner edge of the tub, evidence of male neglect.

She felt sick all over, as though her body were suffering some chemical deficiency. It was more than nausea and worse than mere fatigue. There was soreness but that wasn't the right word. What she felt was complicated and abstract. She tried to think of a better word, an official medical diagnosis, but she could think only in trivializing terms.

The rust disgusted her. On the fixtures in the shower, the knobs and faucets, and on the ring around the drain.

Pain radiated from her core, deeper than muscle and bone, and the spasm in her back like the stiffness in her knees and hips was symptomatic and foreboding, a foretaste of things to come.

The man's vile hairs. His brown towel drooping from a peg. She imagined him standing under the shower, fat-bellied, hawking up spit.

She pressed two fingers against the artery in her neck and counted the beats.

Her phone was in her purse. She reached for it, dialed her mother's number, left a voicemail. "You and I need to talk," she said, and promptly ended the call. She was not calling to verify the facts, a fact-finding mission. Travis had slipped unaware down the slope of full disclosure. The truth was evident. There had been a relationship of some kind, a pattern of sneaking around, sex on at least one occasion. She believed this intuitively and needed no further proof. Travis had no reason to fabricate such a story unless he was delusional, and Virginia was convinced the man was sane. Anyway, it was something her mother would've done. And it explained why in Reno she changed so suddenly, so entirely, why she abandoned one version of herself for another without regard to how it might affect her daughter.

Virginia placed the phone inside her purse with her keys and wallet. She laid the pistol on the counter, closed her purse, and crossed the strap overhead. Coming out of the bathroom she would make her intentions known. Relax, breathe easy, let the gun do all the work. She imagined his head rocking back, in slow motion, his shoulders collapsing, the man falling out of his chair onto the floor.

Thirty years in prison were not enough. Travis had gotten away with it and Virginia could not allow that. She would not allow him to possess an inheritance, a plot of land, not even this shit-hole corner of the desert. His loneliness, his misery, meant nothing to her. He did not deserve the luxury of his own despair, much less the dignity afforded to confession. There were no amends to make, no steps toward reconciliation. Her ruin was total so why should his be any different? It's what she would have told them, the parole board, at the hearing, had they bothered to notify her. The daughter of the deceased.

She would have to remain calm, both now and after the fact. The important thing was to avoid fleeing the scene prematurely. She would wipe down handles and doorknobs and whatever else she might've touched. There was the whiskey bottle and one glass, there was the tabletop, what else? Timothy had touched the walls. In the dust they would find his fingertips. So she would wipe down the walls, although it was probably unnecessary. Timothy was off the grid, anonymous. What could anyone possibly learn from following his mysterious path? Out front there were tire tracks on the driveway. And their shoes, they had dragged dirt into the house leaving footprints everywhere. Virginia would have to dry mop the floor with Travis' towel. The shoes would go into the dumpster at home. But what about her hair, the loose strands that were always falling out? She would examine the chair and kitchen table for stray hairs. She would leave no object behind, not even the tissue, which must be flushed.

In Yucca Valley she would stop for gas under the bright lights, run the car through the automatic wash, use whatever spare change lay in the ashtray to buy a soda from the fountain. Timothy would sleep in the car, unfettered by time and space, emerging finally with no trace reminders of the desert wind or the loud report of gunfire.

The man behind the counter, the gun dealer, told Virginia never to wound anyone. Shoot to kill, he said, and stick to your story.

And the story was simple. Two in the chest, one in the head.

Chapter 20

He was standing at the living room window looking out. Across the desert, as far as he could see, the dust had settled and the scrub had fallen silent. After three wild days, after three days of wild racking madness, the world was quiet again.

His skin felt raw and wiry. Deep inside his inner ear he could hear the drumbeat of his heart. The wind was gone and the air in its absence pulsated with ionic intensity.

There was a story in the gospel, not a story, rather a kind of parable. It was the one about the unclean spirit who goes out of a man, and finding no rest in dry places returns to the man, his former host, where he discovers a house swept clean and orderly. Aggrieved, the demon goes out and gathers seven friends more wicked than himself to storm the man's house, and the torment of that man, Jesus says, is seven times worse than before.

L.T. was recalling this parable when he heard the water flush in the bathroom. He wondered where the boy had gone. No doubt they would find him in one of the bedrooms, L.T.'s room or the other one, curled up on the floor in a deep-water spell, or else standing upright, hard-pressed against one of the walls in a fish-eyed trance.

He heard the woman come out of the bathroom, the lock turned and then the door came unlatched. The only other sound he could hear was the fan outside chirping. Virginia closed the door quietly behind her. L.T. had oiled the hinges and the door no longer creaked when it opened or closed. He could feel the woman's footsteps vibrating on the floor behind him. She paused back there in the dark.

He waited for her to speak, to make her identity known, but it was clear after a long silence she had no intention of speaking first.

"Your father baptized me," said L.T.

It was a thought he had and were it not for the silence he would have kept it to himself. But the game was over now as far as he was concerned and he wanted Virginia to know it. He waited for a response, he listened, but she remained quiet.

"There was a river. Maybe you remember it. They were doing baptisms that day and people were congregated along the water's edge where it was sandy and damp. And your dad was calling for you."

L.T. was looking out at the sky. It was luminous, color-saturated, a red sky all the way across. He looked from left to right, or from the western edge of the horizon eastward. Virginia remained behind him, where it was dark, and did not move.

"I wouldn't do it," she said.

L.T. could feel her back there, the truth of where she was standing. All the years between them, the distances measured in miles and time, were no more.

He said, "Your mother was upset. I went up to the house looking for you. You were in tears and she was upset."

"Because they were mad at me," she said.

"It was your father's idea."

"I was afraid of drowning, of being swept away. You don't get mad at a person, a child."

"He thought you were old enough."

"They were forcing me into it."

"Your mother didn't care one way or the other, the way I remember it."

"You were there," she said. "I disappointed him."

"We had an agreement, you and me. We came to an understanding."

"I didn't agree to anything."

"I offered to go first," said L.T. "I thought if I went first."

"There were flies everywhere."

"You were last in line," he said. "Your job was to hold my towel. And then I was supposed to hold yours. That was the deal."

"There were flies on our towels," she said. "And I was standing in mud."

"You remember that river, how it came rushing under the bridge? It was runoff from the snowpack. I'd never felt such cold water. Your dad tipped me backward and held me under. It came as a shock. I could hear the rocks rolling along the bottom of the river and water roaring in my ears. It must've lasted only a second or two before he pulled me out of it."

"I ran home."

"I know you did," he said with a laugh. "But we had an agreement."

"I didn't agree to anything," she said.

"I felt like I'd gotten the short end. What did I care about baptism? I didn't care about any of it."

"You were a fraud."

"I was broke," he said. "There was nowhere for me to go."

"That's not true. You could've gone anywhere."

"I could've walked away, that's right. I could've hopped a train or hitched a ride somewhere. It doesn't matter where. Up north maybe, up the coast. I've lived my whole life knowing this, Virginia, and regretting it."

He turned slowly to face her. He could hardly make out her features in the dark. What he saw was the gun in her hand and it took him a moment to register this fact. She was holding a pistol in her right hand, the barrel pointed at the floor. He experienced no fear, not at first. She was pointing it down, and he took this to mean she did not want to shoot him.

She said, "You were waiting for my mother to change her mind. You wanted to take her away."

"I shouldn't have told you those things. I didn't realize it was you," he said. "Not until I saw your picture."

"You wanted her and me to go with you."

"That was long ago," he said. "I was different then."

"You would actually do it. You would take us away."

"No," he said. "Not if I could do it again."

He tried to avoid looking at the gun but she caught him doing that very thing and pointed it at him. L.T. showed her his empty hands. He'd had guns pointed at him before. It was important to keep the hands visible.

"You don't have to point that," he said.

It was not yet necessary to raise his arms. The idea was to avoid any sudden movements, any threatening gestures.

Virginia moved forward into the ruddy light of the window. The gun tightened the space between them. A cigarette would help. He thought maybe they could talk about this over a cigarette.

"You mind if I grab a smoke?"

"For years I thought it was my punishment," she said.

"What punishment?"

"I ran up to the house and hid behind the bushes. I couldn't stop crying. I knew he was disappointed, and I hated him for it. I remember running home wishing he would die and leave me alone. Wishing he were dead."

"That's every kid," he told her. "What you're describing."

"I was overcome with shame. The mere thought of it. I was sorry for even thinking it, so I took it back."

"You took it back. The way kids do. They'll say something and take it back."

"I cried," she said. "I begged God's forgiveness."

"You were mixed up is all."

She was starting to cry now. He could hear it in her voice.

"You don't understand," she said.

"Virginia, it didn't mean anything. You were a child."

"Don't say my name," she said.

"You were scared, that's all."

"You're not listening," she said.

"Why don't you put away the gun," he said. "You don't need to do all this. Let's sit down and talk about it."

"I thought he wanted me dead."

"Who wanted you dead?" said L.T. "Your dad? Your own father?"

She calmly wiped her eyes.

"I was afraid," she said. "Not of him."

"I don't follow."

"I was terrified of the punishment," she said. "All the talk of hell and torment. And what my father said about baptism, the part about dying."

"Childhood fears. Everybody has them."

"No, you're not listening," she said. "I had evil thoughts. Nobody knew."

"Christ Almighty," said L.T. "Every child at one time or another."

"You don't see, do you?"

"See what?"

"I did what they said. I prayed, I asked God to forgive me, but it didn't matter."

"Of course it matters."

"And when he died," she said, "I thought it was my fault. I believed it was my punishment."

"It was an accident," said L.T.

"An accident?" she said. "No, not an accident. You killed him. You wanted to take us away. It was no accident."

She was pointing the gun at his chest. He saw himself from her perspective, a large soft target, a slope-shouldered silhouette.

"Wait now," he said.

"I was seven. And I knew, do you understand? I knew he was dead, that it was forever, my whole life looming over me. The judgment, the punishment. And I was to blame."

"It was my fault," he said.

"Even later, after I knew it was stupid and childish, after I knew there was no god. I still blamed myself."

"I'm to blame," he said. "No one else."

"And then to hear you tell me about my mother, that you were in love with her, that the two of you."

"Virginia, wait," he said. "Let me explain."

"I don't want to hear it."

"When I was in prison," he said.

"I'm not interested in your Jesus story."

"I need to tell you."

"You think I care? You think I'm interested in what you have to say? Because I'm not," she said. "I don't care about your dark night of the soul, or whatever you did with your guilt, whatever self-deception."

"I'm not that man anymore."

"Don't say that."

"I'm not the same person."

"Don't say that," she said. "You *are* the same person. The man who killed my father. That's exactly who you are. Nobody can change the past."

"Now, wait a second," he said.

"And if there's a hell, if it's anything like they said, then I hope you burn in it, do you hear me?"

She took a step forward, inching closer with the gun. The shock comes first, he thought, the moment of impact, then you bleed out. And then what?

"There's forgiveness," he said.

"You're wrong, Travis," she said, aiming the gun at him. "There is no forgiveness. I came here to tell you that."

Soon he would be lying on the floor staring up at the ceiling.

"Think about your boy," he said. "They'll take you away like they did me. I can tell you what it's like, Virginia. Think about Timothy."

L.T. motioned toward the bedroom to indicate the boy's whereabouts, although he did not know where he was.

"Do not say his name," she said. "Do not say Timothy."

"It isn't worth it, Virginia. I'm not worth it," he said. "Think of the consequences."

"Get on your knees."

He went down on one knee then the other. It hurt to go down on his knees. He felt the pain in his joints. "It's all right," he said. He kept his hands visible. He was on his knees and she was pointing the gun at him. He understood this was happening. All he had to do was make sense of it. She was the child from long ago. He remembered her sharp eyes. Even then she was as intelligent as she was difficult. He had always been fond of her. Now he was trying to think of the right thing to say or do. He lifted his arms higher.

She said, "It's all your fault. Everything. Even Timothy. His condition, his disorder. I brought him here to show you."

"Wait," he said.

"Because of what I experienced, do you understand? The damage you caused. The suffering and anguish and guilt. It changed me," she said. "A vital change which I passed on to my son. Do you have any idea what I've passed on to him? Look at me. A child in the womb?"

"Tell me what can I do," he said. "What do you want?"

"What do I want? You're asking me what I want?"

"Yes, what do you want?"

"I want my father," she said.

But it was the one thing she could not have. In a moment of heated aggravation and muddled rage L.T. had robbed the man of his life, and not only the man, but also his daughter. And while he had always known this, he had never, in all those years, grieved for Virginia. There was remorse. He had experienced a lifetime of sorrow and misery, but these he realized were exclusively for his own benefit. In prison there was nobody to suffer for him, no one to pity him. He had suffered alone, for himself only, and not for anyone else.

"You've got to understand," he said. "From the time they locked me up it was impossible to think about anyone else. You or your mother. The only pain was my pain, the only loss was my own."

"Then you got what you deserved."

L.T. nodded and stared at the floor. He had convinced himself, many years ago, that he would not fear death when it came. But here it was and he was afraid. And the fear made everything more confusing than it really was. He knew, at the heart of it, that death was a very simple matter. It was good to die. He did not have to understand this statement to accept it as true.

"Yes, and what about us?" she asked. "What about my sister? Look at me. My sister who never knew her own father?"

"Your sister?"

And something made her pause, another thought, occurring unexpectedly. L.T. kept his arms raised. He was not close enough to bat away the gun, or to lunge at her waist. He waited for the next thing.

"You," she said.

"What?"

"You and my mother. Did you know this?"

"Did I know what?" he said.

"That she was pregnant."

"Pregnant?"

"Yes, when my father died. You didn't know this?"

"No," he said.

"Incredible," she said. "You don't see."

"What is it?"

"You don't see," she said.

And then it struck him, the idea she was driving at. The timing, the math, the number of weeks.

"Now listen, Virginia," he said. "What you're suggesting. It can't be."

"Don't shake your head at me. You do see. Yes, you do. Her name is Amanda. My sister. She has twin girls. Think of it."

"No," he said. "It can't be. Your mother, she'll tell you."

"My *mother*? My mother wouldn't tell me the truth. You think she would tell me the truth?"

"I think your mother. She's the one to ask. But, no, it can't be."

"Why not?"

"No."

"Tell me why."

But there were no words. He could no longer speak them. Even as she fired the pistol at point-blank range, even as every muscle and nerve fiber in his body, every gland with its flowing substance, recoiled and clinched in terror at this clamorous verdict of guilt, he knew it was likely true, that he and Vivian had fathered a child, and that whatever wrong they had committed together, whatever law transgressed, having earned no lawful pardon, Travis Lee Hilliard, a most unworthy man, might now enter into life.

Chapter 21

Her intention was to kill him, shoot to kill, but before pulling the trigger, against her better judgment, she decided only to wound his shoulder, and not a wound only, but total destruction of one shoulder. To inflict grievous bodily harm became the objective. To blow apart the socket, to pulverize whatever anatomy of bone and tendon. But in the space of one critical moment, in the half-breath before firing, Virginia aimed the gun away from the man's body and shot out the front window of his house. A single shot fired deliberately, the bullet piercing the window cleanly, forming a hole she could poke a finger through, and then, just like that, a sudden animation of glass crashing down like chains. The guillotine sheets and geometric shards, the blade-shaped pieces, a thousand shiny spines.

Travis remained on his knees, crouched on his heels, trembling in fear. He kept his hands raised in a shielding effort, a weak and desperate act of self-preservation. There was an opportunity here for a lecture or at least some final declaration of rage. Something about her mother's betrayal and the warped aftermath of death and pregnancy. But there was nothing more to say. In the moment when it counted, Virginia had lacked the courage and resolve to carry out the sentence. Anyway, he was right. Not even death could put an end to this travesty. One life for another. It would not bring back her father, would not bind up the mortal wound or resolve the injustice. It would mean imprisonment, interminable separation from her only son, and Virginia could not endure that verdict.

But she soon discovered, when she went to find him, that Timothy was not in the bedroom. She searched the closet and under the bed. He was not there. Coming out of the room she called his name. She glanced into the bathroom and then passed through the living room, gun in hand, on her way to the bedroom at the opposite end of the mobile home. Travis was sitting on his heels. He had not moved except to lower his arms. Virginia searched the second bedroom and found it empty.

"Where is he?" she said.

She opened the front door and ran down the steps. She called out his name, first in one direction then the other. She was not panicking, not yet, even as twilight peaked. All visible shapes, every stone, cactus, and shrub were suffused in a savage glow. Timothy was out here somewhere. He had gotten out of the house, but not far.

She opened the car door and checked the back seat. Looking under the car she saw no one. She called her son by name. The feeling was one of urgency, but still there was no distress in her voice.

Virginia walked over to the shed and opened its doors. Dark inside, it reeked of gasoline and grease. "Timothy," she said, but he was not there. He was not in the toolshed or the backseat of the car, and nowhere inside the house.

She watched Travis come down the porch steps, tottering in a post-traumatic stagger. He called out her son's name in a deeper voice. And then they both waited a moment, not for any verbal response, but for Timothy to emerge from wherever he was hiding.

Virginia searched behind the shed. Then she scanned upward across the rocky slope of the mountain. Her son would scale the rock and then become the rock, tall and monolithic. Virginia climbed carefully up the hillside to achieve a better vantage point.

But it was Travis who finally found him. Timothy was inside the corral where he had been all along. He had slipped out of the house unnoticed and crawled through the fence to join the horse. He did not respond to his mother's voice when she called his name. He was staring up at the horse, captivated by its monstrous features. The horse, guarded and upright, kept one eye fixed upon the small child. They were like two iron figures set against a red desert sky. The boy and the horse alone in the corral.

Chapter 22

L.T. was nailing boards across the broken window under the porch light. He had found a stack of them out behind the toolshed. Old fence boards, sun-dried and splintered. When he saw headlights coming up the road, traversing the rough terrain, an hour or so after dark, he knew immediately whose car it was. He stowed the hammer and nails into a metal toolbox, fastened the latch, and waited as the car approached and came to rest on the driveway.

Timothy was in the front seat of the car. He lay asleep on his mother's lap, unbelted, between her chest and the steering wheel. It was not easy to exit the car with the child in her arms, but she accomplished this without stirring him awake and gently kicked the door closed behind her.

L.T. watched her come up the steps. Her manner had changed. Now frail and soft-spoken, she said very simply, as though she could not suffer another loss, "He forgot his airplane."

That was no reason to come back, but here she was, holding the boy asleep on her shoulder. She glanced at L.T., unsure of herself, it seemed, and then looked down at the myriad fragments of unswept glass scattered across the porch.

"We'll look for it inside," he said.

Virginia nodded and carried the boy into the house. The airplane lay overturned on the floor in the hallway. It was a white jet plane, made of diecast metal, an airline passenger jet with red decals on the wings and tail assembly. Earlier the boy had carried it from room to room. But there were never any takeoffs and landings, no midair maneuvers. In the boy's hand, the airplane was a brave deterrent, all body and contour.

In the hallway, Virginia knelt to pick it up, but as she reached down the boy started to slip from her grasp.

L.T. moved to help her.

"I've got it," she said.

She grabbed the airplane and gave the boy a hitch as she stood up, drawing his frame tightly against her waist. The action startled him. Eyes closed, half awake, he grunted defiantly and started writhing in his mother's arms.

"Stop it," she said.

But he refused to yield. He fought with grinding sounds and fierce contortions. He shoved Virginia's face with his free hand and she worked to subdue him.

"Timothy!" she said, but the boy battled on.

It wasn't until she put the airplane in his hand that he finally surrendered. He clutched it instinctively, with ample satisfaction, and bearing no grudge against his mother he fell slack in her arms.

"Why don't you let him rest," L.T. said. "It's late and the road is unsafe. You can have the bed. There's pillows and clean sheets."

But the idea only aroused her suspicion. Her toughness returned, her hardness toward him. She wrinkled her forehead and started for the door.

"Virginia," he said.

At the doorway, with the child in her arms, she stopped and turned halfway.

"What, Travis?"

"Your pictures."

He motioned toward the kitchen table. Along with the two whiskey glasses half-filled with melted ice, and the saltine crackers, stacked and crumbled, were the three family photographs.

"I don't want them," she said.

Again she turned and started out the door, out onto the porch, and once more changed her mind and came back inside.

"What about my sister?" she asked. "What do I tell Amanda?"

L.T. didn't know. He didn't know what to tell the girl. Maybe the truth, if it could be determined, if they could all bear it. Or maybe not.

"You don't have to decide that now," he said.

He watched the hurt well up in her eyes, the grief she carried, how it surfaced, flooding her face with shame, and the pains she took to overcome it.

"Please, Virginia," he said. "Let's sit down. Come over to the table."

Calmly and without haste he moved toward her, then reached out to comfort her, no more than a touch. He urged her into the kitchen where she sat at the table with the boy on her lap.

From the cupboard, he took down a clean glass. He lifted the handle on the faucet and filled the glass with tap water. It was cold and came in straight from the well outside. L.T. set the glass in front of her and pulled out a chair.

Virginia would not look at him. She wiped her tears with the back of her hand, sniffled and rubbed her nose. Cradling the boy in her arms, she stared blankly at the table for a long time.

After a while, she reached for the glass.

~

The next morning, L.T. was already awake drinking coffee when Timothy opened the bedroom door. The boy had slept fully clothed alongside his mother who was still under the covers. The shades were closed and the room was quiet and dark. Virginia was sound asleep and L.T. had no intention of waking her. Timothy closed the bedroom door, ambled down the hallway, and surveyed the strange living room with its boarded-up window. When he moved to examine the shattered glass on the floor, L.T. gently admonished him.

"Stay away from there," he said. "Come over by me."

But he could not deter the child's curiosity. So he set his cup down, scribbled a note for Virginia, and took the boy outside to look at the horse.

There he looped a length of rope around the horse's neck and walked him in circles around the corral. The boy ran up ahead of the horse and fell in the dirt. He got up again, skipped ahead, and fell. He did it several times, without injury, and then remembered he was small enough to crawl under the fence. Outside the corral he wandered off toward the trailhead at the foot of the mountain. L.T. called after him, told him to come back, but the boy pursued a superior notion.

L.T. unlatched the gate and led the horse over to the trailhead where eventually they caught up to the boy. The path followed a sandy wash and then tracked up the mountain through rocks and cactuses. L.T. led the horse by the rope and the boy either followed the horse or ran up ahead. On the trail he did as he pleased. He tested the cactus with his forefinger.

It was a game to see how close he could come to the needle without touching it. And whenever his finger touched a needle the boy snatched his hand away and shook the injured finger wildly and decried the injustice of it.

The boy did not speak. In this regard he was not unlike the horse. But the horse had a watchful eye, whereas the boy did not regard the horse at all. The horse was massive black. It existed on the edges of perception. It was everything to be ignored. Even so, the horse did not ignore the boy but remained aware of the boy's movements so that he was never startled by anything the boy did. And the boy never touched the horse.

It was early and the air was dusky and sweet smelling. L.T. saw rain clouds moving up from the south. The day would bring showers and muggy sun. It was late summer, when the rain fell hard and fast and made rivers of muddy water. It was difficult to predict where a channel might form. Occasionally storm water funneled across the desert road, washing out the level ground, making it impossible to pass. L.T. did not mind the rain even when it washed out the road. The dark days provided relief from the brimstone heat. Jackrabbits came out of the brush. The wind animated the desert scrub and pushed gray clouds over the mountaintop. When it rained the water poured off the eaves of the house and rinsed the pickup clean.

"It'll rain on us," L.T. said, but neither the horse nor the boy offered any response.

The horse did not like the rain except to drink from the puddles. During a flash flood the horse stood perfectly still in the corral with its rump to the wind.

L.T. never saddled the horse. He had no desire to ride it. He fed the animal hay and food scraps and hosed him down in the heat. It was not a bad horse. At any point throughout the day L.T. might speak to the horse because there was no one else around and because the horse was not as stupid as he first appeared.

"That one's a beavertail," he said to the boy. "Because of how it looks."

He said, "Be careful now. That's a cholla cactus. Don't touch."

Fishhook, foxtail, cottontop. L.T. had no interest in touching the cactuses. The thorns meant they did not want to be touched. But the boy had to learn for himself. He played a game of thin proximity.

L.T. picked up a piece of quartz and tried to show it to the boy. There were plenty of interesting rocks to look at. Some, perhaps, were bone fossils, ancient life forms. He would rather the boy handle the rocks and fossils, but Timothy ignored him. The boy's will was never to interact.

L.T. led the horse up the trail and Timothy walked at his own pace. He wanted the boy to say something. He wanted someone else to speak, even the horse. At least the horse looked him in the eye. The kid baffled him.

Then the rain came. It fell a thousand feet out of the clouds. L.T. saw big droplets hit on the rocks in front of him. He felt rain on his shoulders and head. The horse did not acknowledge this new development. It continued up the trail in a four-footed progression. The boy, on the other hand, made an unpleasant sound. He looked at the drops on his arm and tried to rub them away.

"What's the matter?" L.T. said.

The boy did not like rain. He made a sound to indicate as much. L.T. had nothing to cover him with.

"It's just water," he said. He caught a few drops in his free hand. "Water, you see?"

But the boy was not looking at him. He was trying to rub away the rain.

"We need ponchos," he said to the boy. "You know that word? It's Spanish."

The boy winced and made a growling sound. The rain was making his shirt wet and heavy. He flapped his hands as though he wanted to fly above the clouds. He bared his teeth, wide-eyed with worry, as rain pelted the rocks.

"We had better start down," L.T. said, turning the horse. "Come on, Timothy. Let's get out of the rain."

The boy wore a permanent grimace. He whimpered. This was ultimate frustration. The rain assailed him on the outside and the boy was trapped on the inside. He held his arms close to his chest and flapped his hands. L.T. could see no way out of their predicament. Although they were never far from home, he knew this wouldn't sit well with the boy's mother, and rightfully so. The note he left on the kitchen table would not suffice. L.T. led the horse and the boy down the muddy path.

Then he saw it in passing, an opening in the rock, a den of some kind, with room enough for both of them.

"Here," he said. "Right here, Timothy. Come on inside."

The boy came around the horse and they crawled into the small cave and sat on the dry ground. L.T. added slack to the rope and the horse stood in front of the gap. It was not cold rain, and it would pass before long, but Timothy was shivering. L.T. pulled the boy under his arm.

"You see that?" he said. "We found a place. Nearly walked right past it. I'll bet you saw it before I did." He squeezed the boy and held him. "It's not so bad in here, is it? Kind of quiet. We'll let the rain pass, shouldn't take long, a few minutes. I'll bet an animal lives in this cave. What do you think, Timothy? What kind of animal lives in a little den like this? A coyote, you think, or something else? A bobcat maybe? Or a mountain lion. But we shouldn't think about that. The point is it's ours now. Yours and mine, for the time being."

The black horse stood perfectly tall in the rain. In the distance they heard thunder but the horse did not flinch. The boy huddled against L.T. and trembled there. L.T. was glad they had found a place of refuge. It fit the two comfortably and it was a fine place to shelter. He could not think of a better place to wait out the storm. He hoped Virginia would not wake until they returned home safely. The thought of her son shivering in the rain would send her outside in a senseless panic. She did not know that he was already safe, that an opening had formed in the rock, prepared long in advance of the present age, and that it was appointed for them to enter.

Acknowledgments

I am indebted to Frances Tustin's extraordinary book *Autistic States in Children* and to Paul Ekman and Wallace V. Friesen's *Unmasking the Face: A Guide to Recognizing Emotions and Facial Expressions*.

I would like to thank Dennis Lloyd, Jackie Krass, Jessica Smith, the University of Wisconsin Press, and the following people, past and present, for their encouragement and insights: Janet Akard, Lynne Barrett, Craig Bernthal, David Borofka, James Coffey, Larry Crain, Cynthia Elliott, Steve Hail, Sharon Harrigan, Craig Miles Miller, Don Miller, Kellie Kenedy, Ewa Hryniewicz-Yarbrough, Steve Yarbrough, and Liza Wieland.

I am especially thankful for Susie and Holden, whose love and faith made this book possible.